THE SEASONS THAT FALL

SEASONS DUOLOGY
BOOK ONE

H.E. SHOWS

to my sisters who always made growing up feel like a fight to the death
& to my children whose sibling rivalry has only just begun

AUTUMN
SUMMER
LEGEND
TERRITORY LINES
TREE OF SEASON
CONFORMITY CASTLE
STABLES
CABIN/BUILDINGS
CATHEDRAL
MANOR
GAZEBO
WALL
HILLS
MOUNTAINS
STREAM
TREES
SHRUBS
FIRE PIT

LAND
OF
SEASON

WINTER

SPRING

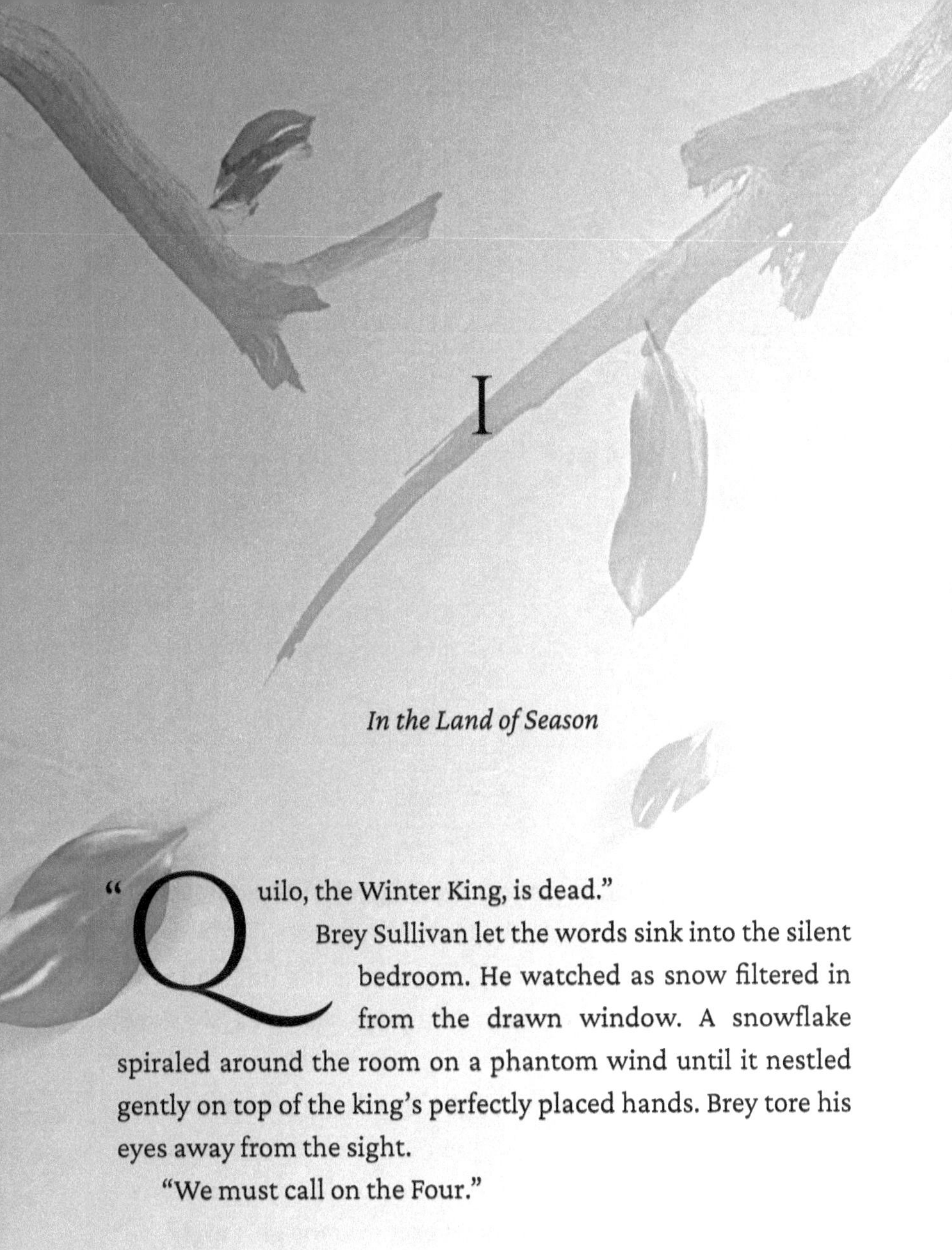

I

In the Land of Season

"Quilo, the Winter King, is dead."

Brey Sullivan let the words sink into the silent bedroom. He watched as snow filtered in from the drawn window. A snowflake spiraled around the room on a phantom wind until it nestled gently on top of the king's perfectly placed hands. Brey tore his eyes away from the sight.

"We must call on the Four."

2

In the Land of Texas

Orla Fletcher sat on the edge of her messy bed. It was dark outside. Little light filtered in from the open window. The flickering of the broken lamp-post on the edge of her parents' house scattered shadows around her room.

A small tick reverberated off the window shutters. She turned her head away from her phone to look out the window. Another tick sounded and then another. Orla stood and carefully padded over to the window to peer into the gray night.

"Shh," she hissed to the two dark figures running up to the house. "You're going to wake up my parents."

"Well, hurry up," Angela called from behind the bushes lining the property.

Orla pushed against the window screen. It popped out easily. She threw a leg over the windowsill and slid out of the window, landing in the flower bed with a scrunch of leaves. She picked up the window screen and gently placed it back over the window. She didn't push too hard, not wanting it to snap back into place and make it impossible to get back in later.

She met her two friends on the edge of the front yard. They grabbed her by the shoulders and squealed with delight.

"Happy birthday, happy birthday, happy birthday to you," Samantha sang close to her ear.

Orla covered her ears to try to beat out the echo of their voices, but it was no use. "Shh," Orla said, holding in a laugh. "If my parents wake up because of y'alls' big mouths..." Orla trailed off.

"No worries." Angela pointed off into the distance.

Orla followed Angela's pointed finger and saw the outline of Angela's car hidden in the woods a few blocks away.

"We have a getaway car," Samantha said with a wicked grin.

Orla ran after her friends. Her heels clicked against the paved road as they snuck away.

Angela hopped into the driver's seat. "You two go push," she said.

"Why do we have to push?" Samantha whined.

"Because it's my car." Angela put the car in neutral and waved to them to start pushing.

"But it's my birthday." Orla rolled her eyes.

"Oh, hush, just push," Angela laughed.

Orla walked to the back of the car. With her hands on the bumper, she and Samantha pushed the car farther down the road away from Orla's house. Once they were far enough away, Orla saw Angela's hand waving from the rolled-down window.

"Get in." Angela cranked the car.

Orla and Samantha slid into the car. Orla looked back at the outline of her house, where her sleeping parents were.

"Let's party," Samantha shouted.

Orla threw a hand over her mouth, and Angela burst into laughter. "Not yet." Orla held in her own laughter.

"Your parents can't hear us in here," Samantha mumbled through Orla's hand.

"Ew." Orla took her hand away from Samantha's mouth and wiped the spit off onto her pants. "And you never know, my parents might have super hearing. They certainly never let me far from their sight." Orla sighed. "Where are we going anyway?"

"It's a surprise," Angela and Samantha sang together.

Orla rolled her eyes and sat back into her seat. "You know I hate surprises," she mumbled with arms across her chest.

She met Angela's eyes in the rearview mirror. "Stop crying. It's going to be a great night," Angela said.

"You bet it is." Samantha wrapped an arm around Orla's shoulder and brought her in for a tight hug. Orla couldn't help but mimic the huge smile on her friend's face. Knowing her two best friends, Orla was sure to have a night to remember.

"It better be for me to risk sneaking out," Orla said, pushing away from Samantha and settling back into her side of the back seat.

"It's not like you don't do it all the time." Angela shrugged.

"Well, if my parents would let me go out like a normal teenager and stop watching my every move, I wouldn't have to." Orla looked out of the window. She tracked the turns they made deeper into town, escaping from her parents' house. Where she felt trapped. She knew her parents loved her. Of course they did. But they were so overbearing. They had waited so long for her, and now they wouldn't let her go. Orla was glad she was a senior in high school. Glad her last year before she could move out was upon her.

A few minutes later, Orla faced a nightclub. The sign at the top of the building blinded her as it displayed *Club Destiny* in a confusing array of blinking colors. It made her head hurt just to look at it. She turned to watch Samantha and Angela climb out of the car after her.

"I hate y'all," she said as her friends each grabbed one of her arms.

"No you don't." Angela squeezed her arm.

"You love us." Samantha beamed at her.

Unfortunately for Orla, they were right. She loved them like sisters. Sisters who knew she didn't particularly like nightclubs.

Orla was pulled to the bouncer, who stood to the side of a big metal door. She took note of the big sign beside the bouncer. *Eighteen and Over.* Good thing today was her birthday. The bouncer took Orla's driver's license and read it thoroughly.

"Happy birthday," he muttered.

Orla watched as he uncapped a black marker and drew a big, bold 'X' on the top of her hand.

"You're officially old enough to get in without a fake." Samantha winked at the bouncer.

Orla let Angela and Samantha pull her onto the dance floor.

"What time is it?" Orla called out over the loud music.

Angela and Samantha were dancing next to her. She wasn't

sure they heard her, but then they shrugged. Orla noted their shoulders lifted in time with the beat of the music.

"Who knows? Just keep dancing," Samantha called out.

Orla closed her eyes and let the music take over. She didn't usually dance when they went out, but it was her birthday. So why not?

"How does it feel?" Angela asked, leaning over to Orla.

"How does what feel?"

"Finally being eighteen," Samantha screamed. "Finally getting some freedom."

"Eighteen doesn't bring freedom. At least not for me. Graduating high school might, though." Orla's throat was hoarse from trying to talk over the music. She looked around the club. It was packed, unusually so for a weeknight. The musk of the air filled her nose, and the strobe lights hurt her eyes. But despite herself, she was having fun. This little taste of freedom. The little bit she took whenever she snuck out or deceived her parents. She wanted more. More freedom to live her life. But she knew her parents would never allow it. Her only hope was to graduate and get into a college far away.

Orla went to close her eyes again, but a sparkle from the ground made her open them wide. She reached down, avoiding the stomping feet of the dancers around her. A small necklace shone brightly against the dark floors of the club. The necklace was warm in her palm as if it had just been taken off someone's neck. Orla looked around as she stood, but no one seemed to notice a lost necklace.

Her eyes got heavy, and her head swam. She stumbled against Angela.

"You okay?" she heard Angela ask through her muddled mind.

She tried to nod or say something reassuring, but a great

wind landed on her chest and throat, making it impossible. Blackness shrouded her vision.

Orla stood in a grand ballroom. The walls were painted in delicate gold and the curtains hung with strands of rubies. She looked around the room, but there was no one to be found.

She walked farther into the room, drawn to a great window. Flickers of snowflakes flitted in. They fell onto the marble floor, intact and whole. A chill ran up her spine. It was cold. Cold enough to keep snow from melting.

A rustling turned Orla's attention to a bed she hadn't noticed before. A huge white drape fell from the ceiling, obscuring the view. She could see through the drape to a figure lying on the bed.

She moved closer slowly. Careful not to wake whoever it was. As she glided across the floor, more figures popped up.

She could just barely make out the outline of four girls surrounding the bed. They were kneeling beside it as if praying. Or maybe waiting for something.

Orla kept walking but got no closer to the four girls or the bed. The room seemed to stretch on forever.

"Quilo, the Winter King, is dead," a muffled voice said from behind her.

Orla turned but saw no one. The words bounced around the room, echoing in her ears. Making her head pound.

"Hey, are you okay?" Angela's voice broke through the mud.

Orla looked up at her from where she had collapsed on the floor. Her heart was beating fast. She could feel each pump of blood in her chest. Her limbs felt leaden. What was that?

She rubbed at her eyes and shook the fog from her head. "What just happened?" she asked timidly.

"You fell," Samantha said, grabbing her arm and hauling

her off the ground.

"No, I just saw a huge bed and some other girls," Orla started. Her knees shook and she stumbled. "Where was I?"

"What are you talking about?" Angela asked.

"For real. Did you have a drink without telling us?" Samantha put an arm around her.

"I wasn't here. Y'all didn't see it?"

"Let's go," Angela said, wrapping her arm around her, too.

They helped her stumble out of the club and into the muggy night. A blast of hot wind woke her up and cleared her head. Angela opened the backseat door and she got in, sliding all the way across so Samantha could get in next to her. The car roared to life.

Orla closed her eyes, her forehead pressed against the window. The car bumped against the dirt road until it hit the pavement. The sound of the wheels against the smooth road calmed her. It almost made her forget the weird vision she had seen. Almost.

"Here." Samantha slid out of the car and held the door open for her.

She stumbled out of the car. Quietly, she made her way through the front yard. She slid a finger under the screen and popped it out of place, climbed inside, then put it back in the windowsill. She closed the window and locked it.

She collapsed onto her bed, trying not to make too much noise but too tired to care much if she did. She couldn't keep her thoughts straight. Her head was too full of weird dreams.

Orla's fingers hovered over the warmth of the necklace she didn't remember taking from the club. She jumped up, eyes wide. Looking in her palm, the necklace seemed to glow. She rubbed the circular necklace mindlessly, tracing the pattern of the tree over and over.

3

Eira Brown shielded her eyes from the onslaught of the sun. It was too bright, even with the shade provided by the bridge she lay under. She sat up and dusted off her pants. What was once a navy blue was now speckled with grains of dirt.

She rubbed a dirty hand through her short hair, stopping at the nape of her neck to stretch out her back. She looked down at the ground. The jacket, the only bed she'd had in a long while, was a crinkly mess much like the rest of her.

She looked around her, taking in the view of the underpass she called home. The stone was cracked and weeds grew through them. The ground was hard and dirty, but it was a lot better than the home she had left many, many years ago. Maybe a little worse than the homeless shelter she got to spend a few months in. But it was what she had, and she made it work.

Eira packed up her few belongings and threw her backpack onto her shoulders. She climbed up the hill and trekked down the highway. It was Friday, and Fridays were bath days.

By the time Eira made it to the house, she was soaked in sweat. Her blond hair was sticking to her forehead. But she made perfect timing.

From a block away, hiding behind the bushes, Eira watched as a family packed up their minivan and drove away from a two-story, blue-shuttered home. Eira knew the home well. It used to be where she lived, but it had never felt like a true home. Nowhere she'd been placed had.

She waited a few minutes before making her way up the pristine driveway. The driveway was lined with flowers, all perfectly plotted and in order. She snuck around to the back of the house and lifted up the big stone vase that sat beside the back door. She picked up the rusty key and unlocked the door.

Eira's foster parents hadn't changed a thing since she'd lived there. Everything was stored in its correct place despite the number of kids that lived there. Her parents, who she never considered her family, didn't let kids out of their rooms except for mealtime. Or when they had guests and had to put on a show. Eira hated the lies. Eira hated the life she'd had under their roof.

But at least now the house was useful to her.

She walked to the stairs in the middle of the open living and dining rooms, and she climbed to the next floor. She stepped onto the small landing and went down the hall of bedrooms. In the back corner of the house was one small bathroom. A bathroom Eira remembered having to share with four other kids.

She grabbed a towel out of the hall closet and brought it to the bathroom. She didn't bother locking the door. Or hurrying through her shower. She knew her foster parents wouldn't be back for hours. On Fridays they dropped the kids off at school and went to spend all of the checks they got from the government. They would come home with bags of new things. But it was never for the kids. Always for them.

Eira shook her head, erasing the thought, and stepped out of the shower. She wrapped the towel around her, packed up her dirty clothes, and left the bathroom. She went to her old bedroom.

Three beds lined the wall. No privacy. No space. Everything was always shared. Eira much preferred her life now, where everything was hers alone.

She walked back down the stairs, toward the back of the ground floor. The master bedroom with the attached bathroom was huge. Completely different from the rooms upstairs with little space to move around. She made her way to the bathroom and threw her filthy clothes into the bathtub. She hunted down the detergent and spread it all over her clothes, washing them with the shower head. Then, she found the dryer and threw them inside to dry.

She left her clothes to finish drying while she went back to the bedroom. She went to her old foster mother's dresser. The top drawer was full of gold and diamond jewelry. *Surely she won't miss it.* Especially since she was probably at the store buying some more. Eira pocketed a few things randomly, putting them in the sides of her backpack. She found a couple of gold plated watches in the other dresser, too.

Her backpack was heavy. She would make good money and be able to get a decent dinner. As if on cue, her stomach growled.

She moseyed to the kitchen where she packed her backpack full of snacks and bottles of water. It was a good Friday.

Eira went back to the dryer and slipped on her damp clothes. They would completely dry with the hot Texas sun. She left the house the same way she came in, through the back door. She left the key in the same spot she'd always found it. It was almost too easy. Wasn't nearly as fun as it used to be. But oh well, she had gotten what she came for. She took off down the road, walking and walking.

Miles later, she came upon a pawn shop.

A bell rang overhead as she walked through the door. The owner, a wrinkly old man with silver hair, looked toward her. "Ah, Eira, what do you have for me this time?" Mr. Sanchez asked.

Eira walked up to the counter and emptied one of the backpack pockets. Two diamond rings, a set of pearl earrings, a matching gold bracelet, and necklace laid on the counter. They glittered against the glass.

"A good bit, I see," Mr. Sanchez said. He picked up the necklace and surveyed it. He put the necklace down and picked up the bracelet.

Mr. Sanchez had known Eira for years. She had often visited when she lived with her foster parents, bringing him many things over the years. He never questioned where she got the stuff she sold him. And she never told him.

"Give me a few minutes," Mr. Sanchez said, turning away from Eira. She nodded even though he couldn't see her.

Eira stepped away from the counter and browsed the shop. A few minutes later, Mr. Sanchez called her back to the counter. He slid a wad of money across the counter. Eira picked it up and counted it. Two thousand eight hundred and fifty dollars.

Eira shook her head. "It's worth more than that."

"Fine. A clean three thousand, then." Mr. Sanchez gave her the extra money with a smile on his face. "You drive a hard bargain."

"No, I just know when you're lowballing me."

"True. Is that all I can do for you today?"

Eira felt the gold watches in the other pocket. "Yeah, that's it for now."

"On your way then. Have a good day," Mr. Sanchez said, waving her out of his shop.

Eira turned and left. The wad of cash burned a hole in her pocket. She needed to hide it and fast.

After eating and grabbing a few things she would need for the week, Eira headed back to her home under the bridge. It was dusky outside, the only light coming from the few streetlights that weren't broken.

She walked by a woman passed out on a sleeping bag. The woman was dirty. Her clothes looked like Swiss cheese. She looked a lot older than she actually was, the sandy dirt turning her hair gray.

Eira knew her. Or as well as Eira knew anyone. Not too long ago, she'd had to kick her out from under the bridge. No one was allowed near Eira. No one was allowed into Eira's home. The only place she called her own.

A shiny necklace caught Eira's eye. It was half-hidden under the woman's sleeping bag. Eira still had the two watches she had stolen from her foster father, but another necklace couldn't hurt. She crouched down next to the lady. Watched her breathe to make sure she was actually asleep instead of just pretending. The lady's chest rose slightly and dropped heavily. She was asleep. Dead asleep.

Perfect. She reached a hand under the sleeping bag and

pulled out the necklace. It was warm in her hand, almost too hot to hold. She stepped away from the sleeping woman.

And then her vision went dark and her body cold. A gust of chilly wind knocked her to the ground.

She pushed herself up on her arms, peering into the darkness. A room with golden walls slowly came into view. "Hello," she called out, but no one answered her. She stood on wobbly legs and walked farther into the room, wisps of smoke fading from view as she passed by the inky clouds.

Suddenly, right in front of her, a great table appeared. She stomped to a stop before running into it. The table was huge, wider and longer than most, and made of stone. On each side there were two chairs. Great, big plush chairs. Each a different color. Eira walked toward the blue chair. She ran a hand along the top of it, feeling where the velvet met the cold stone.

Four inky, black figures appeared. They sat in the chairs. Eira couldn't see their faces. She reached a hand out to touch the figure in the blue chair, but she vanished beneath Eira's fingertips.

A hand pulled Eira away from the table. The room disappeared around her. "We must call on the Four," she heard just before the whole image evaporated.

A tight grip on Eira's forearm pulled her from the vision. Her head pounded, a loud echo bounced around her head. Her eyes barely adjusted before she felt a harsh sting on her face.

"What do you think you're doing?" the woman yelled in Eira's face. Eira looked up at her from the ground.

She yanked her arm away from the woman and put a hand on her hot cheek. She scurried away from the woman, whipping her head back and forth. There were no more inky figures, only the woman staring after her, huffing.

"You tryna steal from me?" the woman screamed, charging at her.

Eira finally got her feet under her and stood just as the woman reached her. She pushed her back. Eira watched the woman fall and knock her head against the concrete. Blood poured from her scalp. The woman's eyes fluttered, not entirely focusing on Eira.

Eira took off running, dirt kicking up behind her.

When she reached her bridge, Eira slung her backpack off her shoulders, unhooked the sleeping bag, and laid it on the ground. Her heart was beating fast, her palms sweaty and sticky with dirt. She shook her hands out but couldn't get the pins and needles feeling to disappear.

In the dark night, Eira felt her way to the edge of the bridge where stone met earth. She ran her hand against the ground. She stopped when she felt a raised section. She dug around, dust flying through the air. She uncovered a small wooden box.

Inside, there were several fine pieces of jewelry she had yet to sell. She rifled through the jewelry until she found an envelope. It was bulging with cash. She placed the money she'd made today with the other cash. It was almost enough. Almost enough to get away from her old life and begin a new life somewhere else. Almost enough to start over.

Eira emptied her other pocket and put the two watches in the box. She looked at the necklace she had stolen from the woman. The one she was sure she had dropped on her run over. It was circular, with a golden tree inside of it. Entangled in the tree's roots were four stones. Yellow, blue, green, and red shone brightly against the golden tree. It was still warm in her hand.

She sat back on her sleeping bag, shaking. The vision—or whatever it was—she'd had earlier came back to her. The necklace dropped from her hand. She couldn't control the beat of her heart. The stench of sweat filled the night air. It was too hot.

"I must really be crazy," she whispered into the dead night with a nervous laugh.

4

Aviva Davis hid behind her black hair as she walked down the crowded hallway of her high school. She scooted around people on her way to the lockers with her head down, eyes on the floor. She stepped over a sticky spot on the floor.

"Oh, watch out, it's the emo girl," a girl said in a high-pitched voice loud enough for everyone to hear.

Aviva shrunk in on herself even more. Tears stung her eyes. She should be used to bullies. They always had snide things to say about her. But she wasn't. And she couldn't stop the tears from falling down her cheeks. She angrily wiped at them and covered her face with the door of her locker. She pushed her textbooks in and closed the door, locking it back.

Aviva stepped around more people, making sure not to accidentally brush against them on her way to the cafeteria. She made it through the lunch line without another incident.

"Enjoy your lunch," the cafeteria lady, Betty, told her as she picked up her tray and walked away.

"Thank you," Aviva whispered.

She went to the far corner of the cafeteria, away from the other students. She sat at a table all alone, like she did every day. She was starved for conversation, but she knew she wouldn't get it at school or home. And she was used to being alone anyway.

She nibbled at her food, slowly putting it in her mouth, all with her eyes down. She never looked up, not wanting to make eye contact with anyone in the room. She didn't want to invite more nasty comments or pretend friendships. She'd had both before, and neither panned out in her favor. Any real friends she used to have disappeared when her foster parents moved her to a new school at the beginning of the year. It was as if their goal was to make her life miserable. And they did a good job at it.

The bell finally rang, but Aviva didn't move. She waited until the cafeteria emptied before getting up out of her seat. She carried her tray to the trash can nearest the door and dumped it.

"Have a good rest of the day, dear," Betty said while wiping a table.

Betty was always nice to her. She wished Betty was her foster mom.

"I'll try," Aviva whispered as she left the cafeteria and walked back to her locker. Luckily, the hallway was less crowded as she made her way to class.

The bell rang just as Aviva slid into her chair. She immediately put her head down in the crooks of her arms, letting her hair fall around her, blanketing her in darkness.

"All right, all right. Time to settle down," Mr. Banks said, waving his hand in the air after the noise died down.

"Beth Castle," Mr. Banks called looking down at his roll.

"Here," Beth said from the front of the class.

"Aviva Davis." Mr. Banks looked up, searching for her.

"Here," she whispered, lifting her head just a smidge to let her voice escape the cocoon she had made.

"Loner," the boy sitting behind her said. He covered it with a cough, but Aviva heard. She always did.

"Speak up, no one can hear you," the girl to Aviva's right said, leaning over into the walkway to get closer to Aviva.

Aviva put her head back down, trying to block out their words. She'd never understood why they were so mean to her. Or what she had ever done to deserve it besides being the new kid.

"All right, that's enough," Mr. Banks said. He continued calling roll, ignoring the students who continued pestering Aviva with comments. Someone from the back of class shot a paper wad. It landed on her desk, right next to her arm. Her skin prickled, the hairs on her arm standing straight up, against the wad.

In the darkness of her folded arms, Aviva let a few tears slip. She imagined she was all alone, back in her bedroom. Though her safety was always in question at her house, too.

"Matthew, that's it," Mr. Banks said walking toward the back of the class where the paper wad came from. "Get up, get out of my class."

"That wasn't me," Matthew said.

"Oh yeah?" Mr. Banks said. "The paper ball that was just on your desk disappeared and landed at the front?"

"Magic," Matthew said laughing.

"Get out," Mr. Banks said, his voice deepening with his anger.

"Yes, sir," Matthew said.

Aviva didn't look, but she could tell Matthew was saluting. He often saluted teachers. The stomping of his feet vibrated next to Aviva's desk as he passed to the front of the classroom. "Good day, classmates," he said as he left the room.

The class erupted in laughter. Aviva still didn't lift her head. Instead, she stayed with her head down in between her arms for the rest of class.

She walked to her next classes with her head down, not making eye contact with anyone. And when she sat at her desk in each new class, she put her head down. She didn't want to bring any attention to herself, not that she ever wanted any. All she wanted was one person to make her feel safe. One person to make her feel like the ball in the middle of her chest could evaporate. One person to make her belong.

Finally, the final bell rang. Aviva left the school, glad for the day to be done. She walked home, glad for the alone time. But with each step that brought her closer to home, her stomach grew weary. A small knot formed in her belly.

Aviva didn't like to be at school, but she disliked being home even more.

She dragged her feet up the small front porch of her home. She'd only been with her family for a few years, but this was the second house they'd lived in since Aviva arrived. She liked the first house better, only because she hadn't had to change schools. She'd had a few friends at her old school. It was nothing like this new school.

She closed the door behind her. It creaked, and she had to push against it so that it would close all the way. It finally closed with a loud click. She scrunched her face and slowly backed away, trying not to make any more noise.

"Aviva," a slurred voice said. Aviva held her breath as she turned and walked into the living room. Her foster dad, Ted, lay on the couch. An empty bottle of beer laid on the ground while he held another open bottle.

Aviva didn't say anything. She knew it was best to keep quiet.

"I don't get a hello?" Ted asked. His eyelids drooped and his words came out slow as if he had forgotten how to speak.

"Hello," Aviva said.

"Come sit down," he said sitting up. He threw an arm over the couch and motioned for her to sit down in the empty space.

"I have homework," Aviva said, inching out of the living room.

"I said," Ted's voice rose in anger, "to sit down."

She nodded and reluctantly sat beside him on the couch. Ted moved his arm from the back of the couch to her shoulders. She shivered in disgust. She hated Ted, hated being near him.

"How was your day?" he asked.

Aviva held her breath, trying not to smell his rank breath.

"Fine," Aviva said, shrugging away.

"Is that so?" he asked, pulling her in close to his side. "Then why did the school call me and say you're having a hard time adjusting?"

"I-I don't know," she said nervously. She could feel the energy radiating off of Ted. She had felt it many times before, and the outcome was never pretty for her.

"One of your teachers seemed pretty concerned. What was his name?" Ted put a finger up to his chin as if he was thinking hard. "Ah, yes. Mr. Banks. Seems like he's taking an interest in your wellbeing."

"I'm sorry," Aviva whispered.

"You're sorry?" Ted asked. He was shaking, and his face was beet red. "You're sorry." He laughed. "You'd rather Mr. Banks be your father, huh?"

"No, of course not."

"I'm the best damn thing to happen to you."

He grabbed Aviva and threw her to the ground. She hit her shoulder on the coffee table, hard, knocking the things scattered on the table to the floor. She grabbed her shoulder and winced in pain.

"You best remember that," Ted said, lying back down on the couch. "Now go to your room. I'm tired of looking at you."

Aviva scrambled to her feet and left the living room. She held her injured shoulder in her other hand and went to her room. She fell onto her bed, exhausted. She was tired of her life. But she knew one day it would get better, right? It just had to. It's not like it could get much worse.

It was dark outside. Aviva had been stuck in her room for hours. She could hear the chatter of dinner and knew she wouldn't be invited down. She hardly ever was.

Instead, she pulled out a box from beneath her bed. Inside were snacks she had stockpiled over the last few months of being in the new house. She pulled out a soda and chips and put them in her backpack. She wasn't going to eat in the confines of her room. No, she wanted to be under the stars with a sense of freedom.

She snuck out of her window and ran to the back of the yard. Her foster parents never knew when she disappeared, even though she did quite often. They never checked up on her. She was just there to give them a check.

Aviva stopped running when she got to the dirt road. She followed it all the way down into the dark night, until she got to a streetlight that barely lit up the park. She'd found this park her first week here. She'd always had to have a place to get away from her family. A place to call her own.

She sat on the swing, letting the warm wind push her back and forth. She opened her dinner and ate in silence, like she always did.

Aviva put her trash back into her bag and held onto the swing. She kicked her feet until she went higher and higher. The top of the swing started bouncing as the force of her weight brought her down hard. Sometimes, she wished she could just fly away. But she couldn't. So she opted to jump instead.

She let go of the swing at its highest point and pushed her body forward. For a moment, she was suspended in the air. But then she came down hard. A lightning strike shot through her feet as she landed on the ground.

Aviva went back to the base of the swing, ducking so she wouldn't get hit in the back of the head. She grabbed her bag and turned to leave. But a spark in the grass turned her back around.

She crouched down to where her backpack had just been sitting. A golden necklace was nestled into the grass. It glowed.

Aviva picked it up. Heat seared through her hand. The heat from the necklace overtook Aviva. She couldn't breathe. She was suffocating, a feeling she knew well.

Aviva stood. It was dark around her, darker than it had been seconds before, and the burning she had felt moments ago was still present. But it wasn't suffocating. She took an easy breath and stepped forward.

Through smoke wafting from the earth, Aviva saw four figures in a circle. She couldn't make them out, but she could see the sparkling colors of the dresses they wore. They stood tall, like royalty. And in between them, in the middle of the smoky circle, there was a burning pyre.

"Welcome," another figure said, walking between the burning corpse and the four girls, "to the Releasing Ceremony."

A burst of light shot into the air. Aviva watched as it exploded into the night sky. She was pushed back hard. The smoke, the girls, the burning pyre disappeared.

Aviva fought to get her feet under her, to see the night sky above her. She put her hands on the ground, rooting herself. She took deep, slow breaths and shook her head. Tears streamed down her cheeks, the earth drinking them in. "What is wrong with me?" she cried. Her broken voice filled the night air.

Moments later, she pushed herself up, wiping her face hard. She took in a shaky breath. And then another. "I'm okay, I'm okay," she chanted.

She slid the warm necklace into the side of her backpack and stood on trembling legs.

"I'm okay, I'm okay."

5

Idalia Gallagher stared at the ceiling of her classroom. The professor droned on and on about some mythological creature Idalia could care less about. The only reason she'd taken the class was because she'd heard it was the easiest of the allowed electives. An easy A, and she'd take all of those she could get to keep her 4.0 GPA. But it was boring.

"Ms. Gallagher," the professor called out as the students around her got up and started leaving. "Please stay back."

Idalia met the professor's eyes. He had a twinkle in his eye. She tried to hide the disgust behind hers. She had heard rumors about him from some of the other girls in her dorm. She had a feeling the rumors were true.

"Yes, Professor Hendrix?" Idalia asked, coming up to the side of his desk.

He was silent until the last of the students left the class.

"I just wanted to inform you that you are failing my class. We haven't been in session too long, but I don't want you to get behind. You need the credits to graduate."

Idalia's eyes widened. "What? How?"

He came from around the desk and perched on the side, sitting so close to Idalia she could smell the whole bottle of cologne he had doused on himself.

"This could be a very easy class," Professor Hendrix said, "for someone like you." He looked her up and down, and her skin crawled. "A little extra credit could go a long way." He raised a hand and let it fall on her bare shoulder.

Idalia stepped back, nervous laughter catching in her throat. His hand fell from her shoulder, and she welcomed the distance between them.

"I can't fail. I have to maintain my 4.0. I have to," she said, brushing her red hair behind her ears.

His hand fell into his lap. "Oh, I can help you with that," he almost whispered, "just a few late nights here and there."

Idalia knew exactly what he was talking about. The rumors were right, but then again, she couldn't fail. She needed this class. Needed a perfect grade. Needed a perfect semester.

"I'll think about it. I gotta get going though. Have to study." A small laugh played on her lips.

Professor Hendrix licked his lips. "Oh, of course." He grabbed her forearm and squeezed. "Have a good night."

Idalia didn't say anything. She turned and left, rubbing a hand over her arm where he'd held her. Small red fingerprints popped up on her skin, and she knew it would bruise. Like she needed any other reminder of the disturbing experience. Her skin crawled.

She turned a corner and stopped short, right in front of Professor Hendrix's wife. She looked just like the picture he had on his desk. "Oh, sorry," Idalia apologized, not making eye contact with the wife of the sleazy professor.

"It's okay, dear," Mrs. Hendrix said. "Would you happen to know where Professor Hendrix's class is?"

"Yes ma'am, just right around that corner. Room 215," Idalia said, pointing to the corner she had just come around.

"Thank you. I get so lost in these hallways," she said smiling. She was beautiful. Idalia wondered how someone like the professor could get her.

"So y'all were right," Idalia said when she fell into the seat across from her friends in the dining hall.

"Well, of course we were," Brittany said looking at Katie and shrugging. "But about what?"

Idalia watched as Brittany took a big bite out of a burger, the juices running down her hands. Her face contorted at the scene. She picked fries off her plate and plopped them into her mouth. "Professor Hendrix. He made a move."

"Oh, yeah. He always does," Katie said.

"What did you do?" Brittany asked, taking another big bite. She seemed to swallow the thing whole.

"He said I was failing his class, but I don't see how when we haven't gotten anything back yet," she said, biting her cheek. Frustration seeped through her words. "I said I'd think about it. I don't want him to fail me on the spot."

"It's only a couple times, no big deal," Brittany said, shrugging.

Idalia's mouth dropped, a fry falling to the table.

Katie turned to her with wide eyes. "Why on earth—"

"You slept with him?" Idalia said, her voice rising, as her hands came to her mouth in shock.

"Shh," Brittany said, jumping up and bumping the table with her legs.

"That's disgusting," Idalia said from beneath her hands.

Brittany shrugged again. "I didn't feel like taking the class. It was boring." She shrugged.

Idalia was sure her shoulder would get stuck near her ears with how often she shrugged.

"That's just wrong," Katie said, shaking her head.

"He has a wife," Idalia whispered.

"I know, she's nice," Brittany said nonchalantly, plopping back down into her seat and taking another bite.

"Oh my gosh," Idalia said, putting a hand to her forehead. She peered around her fingers to look at her friend.

"What?" Brittany shrugged. "You think she doesn't know about him?"

Katie and Idalia stared at her blankly.

"She most definitely knows what he does around here. Why else would she come to campus all the time?"

Idalia and Katie shrugged, mimicking Brittany.

"Look, all I'm saying is do what you gotta do." Her shoulders lifted. "It was the easiest way for me, but I only had him for one class. You'll have a lot of his classes, so might not want to give it up just yet," Brittany laughed.

"Or never," Idalia said.

"Your choice," Brittany said.

"Can we change the subject?" Katie asked, pushing her plate away like she was disturbed by the conversation.

"What? Are you jealous you've never been propositioned?" Brittany asked, bumping her shoulder.

"Not even."

They all laughed. "I gotta get back to my room. I have to study," Idalia said.

"Wouldn't have to study if you took Professor Hendrix up on his offer," Brittany said.

"Ew, no. I'm good with studying."

"Your loss," Brittany said, getting up from the table and throwing away her food. Idalia and Katie followed her and they all walked out into the night together.

"Bye, losers," Brittany said, hugging them and then walking away in the opposite direction.

"I can't believe her," Katie said.

"You're telling me. But that's her. Taking the easy way out instead of using her brain," Idalia said. She could see the outline of her dorm against the black night.

"What brain?"

"Who knows." Idalia laughed. "See you tomorrow."

"Okay," Katie said, heading toward her dorm.

Idalia walked up the stairs and unlocked her dorm room. She looked down at her welcome mat. Sticking out of the corner was a gold chain. She reached down and pulled on it. A necklace appeared from under the mat. There were four stones entangled in the roots of a tree encircled with diamonds. It looked expensive. Idalia looked around to see if anyone was around who could have lost it. But it had been stuck under her welcome mat. No one could have dropped it there by accident.

The necklace was hot in her hand. Her body burned up until a scream was at her throat. But nothing left her mouth. She was stuck in a pitch black, burning hole, with only the necklace as a tether.

Light filtered back into Idalia's vision.

In front of her, in a big wide open room, there were five thrones. On top of each throne was an elegant crown woven into the chair. The throne in the middle had the most significant crown. It rose high above the rest. The different colored jewels shone so brightly Idalia was forced to cover her eyes.

The jewels were the same color as the stones on the golden necklace that Idalia still felt hot in her hand.

She walked farther into the room. Trying to get a better view of the thrones. But as she walked and walked, nothing changed. She was still far away.

Slowly, inch by inch, four figures came into view. They sat on the outer thrones, their faceless shadows all Idalia could see. No one dared touch the middle throne.

Idalia's eyes were drawn to the left of the middle seat. She watched as the throne erupted in fire. She jumped back, putting an arm over her face to shield herself from the intense heat.

She dropped her arm. But the thrones were gone. Only the wooden door to her dorm was before her. She pushed the door open and walked through quickly. The heat of the flames still burned around her. She fell back against the door, her knees wobbling. She slid down the door into a puddle on the floor.

She shook the necklace out of her hand. It clinked when it toppled to the floor. She scooted it away with her foot, staring at it with wide eyes.

6

In the Land of Season

Queen Quinn sat beside King Quilo's bed. She was like a stone, frozen in time. She hadn't moved an inch since Brey had announced the death of her husband. Not as King Quilo took his dying breath, and not after everyone who looked on finally parted ways. Quinn was all alone. Just how she liked it.

"My queen," a whisper of a voice said from behind her.

She turned, slowly, her muscles aching from sitting so long. She rolled her shoulders, straightened her spine, and looked up at Brey.

"Yes, Brey?" Quinn said in a voice that couldn't hide her irritation. She only wanted to be alone, for once. Was it too much to ask of her subjects? To leave her with the dead king?

"We must call on the Four," Brey said, repeating the words

that still hung heavy in the back of Quinn's mind. She had heard him the first time. And she heard him this time.

"Must we right at this moment?"

"It is protocol," Brey said lightly.

As if she needed a reminder of the protocol that ran her life minute by minute.

"There is no protocol for the situation my dear late husband has put us in," Quinn snapped. She stood from her seat by the bed. The black silk ruffled around her as she moved away from the king. She shook her head. "But if we must call on them, we may as well do it someplace else. There's no need for them to see the king in this state."

"Very well, my queen."

Quinn could hear his footsteps behind her. She led him out of the ballroom where the king had been on display. It was customary for the last breaths to be viewed by many. So there was assurance that no ill will had been bestowed on the king.

"Here," Quinn said, stepping aside.

Brey pushed open the huge doors, holding them for her. She walked around the room, to the large stone table in the center. She stopped short of the head of the table where two chairs were stationed. She called over a servant.

"Get rid of it," she said, motioning to the chair she used to occupy. The smaller chair, the less sturdy chair.

Quinn watched the servant cut a glance toward Brey. Brey answered with a curt nod. She smiled. It was her way now. Whatever she said was obeyed.

The servant picked up the plush chair and moved it out of sight. Quinn sat at the head of the table, in the golden chair. In the king's chair. "Hurry up, Brey. We don't have all day," she said. She rubbed her eyes and settled back into the chair, trying to get comfortable. But it wasn't meant for her. The impression the king had made in the plushness of the chair made her want to call the servant back to return her chair. But no, she was ruler now. And she would sit where rulers sat. No matter how uncomfortable it might be. It would conform to her, just like her subjects would.

Quinn leaned forward in her chair as Brey laid a pendant on the table. It was circular, a row of diamonds encasing a golden tree.

"We call on the Four. Return to Season. Return home," Brey said, loud and clear.

Quinn sat back as the pendant lit up. The yellow, blue, green, and red stones shot brilliant light into the room. A gust of wind, a chill, an earthy smell, and a burning sensation filled the room in one instant.

A loud *pop* sounded. And then four bodies appeared.

"Welcome to Conformity Castle, the heart of Season," Brey said into the dead air.

Four pairs of eyes looked at him. The stench of fear filled the room.

Quinn smiled.

She nestled back into the chair, watching Brey bow to the girls. She hoped the hat that sat on top of his brown mop of hair would topple to the floor with the sudden downward movement. But he stood straight, running a hand down his silk shirt, and managed to not look like the fool Quinn knew him to be.

"My name is Brey Sullivan. I am the late King Quilo's Hand." He turned to glance at Quinn. She did not smile as he made the introductions. "And now Queen Quinn's."

The corner of her mouth turned up when four pairs of eyes skittered toward her with confusion. Quinn noted the lack of recognition on their faces. As if the words being said were a language they did not know. And it might as well have been. They knew nothing. Thanks to her dearly departed husband, they had been left blind to their destiny.

One by one, Brey called each daughter. Eira, the oldest of her daughters, the one that resembled her closely with her blond hair and blue eyes, sat to her right. The fiery redhead, the one that looked neither like her or her husband, sat to her left. Orla, an exact replica of Quinn's beloved, sat next to Idalia. Which left her youngest, smallest, weakest child to scrounge up to the last chair.

"It's nice to see you all again," Brey said, pacing back and forth around Quinn.

She tried to keep her eyes from rolling, but Brey was fraying her nerves. She couldn't get a clear picture of all her daughters sitting before her with him moving incessantly.

"Again?" Orla asked, leaning toward Idalia, who only shrugged.

"Where are we?" Eira demanded, rising to her feet and hitting her fists on the tabletop. Quinn admired her tenacity. She saw fire in her eldest daughter, fire she'd also once inherited. Before her husband zapped it out of her, stolen it from her.

Quinn sat still, bored with the pleasantries. "If King Quilo hadn't made such a mess with things, we wouldn't be having this conversation," she murmured.

She watched as Brey struggled to control his face. His eye twitched as he turned his back to her. She smirked. At least pestering Brey, Quilo's trusted Hand, didn't leave her bored to tears.

"You four are the daughters of the late King Quilo of Season. With his death, you have been called back home. One of you," Brey said, meeting the eyes of each girl, "will be the next Queen of Season."

"Wait," Eira said, "We're all daughters of this supposed king?"

Quinn appreciated the sarcasm coating her voice.

"And what about this queen? What happens to her?" Eira let out a sharp laugh, pointing a finger toward Quinn.

Quinn turned a blue eye on Eira, looking her over. Unease settled into the room.

"Queen Quinn is only here until one of you rises up," Brey said.

"And if none of you prove worthy, I am here to stay," Quinn snapped. She didn't have time to waste on this foolishness, nor Brey's snarky attitude. She was Queen of Season. And it would stay that way.

"So we're sisters?" Idalia spoke up, waving a hand about the room as if to include a multitude of people.

"Yes," Brey answered. "This was the first time the Four were sent into a new realm to be raised. Your father, the king, thought it best if you did not reside in Season for your upbringing. So that only true leadership would be born from his death."

"Or be the end of us all," Quinn quipped. "Get on with it, Brey," she said, motioning to the pendant that called the girls home.

"Ah, yes. The necklaces," Brey said. "They are what brought you all here tonight. And it will continue to beckon you until one is chosen and remains permanently."

Quinn monitored each girl. Orla brought her hand to her throat where her necklace hung. Eira stuffed her hand in her pocket, making a fist around it. Idalia turned the necklace over in her palm, again and again. And little Aviva kept her eyes down in her lap.

"Is this a choice?" Eira asked, her voice pitched low like she didn't have a care in the world.

"No, unfortunately, the only choice you have is if you're willing to do what it takes to become queen. Because it is a hard choice. A life or death choice." Brey finally stopped pacing. Quinn breathed a sigh of relief. "The next Queen of Season will have no competition. She will have defeated any and all who stood in her way. Only one of you will survive."

A deathly silence froze the girls in their seats. Aviva looked up for the first time, meeting Quinn's eyes.

"You're joking, right?" Eira said, a boisterous laugh leaving her mouth. The laugh seemed out of place in the dead room.

Brey said nothing.

And Quinn finally had a look on her face that wasn't anger or annoyance. Instead, it was joy. Joy that she hadn't had to endure what her daughters would have to. Joy that it only took a marriage and a death to put her on the throne.

"I don't know what kind of joke this is," Eira continued, rising from her seat, "but I'm out." She pushed the chair backward and headed for the door.

"Leave if you must. But you will return. You all will." Quinn's voice floated over them all.

"I must be tripping on something good," Eira said as she opened the door of the room and escaped into the hallway. A whisper of a haughty goodbye fluttered into the room.

"It is time you go back now. You will be summoned again, once the funeral arrangements are finalized." Brey didn't give them time to answer. He waved his hand over the pendant.

Quinn watched as they disappeared in a black cloud. Screams were all she heard as her daughters returned to the world they grew up in. The world that would give her the advantage to take the throne for herself. Her husband had thought sending them away would benefit them. Little did he know, her whispering in his ear, pleading for their safety, was all it took to ensure her place as Queen of Season.

7

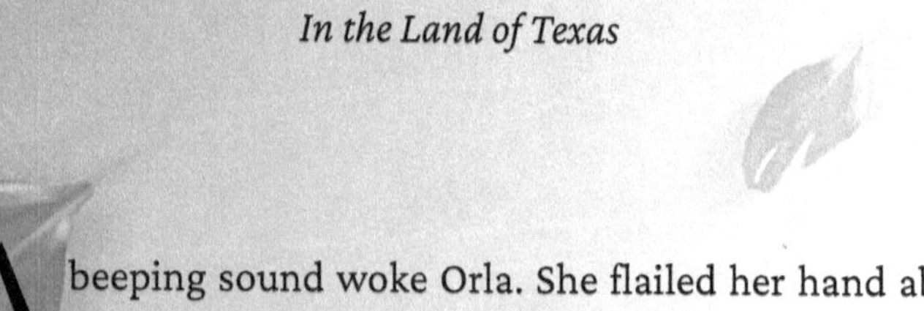

In the Land of Texas

A beeping sound woke Orla. She flailed her hand about the nightstand to find her phone. The phone flew across the room, pulling free from the charger. She sighed heavily and pushed herself up into a sitting position.

Orla rubbed her eyes, and black mascara smeared on her hands. "Ugh." She sighed. It was going to be a great day, she thought sarcastically, rolling her eyes.

She stood and found her phone on the floor by the end of the bed. She clicked the alarm off, and the beeping ceased. She scrolled through her messages on the way into the adjoined bathroom. She put her phone down on the counter and stared at her reflection in the mirror. A raccoon mask surrounded puffy brown eyes. Her usually full, wavy brown hair lay flat against her head. She looked as terrible as she felt. And it felt like she hadn't slept in days.

Orla jumped into the shower and washed off last night, trying to wash off the extremely real-feeling dream. It took her almost thirty minutes to get ready for work, something she definitely was not looking forward to.

A few hours went by as Orla took order after order at the coffee shop. Her coworker, Maddy, came through the door. "Glad to finally see you," Orla said with a roll of her eyes.

Maddy held up the cup in her hand. "I had to get a smoothie," she said with a laugh.

Orla's laugh abruptly died as the ding of the bell rang, and in came a redheaded girl. It was the same kind of red with light blond woven throughout that one of the girls from her dream had. But it couldn't be.

The redhead walked up to the counter, looking over the menu that was pasted on big chalkboards behind the bar. She looked down and saw Orla for the first time.

"Idalia, right?" Orla said shakily.

"Orla?" she asked, her voice just as shaky as Orla's.

Orla nodded.

They stared at each other over the counter, in an awkward moment of silence.

"So it was real? We aren't insane?" Idalia whispered.

Orla pulled the necklace out from under her work shirt and showed it to Idalia. "I guess so, but I think it still makes us insane," she said.

Idalia took her necklace out of her pocket. They shook their heads simultaneously. "This is crazy. There's no way any of that was real. I thought it was a dream."

"I know," Orla whispered, still too shaken to form more than a few words at a time.

Idalia's brown eyes sparkled. The same brown eyes Orla had seen earlier in the mirror. "So we're like sisters?"

"Seems so," Orla said, shrugging her shoulders.

"Orla, dear, you can go on your break now," Lizzy mentioned in passing as she swirled about the bar fixing drinks.

Orla could only nod.

"What are you doing here?" she asked as she walked out into the shop after grabbing her lunch, leaving the coffee bar behind her.

"Oh, I come here all the time. I go to the college down the street. It's the closest coffee shop."

"No way." Orla put a hand to her head. Dizzying thoughts swam in her mind. Maybe she had fallen asleep at work. That wasn't too far-fetched. She'd done it before. Maybe this was all another elaborate dream. Or maybe she was crazy. Maybe they both were. "I've worked here for a few months."

Another moment of silence passed between them.

"How have we never run into each other before?" Orla asked.

"We probably have. Just never stopped to notice," Idalia said, a nervous laugh escaping her lips.

Orla found an empty table and waited while Idalia ordered her coffee. She pulled out her sandwich, unwrapped it, and didn't touch it. Her stomach was in knots. Bile crept up her throat as she watched her supposed sister grab her coffee from Maddy and swerve through the shop to her table.

"I have to go, but we should get together sometime. Let me get your number."

They exchanged numbers, and Idalia left the shop, leaving

Orla shaking her head. If Idalia was real then everything Brey had said was true. And Season was real. And the queen. And the dead king. What was happening?

Orla put her head in her hands, hovering over her uneaten sandwich. The ticking from the clock sounded louder and louder with every click of a second.

She jumped up and bolted from the shop.

8

Idalia left the coffee shop, feeling overwhelmed and caffeinated. What she thought had been an intricate dream was reality. Even though she was studying mythology and folklore, she didn't believe in the unbelievable. Until now, anyway.

Orla was real. So, Eira and Aviva must be, too. But where were they? It couldn't be a coincidence that she and Orla happened to be in the same exact town when they were finally called to Season. Could it? Brey or Quinn should have told them more before sending them away. They should have helped them.

"Hey, Idalia, wait up," someone called from behind her.

She rounded the last corner street to get to the college. She could see the beginning of the classroom buildings pop up through the hedges that lined the campus. She turned and looked for the voice.

Orla ran to catch up to her. "Hey," she repeated when she reached her.

"Hi?" Idalia's eyebrows rose in confusion. She began

walking again, getting closer and closer to the school. She watched as cars flew by on the road separating her and the college.

"I'm sorry." Orla breathed hard. "I just can't wrap my head around this."

Idalia focused on her breathing, making sure her breaths were even. *In. Out. In. Out.* She finally met Orla's eyes. "Me either. I don't even know how—" She stopped mid-sentence, unable to formulate a complete thought.

"Same." Orla nodded. "In what universe does this make any sense? We don't live in a fantasy world where these things happen," she said, her hands raising into the air.

"Apparently we do."

Orla snapped her mouth shut.

"Apparently we weren't even born in this realm," Idalia said, quoting Brey from the night that seemed so far away. Idalia looked across the street at her dorm. "I'm sorry, but I really have to go."

"Yeah, no, I get it." Orla stepped away.

Idalia gave her one last look before crossing the street and following the walkway to her dorm. She scrubbed the start of tears from her eyes, inhaling deeply. She couldn't believe it. She'd been born in a fantasy land. No wonder she had never felt like she belonged here. No wonder she had always felt like she didn't measure up to the standards here. She wasn't from *here*.

But that didn't matter. What mattered was figuring out exactly what was going on with her life now.

9

Aviva stood in her living room, silent. She had been waiting for Ted and Kathy to come into the room for what felt like hours. They were running late for church, and even though it wasn't her fault, Aviva knew she'd get the blame.

"Ted, honey," Kathy called when she finally walked into the living room. "Let's go, we're going to be late." Kathy looked in the mirror. She scrunched up her hair and pulled little wisps behind her ears.

Ted's stomps thundered through the house as he marched into the living room. His face was beet red with anger. "It wouldn't have taken so long if my shirt was ironed like it was supposed to be," he practically yelled. He flattened the shirt underneath his hands and stepped toward Aviva.

Aviva took a step back. She felt the door on her back. Blood rose to her face.

"We don't have time for all that," Kathy said with a dismissive wave of her hand.

Aviva let out the breath she'd been holding. But then she met Kathy's eyes.

Kathy looked her up and down with a disapproving sneer. "Ted, get me the hairbrush," Kathy said in a sickly sweet voice. It made shivers run up and down Aviva's spine.

Ted went into the bathroom and walked out with a hairbrush. He handed it to Kathy. Kathy walked toward Aviva, cornering her, giving her no room to escape. "Now, you know you can't have your hair like that at church."

Kathy grabbed Aviva around the shoulders and forced her face into her chest. She pulled the brush through Aviva's hair, ripping the hair straight from her scalp. Aviva fought tears and screams as Kathy repeatedly yanked her head back and forth. What was once a slightly teased hairstyle was now completely straight against her throbbing scalp.

"Let's go," Kathy said, dragging Aviva and Ted out the door.

Before leaving, Aviva saw the hairbrush lying on the counter. It was full of her tangled black hair.

The car ride to the church was silent. Aviva relished the silence. It meant no one was going to hurt her, at least not yet.

"You better be on your best behavior," Ted said, turning around to look at Aviva.

She nodded. She knew what would happen if she wasn't on her best behavior. But then again, Ted and Kathy always came up with a reason to punish her.

Kathy stepped out of the car and opened Aviva's door as if she couldn't do it herself. A smile was plastered on her face. She reached a hand into the car, and reluctantly, Aviva grabbed it. Kathy helped Aviva out of the car with a strong grip on her hand. It hurt.

Kathy patted down Aviva's dress, making sure to get out all the wrinkles the drive had caused.

Aviva was uncomfortable. She didn't like dresses or having to pretend to be someone she wasn't. But at least she had her hair to hide behind. That was a plus.

Ted came around the car and met them. Kathy pushed Aviva's hair behind her ears, and her only peace was gone.

Ted put a hand on Aviva's hurt shoulder. She wanted so badly to shrug it off, but there were too many eyes on them, and she knew it would make Ted mad. She dealt with the pain as they walked up to the church, stopping every so often to talk to people.

"Oh, Aviva, you look so lovely," an older woman said, stopping them at the door.

"Thank you," Aviva said, barely meeting her eyes. *Save me,* she wanted to say. But she kept her mouth shut, just how Ted and Kathy liked it.

"Doesn't she, though?" Kathy asked, playing the part of the doting mother wonderfully. She had everyone fooled. They all did.

"I'm so glad y'all have finally made it back here. We surely missed you," the older woman said with a sweet smile. She held the door open and let the three of them walk in before her.

"Yes, Aviva is finally feeling better," Ted said, squeezing her shoulder.

Aviva winced. Ted coughed to cover up the painful sound and glared at her. He dropped his hand to his side. She felt as though a great weight had been lifted. If only someone would take Ted and Kathy away.

"That's wonderful to hear," the older woman said.

"Go grab us a seat, dear," Kathy said to Aviva, pushing her out in front of them.

Aviva didn't say anything. Instead, she quickened her steps and put space between them. She slid into an empty pew and breathed a sigh of relief. She always felt suffocated around them.

Ted and Kathy stopped at the end of the pew, a few feet away from Aviva. The older woman had walked off to sit down in the front of the church. A man about the same age as Ted walked up to the pair. "Good to see you again," he said, grabbing Ted's hand and shaking.

"You too," Ted said.

Aviva wondered if the man could smell the alcohol on Ted's breath. If he did, he made no mention of it.

"Hello, Aviva," the man said, calling down the pew.

Aviva nodded.

"I still can't believe y'all took her in. I have a few teenagers myself, and I'd give them up." He laughed.

Aviva knew he was joking. The size of his laughter made it clear. He was full of joy and love. Something Ted would never be.

"I'm just so grateful we were able to provide," Kathy said.

"Of course, of course," the man said.

Aviva wanted to scream at him, at everyone in the church. Someone should've noticed by now. Someone should actually save her. But they all thought she had already been saved. They were wrong. Dead wrong.

IO

Old habits die hard, Eira thought as she stuffed her pockets with food from the convenience store. She could have easily paid for everything, but she couldn't resist. It was such a thrill, taking things that weren't hers. And she needed a thrill after the weird few days she'd had.

No one questioned her as she draped her baggy shirt over her pants to mask the bulge of stolen food. She walked to the front of the store, passing the man at the cash register, and out into the busy street.

Shuffling feet sounded behind her. "Hey, hey," the man at the register called after her. "Get back here. She stole from me," he yelled in frustration as Eira ducked in between people and melted into the crowd.

She kept her head down, looking at the sidewalk, skipping around people's feet. Suddenly, she jerked to a stop. What felt like a boulder stopped her in her path.

Eira looked up into the face of a cop.

"Where are you off to?" The cop raised an eyebrow. He was young, probably only a few years older than she.

Eira tried to step around him, and he almost let her.

"Stop her, stop her," the guy from the store yelled down the street. He pointed crazily in their direction. "She stole from me," the guy yelled.

The cop glanced at Eira, who had managed to step to the side, a little out of arm's length. Eira took off and was violently jerked back to a stop. "Oh, no you don't," the cop said with a tight grip on Eira's upper arm.

The store owner finally made it down the sidewalk. He was dripping with sweat and out of breath. He hunched over, putting his hands on his knees. "Th-thank you," he muttered between ragged breaths.

"She stole from your store?" the cop inquired.

"Y-yes, sir," the owner said, making a great deal of effort to stand up straight. "Ch-check her pockets. I have it on camera."

The cop eyed Eira. She tried to turn her scowl into a friendly smile. But she felt how fake it was, how her muscles denied stretching up.

"Let's go back to the store and sort this all out," the cop said. There was no room for disagreement. He kept a solid hand around Eira's arm the entire way.

Once they reached the storefront, the cop turned toward Eira. "Did you steal merchandise from this store?"

A look of confusion crossed Eira's blank face. "Of course not," she said, trying her best to sound high and mighty. But it didn't work, not well with her baggy clothes and unkempt hair.

"Show me the tape," the cop said to the owner.

"Gladly." The owner rolled back the tape and played the

security footage. A few seconds later, Eira appeared on screen in the aisle, stuffing her pockets with items.

The cop turned an eye toward Eira as if disappointed she would lie to him. She only shrugged.

"On the counter," he instructed.

Eira dumped her pockets out on the counter. The owner stood with a smug look on his face. Eira wanted to wipe it away for him.

"Is that all?" the cop asked Eira when her hands finally stopped digging into her pockets.

"Of course, officer," she said.

The cop eyed her, but he must have believed her because he didn't question it. "How do you want to proceed?" the cop asked the owner.

"Take her away," he practically yelled.

Eira covered her ears.

"She stole from me. She should go to jail."

"And if she agreed to pay for the items?" the cop said, looking at Eira.

"No, not enough." The owner crossed his arms.

"Very well," the cop said, stepping away to make a call on his radio. He kept an eye glued on Eira the entire time, as if she'd bolt out the door with him standing right there. But she couldn't lie, she was definitely considering her chances of getting away.

Yes, the cop was a big guy, but Eira figured she was faster. And if not, she could catch him by surprise and knock him off his feet.

A few seconds later, Eira heard sirens off in the distance. They were coming for her. And this time, they weren't going to let her go so easily.

II

In the Land of Season

Queen Quinn, with Brey at her side, waited for the Four to appear. Slowly, inch by inch, they fluttered into view. She watched as her daughters, her four perfect strangers, opened their eyes.

"We're back," Orla whispered. Her voice floated around the room, bouncing off the delicate gold walls.

Aviva stood, wide-eyed, staring at the scene. She looked shocked; a paleness washed over her face as if she had seen a ghost.

"In Season?" Eira asked. "Seems so," she answered her own question. She stepped to the side, going toward the huge window. She reached down and grabbed a snowflake. It stayed intact, not losing one piece of its intricate design. She crushed the snowflake and walked back to the other girls.

"No," Orla spoke again, her voice louder. "In this room."

"You've been here before?" Idalia turned toward Orla quickly, spinning on her heel and raising an eyebrow.

"Yes, I believe so," Orla said, confused.

"We've all technically been here before." Eira rolled her eyes.

Queen Quinn watched her girls with a bored expression on her face. She didn't feel like a mother, especially their mother. Emotions she remembered having while raising them as bright, happy toddlers evaded her. They were each so different from her. The love that should have filled her at the sight of them, after finally getting them back, was nowhere to be found. Oh, well. They had been taken away from her, and now she had them back just in time for them to watch her become the true Queen of Season.

"Come," Brey said, interrupting her thoughts. "We have much to do." He marched out of the room, not waiting to see if the girls followed him.

Quinn scowled daggers in his back.

All four of the girls stared at one another for a moment, as if suspended in time. They looked up at Queen Quinn. She waved a hand, dismissing them, and they broke apart and caught up to Brey.

She rose from her chair, grabbing the hem of her billowing skirt and walked to the door. She watched as her daughters chased helplessly after Brey. As if he were in charge. As if he held all the answers.

They caught up with Brey outside of the ballroom, in the large entrance hall. A set of magnificent stairs was situated in the middle of the antechamber. The stairs spiraled up into the ceiling, farther than Quinn could see at her vantage point.

She saw Brey make his way to the stairs, carefully climbing them so as to not disturb the rug that ran along the stairs.

Soft wool laced the stairs' railing, intertwined between each post. They climbed higher and higher, going in circles until Quinn could no longer see them from the ground floor. She turned, whipping her skirt behind her, and slammed the door shut.

"Your chambers are here. Typically, had you grown up here, you would be very familiar with this floor. But as it is," Brey said, walking toward the first door.

The first door had a small blue water droplet situated in the middle of the panels. "Eira," Brey said, opening the door.

Orla peeked her head inside. The walls were sapphire blue with intricate lace designs throughout. White fur adorned the floor. Sapphires hung from the ceiling, sparkling in the midday light. The bed was made up of blue silk sheets and a white fur blanket.

"Wow," Orla breathed. "That's one magnificent room."

Eira sneered, her nose scrunched up in what Orla could only discern as disgust.

Brey continued down the hallway. A small flame insignia was painted on the second door. "Idalia," Brey said, pushing open the door. He didn't stop to let the girls admire Idalia's room. Instead, he pushed open the two remaining doors. One with a delicate feather and the other with a harsh bolder.

"You must prepare for the Passing and Releasing Ceremony," Brey said, a hint of sadness in his voice. "Go to your room. Your handmaidens will be there shortly to assist you."

The girls stood in the hallway after Brey disappeared down the stairs. "Is it just me, or are we stuck in some sort of crazy dream?" Idalia broke the silence.

"Not just you," Orla said, looking around herself. She had never been in a place of such magnitude before. Even in her wildest imaginations, she wouldn't have been able to come up with such a grand place.

Aviva didn't speak, but she agreed with a nod of her head.

Eira turned away, heading back down the hall. "Better listen to the little man," she said laughing. "Who knows what crazy things he may be able to do?" Her laughter was cut short as she closed the thick wooden door behind her.

Orla stared at the closed door. "She's odd."

"But might be right," Idalia mentioned. She took a step down the hallway, toward her room.

Aviva shrugged and did the same. Orla turned and crossed the threshold.

The room was adorned with sparkling yellow curtains. They were pulled to the side of a massive window that over-looked the castle's land. A big, heavy fur blanket lay on the bed, pulled back to make the golden sheets noticeable. The tall bed posters reached up to the ceiling, the black metal woven intri-cately to create the same look as the tree's roots in the necklace she'd found.

There was a box laid perfectly in the middle of the bed. Orla padded over to the bed, across the fur rug, and pulled the box to her. It was a garment box. A big bow was tied nicely on top. A small envelope was tucked under the bow.

Orla, it read in impressive cursive. She opened the envelope to find more cursive lettering.

For the funeral. Be prompt.

It was signed by Brey. Orla threw the note onto the nightstand and pulled one end of the ribbon from the bow, detangling the whole thing. Slowly, she lifted the box's top. The tissue paper wrinkled as she moved it aside to get to what was underneath.

Orla gasped. The sound hung in her ears, reminding her she was alone in the room.

A golden dress, sewn with strands of citrine, lay before her. She carefully removed it from the box. The light filtered in from the window onto the citrines, making them shine even more. The dress was long, falling all the way to the floor with a soft train. The top of the dress was bare except for the few gems that made a filigree pattern over the shoulders. It was beautiful. Breathtaking.

A knock on the door woke Orla from the daze she was in. She broke the stare with the dress and walked to the door, still holding the dress in her hands.

"Yes?" she asked, opening the door to see three little ladies standing outside.

The one in the front spoke in a soft voice. "Lady Orla, we've been instructed to help you prepare for the Passing."

"Oh, okay." Orla moved to the side to let them pass. All three of the ladies were shorter than her, a feat hard to accomplish with her small stature.

The last lady to pass through the door wound an arm around Orla and pulled her into the center of the room. The lady let go of her and went to the closet Orla had yet to notice. She pulled out a stepping stool and brought it to Orla's feet.

"Undress," she huffed. Her voice was the complete opposite of the first lady's. It was rough and fast.

Orla did as told and began to undress. Orla looked wildly around the room as the other two ladies set up in the bathroom. Cold hands turned Orla's face away.

"Pay attention," the lady said, her harsh breath smothering Orla.

Orla nodded and completely undressed in front of her. A lady she didn't know. "Do you have a name?" Orla asked, wanting to familiarize herself with these ladies if they were going to see her naked.

"Of course I have a name," she said, throwing her head back in laughter. "You can call me Pete. Her name," Pete said, pointing to the first lady who had entered the room, "is Clary. And she is Robin." Pete pointed to the last one.

Orla nodded. "I'm Orla, but I guess you already know that." Orla laughed nervously, the sound dying away as Clary and Robin ran the water in the bathroom sink.

Pete roughly shook her head. She grabbed the dress and stepped on the stool. "Bend," she said.

Orla bent at the waist so Pete could fit the dress over her head. She pulled the dress down harshly. Orla stayed silent, but she was glad the ladies were with her. It would have taken her ages to put the dress on. Apparently, the dress didn't need the careful attention Orla had previously thought.

"Stand," Pete ordered.

Orla stood up tall. Even with Pete standing on the stool, she managed to be shorter than Orla.

Pete got off the stool and walked around Orla, tugging the dress down at random times. "Perfect," she whispered. "To the bathroom," she said, pushing Orla toward the other ladies.

Orla almost tumbled to the ground. The dress was tight throughout the body, only letting up at the very bottom. It took a few steps to get accustomed to walking with her feet so close together.

Pete guided Orla to the bathroom and instructed her to sit in the chair Clary and Robin had set up. She did, grateful to be sitting. Clary pulled the stool from the room into the bathroom and climbed onto it. Orla could see her in the mirror. She tried making eye contact, but Clary averted her gaze and plastered a simple smile on her face. She didn't speak.

Orla tried keeping her head straight as Clary bundled her hair on top of her head and looked in the mirror. She nodded and let the hair fall. She went to the sink where they had lain out a ton of bottles. She grabbed a few, stuck them into the big pockets of her apron, and made her way back to the stool. She began working on Orla's hair.

Robin stared at Orla. She awkwardly stared back as Robin moved her head left to right to see each angle of her face. She took a few things out of a makeup bag and placed them on the counter. After wrapping a towel around Orla's shoulder and holding up a few shades near her face, Robin set to work on putting makeup on. Orla had never in her life been pulled and prodded so much as she was by Robin and Clary.

"Done," all three of the ladies said at the same time.

Orla stood from the chair when instructed; her legs were sore from sitting still for so long.

Pete ran back into the room and grabbed golden slippers. Luckily, they didn't have heels. She dipped down to the floor, moving Orla's dress, and slipped them on Orla's feet. They carefully walked back into the room to look in the floor-length mirror.

Orla didn't recognize the reflection.

The dress hugged her body in all the right places. It was as if Brey, or whoever ordered it, knew her exact measurements. Her hair was piled high on top of her head in an intricate bun laced with braids. Golden dust was sprinkled randomly throughout her hair, matching the shine of the dress. Her face was far from how she usually wore it. It looked natural to an extent but with exaggerated eyes. A shiny golden eyeshadow made her brown eyes pop even more. It was truly amazing, the work her ladies did.

A knock on the door tore her attention away from the mirror.

Pete padded over to answer it.

"Come, come," she said, opening the door wide.

Brey stood outside. Aviva stood behind him in an identical, but emerald, dress.

Orla moved her feet slowly so she wouldn't stumble and followed Brey and Aviva to the other girls' rooms. Orla noticed the sad bend of Brey's shoulders and the silence he offered.

He led the girls to the stairway, walking down the stairs gracefully. The girls paused at the top. It was hard enough walking on flat ground with the dresses they wore.

Aviva grabbed the rail first and began slowly descending the stairs. She looked back at the others as if to say it was safe. Orla followed her, being careful not to spread her legs too far in case the dress ripped in half. Idalia and Eira descended after her.

Orla kept her mouth in a tight line, trying to hold in the laughter she felt bubbling in her throat at the expletives Eira kept muttering all the way down the stairs. Orla wasn't used to dressing like this or being in a place like this, but she knew Eira was even worse off.

"I know there is much still to be said," Brey began, taking in each girl when the last foot fell on the marbled floor of the entrance hall. "And when time permits, I will say it. For now, all you must know is it will be crowded at the ceremony. People from all over Season have traveled here to stand and show their support for you in your conquest of the crown. The people who stand behind you are your people, and you are their queen."

Brey took off outside to the courtyard. When Orla passed under the archway at the entrance of Conformity Castle, still following behind Aviva in their age-order line, Pete slipped on a big white coat.

The frigid wind slapped her in the face, but the coat kept her warm enough. As did the fire burning in the middle of a huge circle of people. The people parted as Brey walked up.

Orla's heart skipped a beat as hundreds of eyes turned toward her and the others as they trod through the snow.

There were four distinct sections within the circle of people. Each identified by the colors the people wore. Brey stopped and placed Aviva in front of the first section. The people wore different shades of green to match the emerald dress she wore.

Orla made her way to stand in front of people wearing yellow. She watched as Idalia kept walking until she was in front of the people in red. And Eira took her place at the last section, closing the circle, in front of shades of blue.

"Here, before us," Brey spoke, his voice easily projecting around the circle, "stands the next generation of Season. The next queen. Aviva, Princess of Earth. Orla, Princess of Air. Idalia, Princess of Fire. Eira, Princess of Water."

Clapping and shouting erupted as he called out each of their names. The noise was deafening. Then, the sound of trumpets started playing. A slow melody filtered in around them as Orla watched Brey pace back and forth.

"Each of you have a responsibility to your people," Brey said, taking turns looking at each of the girls. "Just as your father had a responsibility to his, and then to everyone of Season when he became king."

He paused, taking a breath. "King Quilo's reign has ended."

Orla whipped her head around, trying to find the source of the music as it picked up, a thudding sound emerging from the depths.

"But his sacrifice makes way for new life and new ways. Let us honor our fallen king and prepare to welcome our new queen."

The thudding sound rose louder and louder. The circle parted, and men in fur bounced into the ring. They carried a long piece of carved wood on their shoulders. Orla could just barely make out a long shape wrapped in white on top of the board. The men in fur brought the board to the edge of the fire and placed it on the snow.

Queen Quinn stepped out from within the mass of men in fur. Orla gasped at her sparkling black dress and black fur coat. It matched hers perfectly. Shadows were thrown across Quinn's face from the flickering fire. She looked regal. And deadly.

Quinn moved across the snow in a smooth sweep, stopping only when she reached a lone throne at the edge of the circle. She took a seat. Orla tried meeting her eyes, but she looked straight ahead.

Brey opened his mouth once more. "Farewell to King Quilo."

"Farewell to King Quilo," everyone echoed.

Orla was drawn away from Quinn as one of the men in fur took a torch and lit it with the fire. After a moment of silence, he laid the torch on top of the board. It burst into flames. Orla's hand went to her mouth, her eyes wide. As the sheet burned away, she could see what lay beneath. The crackling of burning flesh overtook the trumpet sound. It was all that she heard as she watched her father burn.

The fire burned bigger and brighter as she stared into it. She couldn't tear her gaze away. Orla couldn't make sense of their new world, the one she had been thrown into. The one she had been born from. What was real? She couldn't even answer that anymore.

"Welcome," Queen Quinn said amid the silence, her words barely registering to Orla, "to the Releasing Ceremony."

A great white light shot into the sky from the middle of the king's body. Once it reached its peak, far above the crowd where Orla could barely glimpse it, light shot out in four directions, dividing the night sky into sections. Each section took on a different hue. The four colorful streams of light fell back to the earth.

Orla tried to run, but she couldn't move. She was frozen in place as the streams of light headed straight for her. She could only watch as the light exploded into her skin. Her body burned as the light overtook her senses. She couldn't see or feel anything except for it. She had become the light. There was no distinction between the two.

It stopped.

She blinked hard. Her vision slowly came back. The fire had died down; just the ashy remains of her father scattered against the snow lingered.

12

In the Land of Texas

Alarms sounded around Eira as she faded back into the holding cell. Cops were running around the station in an uproar, yelling at each other. Eira sank back against the wall, watching the chaos with a small smile on her face.

"Captain," a cop called from the front desk of the station. "There's no way she could've escaped."

"Then where is she?" a stern voice asked.

Footsteps bounced around the station, echoing off the walls. Someone was coming to Eira's cell. She sat on the metal bench, her knees and arms crossed. A smug smile spread across her lips.

A man in a police uniform stormed up to the cell. He peered through the bars. "You," he said, pointing to Eira.

Eira pointed to herself. "Me?"

"Yes, you. Come here."

Eira stood and sauntered over to the bars. Her face was cascaded with light.

"Is this not the runaway?" the man asked the group of cops standing down the hallway.

One of the cops peered down at a picture in his hands. He shook his head, but no one wanted to admit they had been searching for hours for her.

"Yes, Captain," one of the women said.

"Incompetent," the captain spit.

The captain slid a key into the cell and grabbed Eira by the arm. "Come with me," he said, leading her down the hallway. He opened the door to an interrogation room. "Someone will be with you soon."

Eira sat in the room with white walls for what felt like hours before the door finally opened. Two detectives walked in. "How's your night going?" the male said, sitting in the chair across from Eira.

"Fantastic." Eira sneered. "Best night of my life," she said. It had been the most comfortable place she'd been in a while. She was inside, under a quiet air conditioner. Instead of her usual spot outside in the sweltering heat.

The woman shook her head sadly. "I'm Detective Harrison," she said. She pulled a chair out from under the table; it squeaked against the floor. "And this is Detective Williams." She jutted a finger toward her partner.

Detective Williams sat back in his chair, looking relaxed.

Detective Harrison leaned over the table, crossing her arms in front of her. She peered at Eira as if contemplating what to say next. As if they didn't have the whole thing mapped out already. Eira was familiar with the setting. She'd been here before.

"So, we ran your fingerprints. Want to know what came up?" Williams asked, putting his chair back on all fours and opening the folder he'd been carrying.

Eira shrugged. She knew what it would say, which is why she'd always been careful not to get caught.

"Grew up in the system, bounced around for years, until one family decided to take you in. And what do you do? You steal from them," Williams said, reading off of the papers.

"You have some sticky hands, huh?" Harrison asked, still peering at Eira.

It made Eira's skin crawl, the way Harrison was staring at her, but she tried shrugging it off.

"But that's not even the worst part," Williams chided.

Harrison looked over and glanced at the file.

"Eira, Eira, Eira," Harrison said with a shake of her head.

"Why did you murder Samuel Smith?" Williams asked, looking her dead in the eyes.

Eira didn't even blink. "I didn't."

"Then why were your fingerprints found on the murder weapon? And DNA found at the crime scene?" Harrison chimed in.

"Probably because I lived in the house." Eira shrugged nonchalantly on the outside, but on the inside, she was frozen. She didn't like to remember her time with her foster parents, any of them, but especially her last set. And she definitely didn't like to remember Samuel Smith. Samuel had been the best brother she could have ever asked for. The best anything she could have asked for. Until he wasn't.

"Right, of course," Williams said, filing through the papers in the folder. Looking for something else to use to get her to talk. But there wasn't anything else. Eira was a master of staying silent and giving nothing away. Years and years of practice honed her skill.

"And who else lived in the house, besides you and Samuel?" Harrison asked.

Eira didn't speak.

"Your foster parents, Mr. and Mrs. Knightly," Williams answered her question.

The detectives watched her reaction closely, so she tried her hardest to sit still, not to fidget uncomfortably. She still didn't speak, as if she could even muster words at that moment.

"That's all for now," Williams said after a few minutes. "But don't worry, we'll see each other again very soon." He almost winked at her as he stood and knocked on the door to the room. Harrison followed him, leaving Eira alone again. She finally breathed again, her breath ragged and harsh. She knew they were still watching her. She could feel their eyes on her through the wall. She took deep breaths in, trying hard to act normal.

An officer walked into the room, snapped cuffs around her wrists, and brought her back to her cell. He didn't speak, and Eira was glad for it.

He sat down at his desk, a few cells away from Eira. No one was watching her in the cell. She let out a shaky breath, ran her hands through her short hair, and shook her arms to try to rid the prickling sensation taking over.

She tried laying down, making it through just one night, but she couldn't. She paced and paced.

Samuel. Eira hadn't thought of him in so long. She actively tried not thinking of her foster brother. The best foster sibling she'd ever had. Samuel. They loved one another as much as children who grew up in sketchy foster homes could love each other. A tear slipped down Eira's cheek as the image of Samuel entered her mind.

She wanted out, needed out, badly. She wrapped her hands around the cell bars, peering down the hall to see the officer with his head down on the desk, snoring.

If only she could escape. She needed to escape.

Her hands were freezing. The cold metal bars felt like ice. She wanted to shake them away, but she didn't want to wake up the guard. So she stayed silent, with her hands on the bars, waiting. Waiting for a plan to jump into her mind.

A *pop* sounded. She felt the crumble of the bars beneath her hands.

She looked down, metal encased in blocks of ice lay broken at her feet.

She didn't wait. Eira ran. Past the guard who had started stirring and through the exit of the jail. They weren't going to catch her, not again. She burst into the night.

I3

"Where'd you disappear to?" Angela asked Orla when she walked into the living room.

"What? What do you mean?" she asked, sitting beside her friends on the couch.

"You missed the whole movie." Samantha rolled her eyes and pointed to the TV screen where end credits rolled. "And you're the one who picked this dumb movie."

Orla shook her head; it was a muddled mess. She couldn't tell how much time she had missed while in Season. Enough to notice being gone but not long enough to cause worry. Time must work differently, she hoped anyway. Hoped Brey or someone would finally give them some answers the next time they were literally pulled from their lives.

"Sorry," she said. "Fell asleep in the room. You know going to school every week and then working every weekend is tiring." She didn't like lying to them. They were her best friends. The first friends she'd ever made. But they wouldn't believe her if she did tell them where she'd actually disappeared to. She hardly believed it herself.

"You work every weekend? Yeah, right." Angela laughed.

Orla shrugged. "I'm on the schedule for every weekend." She laughed.

"Girl, please, you skip work more than I skip school. And that's a lot," Samantha chimed in.

They burst into fits of laughter, clutching one another. Orla relished the moment. The normal moment with her friends. The carefree moment.

The TV screen went black as the movie finished. "I gotta go," Orla said, standing up. "Y'all know my parents are going to flip out if I'm one minute late."

"See you tomorrow," Angela called as Orla walked herself out.

"Yeah, see you tomorrow. If I feel up for it," Samantha said with a pointed cough.

Orla shook her head and walked outside with a smile. It wasn't too far of a walk. Just a few blocks home, which was the only reason her parents had even allowed her to go to Angela's for a movie night. She'd had to plead with them not to drive her or pick her up. She wasn't a baby anymore. She was almost an adult. It was about time they let her live a little.

She enjoyed walking in the night air, even though it was still sticky with humidity.

Rustling behind her made her stop. She turned her head to look around.

It was dark, her vision skewed, but she saw the outlines of three men coming toward her. They were big, their shoulders protruding.

Her body revolted in shivers. There was no escaping them as they closed the distance easily in a few strides. Orla was stuck with nowhere to go. She harshly wiped tears from her face. They were closing in, each step echoing off the brick walls of the nearby buildings.

Orla needed to move, to get out. But she was frozen in the middle of the sidewalk.

The first man reached her. He tried touching her arm, but she skirted away. His laugh filled her ears. It was all Orla could hear.

This was a game, Orla realized. To all of them. And she was going to lose.

Orla backed away as far as she could as the men kept approaching. Two of them came up on her side, and one stayed in the front, blocking her view in every direction.

She felt the brick wall at her back and knew she had gone as far as she could.

"Come here, pretty lady," one of the men said.

"We got you now," another said.

They were closing in. Orla could feel the warmth radiating off them as they got closer. They tried reaching out, trying to put a hand on her. But she shrank back against the wall so they wouldn't touch her.

Orla threw her arm out. "Get away," she screamed.

A big gust of wind swept the street, throwing the men back into the buildings. Orla took her chance and ran past them. She didn't stop running. Her heart beat hard, and her breaths were coming too fast. But she didn't stop. Couldn't stop. Not until she saw the light fixture outside of her house.

Orla wrestled with the keys and finally managed to get the key into the door. She stepped inside and leaned heavily on the wall. Finally, she was able to breathe.

"You okay, honey?" Orla's mother called, jumping up from her seat on the living room couch.

Orla ran into her arms, tears streaming down her face.

14

Idalia left her class. She had a few hours to kill before her next one. And she wasn't looking forward to it at all. She did not want to see Professor Hendrix or hear his voice. Didn't want to feel his eyes on her or awkwardly avoid his eye contact throughout class. She wanted to get through his class and never see him again. But that wasn't going to happen.

She left the building and walked outside to the courtyard. She was searching for a friend. Either Brittany or Katie to pass the time with. But she found no one.

Idalia kept walking until she got to the dining hall. She went inside, grabbed some food, and sat at an empty table. She pulled out a textbook so no one would bother her. It was only a few weeks into the semester, but she had some studying she could do. And if Professor Hendrix intended on failing her to get what he wanted, she wasn't going to make it easy for him. She wasn't going to take the easy way like Brittany had. She was going to study. She was going to make straight A's like she'd done all her life. She was going to prove to herself and anyone else that doubted her that she was the smartest one in that class. He wouldn't be able to fail her. She wouldn't let him.

An hour passed. Her empty plate had been slid to the side of the table so that she could have more room. She had her textbook, laptop, and highlighters all laid out in front of her. She leaned back in the chair, taking a break.

She shook out her hand; the cramps from writing out notecards slowly dissipated with each shake. She put the chair legs back on the ground and picked up her stack of freshly written, color-coded notecards. Slowly, she went through them. One by one, she recited the definition on the back and memorized the word on the front. With each correct answer, her stack lessened. Until only a few remained.

She gritted her teeth and clenched her fist when she got the word wrong. Again. And Again. "Ugh." She banged her fist against the table lightly. "Come on, Idalia. It's not that hard to memorize this stuff," she muttered to herself.

She tried again. And again. But still, she couldn't memorize the last five cards. She stared at the cards, burning a hole through them. Maybe just staring at them long enough would help her stupid brain to memorize it.

The cards burst into flame in her hand. She dropped them to the table, took the lid off her cup, and splashed it over the growing fire.

She felt a million eyes on her.

She grabbed her backpack, unzipped it, and chunked all of her stuff inside. It was soaking wet from the drink. Without meeting anyone's eyes, she cleared her table and darted from the dining hall.

15

"Oh, you better be careful. She might bite," a girl said, pulling her friend away from the table Aviva sat at alone. They laughed and walked away, barely giving Aviva a second glance.

Aviva was alone, as normal, sitting in the cafeteria of her boring high school. The day was only half over, and she was so over it. She wanted to go home. But then again, she didn't. She had nowhere to go.

Aviva bowed her head low over her tray of barely touched food. She should be used to this, to being the outcast. But she wasn't, and she didn't know if she ever would be.

"Hey," a boy's voice said from beside her. She heard the rustling of his pants as he slid next to her and the loud bang of his tray as he put it on the table.

Aviva looked up, wide-eyed. Someone was speaking to her. And sitting with her. She couldn't form words in her brain, and even if she had been able to, she couldn't get her mouth to cooperate.

"You looked lonely." The boy shrugged. "And I saw those

girls pick on you." He waited for a response. "Some people are so rude," he said when he didn't get one.

Aviva only nodded.

"So you're new here?" he asked. "I'm Zach, by the way."

"Aviva," she whispered.

"That's a different name. I like it," he said with a smirk. He looked away from Aviva across the cafeteria to a group of boys laughing and jumping around.

Aviva hated how obnoxious the kids her age were. They didn't know how to behave. They hadn't been taught to sit and be quiet. Not like she had. She went unnoticed. It seemed like everyone else's goal was to be noticed.

"What are you doing after school today? Want to hang out?" he asked.

Aviva looked at him blankly.

"We could get to know each other." He placed a hand on her leg.

She shot away from him, skirting to the edge of the cafeteria bench.

"What's your problem?" he asked, scooting closer. He looked over at the other table, and nodded his head at the obnoxious boys. They erupted in another fit of laughter.

Aviva wanted to scream. Instead, she started shaking.

"Or not," he said, finally standing up. He leaned down next to her ear and whispered, his hot breath blowing all over her face. "You're not pretty enough for me. Or anyone, for that matter. You should just go back to where you came from."

He walked away, laughing.

Aviva sat still, so very still. Outside, she watched Zach saunter over to the other table. He high-fived a couple of the guys. They kept looking back at Aviva and laughing. As if she were some kind of punch line to a hilarious joke.

But inside, inside Aviva was seething. She was tired. Tired of feeling unwanted, like a waste of space. She was mad. Mad at everyone who had ever done her wrong, and that was a whole list of people.

She wanted them to hurt, to feel the pain she felt every day. Wanted them to know not to mess with her anymore.

A loud crash sounded around the cafeteria, followed by screams. Aviva watched as a huge tree branch flew through the window near Zach's table, shattering it to pieces. The students jumped up and away from the broken glass. Zach's eyes were wide, and he pinched his face together, looking like he was about to cry. Aviva smiled at the scene.

She felt powerful. And she didn't want the feeling to go away.

16

In the Land of Season

Queen Quinn sat on a bench, staring at herself in a mirror. Behind her, a servant brushed the tangles out of her long blond hair. The servant wasn't gentle, but Quinn was used to it. She had grown up in Season, and though it was a lovely place, it was tough.

Season had hardened her heart. Or maybe it had been her late husband that changed her. Either way, she was not fond of the way Season had always done things in regard to its royalty. And now, with the king gone, maybe she could make the changes needed so she could be the queen she always knew she should be. Maybe now her daughters wouldn't inherit the crown simply because it had always been done that way. Maybe now she would be able to rise.

A knock on her door took her out of her harsh thoughts.

The servant put the brush down beside her and sauntered over to open the door. Quinn barely turned to see who had entered her chambers.

"My queen," Brey said with a low bow. "You've summoned me?"

"Yes," Quinn said standing up from the bench. "I was hoping to check in with the Four. See how they are after the Releasing Ceremony. It's a hard thing to withstand while being brought up in Season. I can only imagine the confusion they must feel," she said, trying her hardest to sound sincere.

"Of course, my queen," Brey said, stepping farther into the room. "Do you mind?" he asked with a point of his finger toward the mirror that still held Quinn's reflection.

"Oh, no. Whatever you need, Brey," she said. The sweetness in her voice could kill.

The servant girl closed the door after Brey entered the room fully. Brey walked across the room and stood in front of the mirror. Quinn could no longer see her reflection. He dug in his pocket and pulled out the pendant.

Quinn watched Brey curiously. She had never learned how to use the pendant. Or how to contact the Four. King Quilo gave only one person that power. And it wasn't his wife.

Brey hung the pendant on the mirror. The tree and stones facing the glass. "We call on the Four. Let us see into your eyes."

The pendant's stones lit up, bouncing back and forth between the mirror and the pendant. A *crack* sounded through the room. The mirror broke, shattering into a million pieces. Quinn jumped despite herself.

Left hanging on the wall was a ball of light. Slowly, within the light, images came into view.

Brey stepped back from the portal. Quinn stepped closer. She watched as, one by one, her daughters' images emerged.

Orla blasted men three times her size away. Eira froze the bars of her cell off. Aviva brought a tree through a window. Idalia burned cards with a single thought.

Queen Quinn smiled. She was proud of their powers. Something she'd helped create. But most importantly, she was proud of their chaos.

"They are strong," Brey said, mostly to himself.

"What did you expect from King Quilo's children?" Quinn asked, unable to tear her eyes away from the portal.

"Nothing less," Brey said.

Slowly, the light of the portal died. And with it, the images of the Four.

Queen Quinn finally blinked and backed away from the wall. She took a seat on the bench again. Brey took the pendant down and slid it into his pocket. It was never out of his sight and never away from his body. Quinn wished there was some way to relieve him of it. Just a peek was all she needed.

"Clean it up," Quinn quipped at the servant girl who had remained by the door.

She scurried over to the broken mirror and began picking it up, piece by broken piece.

"Would it not be best to bring them here permanently?" Quinn asked, looking at Brey.

Brey shook his head. "King Quilo didn't want that."

"The king is dead," Quinn said as if he needed a reminder. She gripped the armrest of her chair. Her fingers curled around the wood.

"His laws still remain."

Quinn took a deep, audible breath. She let it out harshly.

"Please explain to me the purpose of his laws. What good was it to send them away?"

"Did the king not tell you himself?"

The queen stood. She put a hand on Brey's shoulder, bearing down. "If he had, do you think I would be asking you?" she said through gritted teeth.

"Very well," Brey said.

Quinn removed her hand from his shoulder and went to her closet. The servant girl quickly threw the glass in a bin and followed Quinn without so much as a beckon by the queen. The girl knew her place, and it was wherever the queen was. At least she held some semblance of power.

"Season is weaker and has been getting weaker with each term of the Four. King Quilo decreed his Four would be sent away in hopes of making them stronger, self-sufficient. It was fate that brought them to one central place. Fate that pulled them together through sheer will," Brey said, turning away from the closet as Quinn undressed.

"Did he not realize he was naming himself weak?" Quinn laughed. She bent forward as the servant helped her into a new gown.

"He did. Because he was," Brey said. "He was not ashamed to name himself weak if it meant Season would have stronger leaders in the future. It was his hope that in his heartache, Season would live forever."

Quinn rolled her eyes at the admiration in Brey's voice. A weak king had never garnered so much loyalty as King Quilo had.

"King Quilo wanted to give Season its best chance. And Season's best chance is his four daughters." Brey paused. "He was selfless, and it seems to have paid off. Wouldn't you agree?"

"Yes, I suppose so. Our daughters are strong. But they are ill prepared and unfamiliar."

"That is easily reconciled."

"Then so be it," Queen Quinn said, coming out of the closet in a tight-fitting gown. Her servant girl followed close behind her. "But if they fail and Season dies, it is on you and the king." She said, staring daggers at Brey.

"I'd see it no other way."

17

In the Land of Texas

Orla jumped back from the shattered window. She watched as a frenzy broke loose. Students ran away from the broken window and toward the cafeteria doors.

In the back of the cafeteria, Orla saw a small black-haired girl staring at the tree branch on the table. "Aviva?" Orla called pushing through the crowd of people to get to the other side of the cafeteria. "Move, get out of my way," she said over and over again as she waded through the crowd. Finally, she made it out and to the back of the room where Aviva sat alone.

"Aviva?" Orla said again, coming up to her side.

Aviva didn't break her stare with the tree branch. Zach was frozen, still standing amid broken glass.

"Hey," Orla said, shaking Aviva's shoulder.

Aviva finally looked up.

"Orla?" she blinked.

Aviva's voice was different than Orla thought it would be. Instead of being soft and shy, it was strong and powerful. Aviva wasn't a little girl anymore. She had already changed so much from the first time they'd met.

"Yeah," Orla said awkwardly. "I didn't know you went here."

"Just moved this year."

They both turned toward the cafeteria doors. The principal came strutting in, all high and mighty. He investigated the window, as if to see if it was actually shattered or if the students' yelling was some kind of joke. He looked angry as he turned and stalked out of the cafeteria, the blood boiled up to his cheeks.

"Was that you?" Orla asked, nodding toward the fallen tree branch.

"How could it have been?" Aviva asked with a raised eye.

"Trust me, it could have. Weird things are happening. At least to me," Orla admitted. She remembered the immense surge of power she had felt when the guys tried to get her. The kind of power she'd felt when the light from her father's body exploded in the air. Anything was possible now. Anything could happen.

Principal Thomas stomped back into the cafeteria. Students made a huge path for him to get through, not wanting to be close to the seething man. He held up a megaphone. "Classes are canceled for the rest of the day. Go home," he yelled into the megaphone.

Students erupted in cheers and high-fives, glad to have an excuse for a half day.

"I don't want to go home," Aviva said.

Orla glanced at her, but Aviva wouldn't meet her eyes. "You can come to my house." She shrugged. "My parents won't be home for a while. And I can text Idalia to see if anything weird has happened to her."

Aviva paused. Orla could see her working through things. What, she didn't know.

"Yeah, okay," she finally said.

Idalia knocked on the door and waited. She could hear the rustling from inside as the lock unclicked. Idalia expected to see Orla standing in the doorway; but instead, Aviva opened the door wide.

"Oh, hey," Idalia said in surprise.

"Hi," Aviva said, letting Idalia pass by her.

Idalia stopped to let Aviva close the door behind her. They walked into the living room together.

"Orla's using the bathroom," Aviva said, awkwardly filling the dead air. She sat on the couch.

"Okay," Idalia said. She walked around the living room. Family pictures hung on the wall and filled frames set out on every available tabletop. It reminded her of her house. And how long it had been since she'd gone home to see her parents. She missed them, but she never felt good enough for them. Always felt like they deserved a better daughter.

"Embarrassing, right?" Orla said, walking into the room.

"It's nice," Idalia said.

"You got here quickly. Thought you might be in class." Orla sat in the recliner.

Idalia took a seat on the opposite end of the couch from Aviva. It still felt odd to be around each other. Knowing they were sisters didn't help matters. There was a great expectation looming over their heads to get along and be close. But she didn't feel it. Not yet.

Idalia shrugged. "I skipped."

"Can't wait to be able to do that." Orla leaned back in her chair and sighed.

"Yeah, I don't do it often."

Orla scoffed. "Shoot, I'd do it all the time."

Idalia shuffled uncomfortably in her seat. A small cough escaped her lips. "So what's going on? You didn't really explain in your text," Idalia said after a moment.

Orla glanced at Aviva, who sat with her hands clasped in her lap. "Strange things have been happening to us." Orla pointed between herself and Aviva. "Anything strange with you?"

Idalia sat still for a moment. She didn't know whether to tell them about the fire. They weren't that close, and she wasn't sure how they'd react. Plus, it could've been a coincidence that her notes caught on fire when she got upset. Somehow. She wasn't one hundred percent sure she had anything to do with it. "Uh, kind of, I guess," she said slowly.

Aviva looked up from the carpet. "Like what?"

Idalia scratched her head nervously. "I kind of, um, burned my notecards while studying. Well, I think I did. I got mad because I couldn't get a few definitions to stick in my brain. And before I knew it, the cards were in flames." Idalia couldn't meet their eyes. She felt silly saying it out loud. Felt even sillier realizing she was the type of person to get mad at herself while studying.

"Really?" Aviva asked, her voice spiking in excitement like burning something was a good thing.

"Yeah? What about you guys?" Idalia asked.

"I made a tree branch crash through a window next to a group of bullies," Aviva said. "At least I like to think I did."

"And I blew three men away who were trying to attack me last night," Orla added quickly, in one breath.

"Oh, my gosh," Idalia said, scooting to the edge of the couch. "Are you all right?"

Orla nodded. "Yeah, I told my parents when I got home. Not about what I'm assuming are powers, but about the men. They're taking care of it with the cops. I'm fine."

Idalia opened her mouth to speak.

"I'm fine," Orla repeated with a dismissive wave of her hand.

All three girls grew silent. Thinking.

"Anyone know how to reach Eira? Maybe something happened to her, too?" Aviva said.

"No." Idalia shook her head. "She hasn't really been forthcoming with personal information."

"Do you think this has to do with the shot of light at the funeral?" Orla asked.

"Yeah, it was called the Releasing Ceremony. Maybe releasing the king's powers," Idalia said. "What else could it be?" It was the only logical explanation. Though nothing about any of this was logical. They had moved so far away from logic that Idalia was unsure if she was trapped in some dream, or an alternate universe, or something else entirely.

"But Brey never said anything about powers. And neither did Queen Quinn," Aviva said.

"They haven't said anything about a lot of things." Idalia shook her head. None of it made any sense to her. And for the last nineteen years, it had been her mission to make sense out of everything. That was the one thing she could always count on. Things making sense. Things happening for a specific reason. Not this make-believe fate or destiny or whatever it might be.

"Do y'all know how weird this is? We're talking about powers. And a queen of some far away land. This is crazy." Orla threw her hands up in defeat.

"You got that right." Idalia leaned back into the couch and took a big breath. She tried to rid herself of the slowly building knot in her stomach that had appeared from the moment she first encountered the necklace. The knot of uncertainty.

"Can I use the restroom?" Aviva asked Orla.

"Yeah, sure. It's just around the corner, down the hall," she said, motioning to the hallway.

Aviva disappeared around the corner.

"Third door on the right. No, the left," Orla said with a hiccup of a laugh.

Orla turned toward the TV, flipping through the channels. Idalia sat uncomfortably in her presence. They didn't speak. What was left to say, anyway? They didn't know each other. They had only been thrust into this crazy new world together upon coincidence. They had nothing in common with one another.

"Turn that up," Aviva said, coming back into the room. She stared at the TV, watching the news channel Orla had stopped on.

Orla clicked the volume up.

On the screen was a reporter reading from a script. And to the side of her a picture of a girl. Blond hair, blue eyes.

"This just in," the reporter said. "Eira Brown, serial thief, suspected murderer, broke out of county jail last night. If you see this girl, do not engage. She is dangerous."

Idalia, Aviva, and Orla leaned in closer to the TV.

"Cell bars had been frozen off and forcefully removed. We do not know at this time if she has an accomplice," the reporter said.

"Well, I guess something happened to her, too," Idalia whispered.

18

"Welcome back," Brey said to the girls as they appeared before him. He gave them a moment to settle in. Limb by limb, they came into view until they were fully opaque.

"Do we just randomly disappear from Texas when we're here?" Eira asked as soon as she got her mouth to work.

"Yes, in a way."

"Oh, that's perfect." A broad smile broke out on Eira's face. "I might just have to stay in Season then," she said.

Idalia, Aviva, and Orla shared a knowing look but said nothing.

Brey waited until all four sets of eyes were on him. "We've been watching you," Brey said, gesturing to Queen Quinn, who sat on her throne at the head of the stone table.

"Because that's not creepy." Eira laughed. She made her way around the table to the plush blue chair. The other girls found their seats.

Everyone ignored Eira's snide remark.

"We see that you've come into your powers," Queen Quinn said. Her voice was proud, but her face showed no emotion.

"No one thought to mention we would get powers?" Idalia asked. "That would've been nice to know ahead of time."

"Yes, well, there is a lot you do not know. It is what King Quilo wanted," Brey said.

"That's kind of stupid," Eira said.

Queen Quinn gave her a slight nod.

Brey fought the anger rising in him. The disrespect the Four showed their late father was almost excusable. They did not understand the customs of Season. They did not understand anything. But Queen Quinn understood.

Brey pushed the disloyal thoughts away. "King Quilo hoped to have four strong, independent contenders for the throne. And I believe he will. But first, you must practice."

"Practice for what?" Aviva asked, speaking for the first time in Season.

"Why the Showcase, of course," Quinn said, rolling her eyes. "If your father would have let me raise you as was customary, you would know all of this." She scoffed.

"He needed to assure your strength," Brey explained, keeping his focus on the girls and away from the queen that lured so many foul emotions from him.

"Showcase?" Orla asked for all of them.

"Yes," Brey answered. "A showcase of your strength and power. The people of Season will come out to watch each of the five trials. And by the end of the Showcase, Season will have its queen. Undefeated and uncontested."

Silence filled the grand room.

"Come," Brey said with a wave of his hand as he headed to the door. "We must prepare."

Brey led the girls out of the room, down the staircase, through the back of Conformity Castle, and out into the garden. They trekked through snow, across a bridge, to an archway. Brey had walked this walk so many times in his life that his mind was left to wander as his feet guided him.

He hardly noticed the missing stone pieces of the archway or how it sagged with sadness. Snow piled in the crevices but couldn't hide all of the cracks embedded into the stonework. He hardly saw the completely missing parts of the arena wall as they walked under the arch and made their way to the middle. He pushed the snow with the toe of his boot and remembered the many times he had seen the arena. What felt like a lifetime ago, King Quilo had brought him to the arena, a magnificent field where he'd watched the king become King of Season. He longed for his king. For the kind and gentle man that ruled with a firm hand but intelligent mind. He longed for the loyalty he did not feel toward the king's wife. But he knew that loyalty was now with the king's daughters, as was entrusted upon him. He was to prepare the Four in the king's absence. He would be the reason the king's dream of stronger leaders would fail or succeed.

In the middle of the field was a huge, glistening golden tree. The tree was the only thing that remained intact from years of disuse. It still shone just as big and bright as it had since the day it had erupted from the earth and Season became whole.

"The Tree of Season. You know it well," Brey said, nodding toward the girls as they looked at their identical necklaces.

The Tree of Season had four large roots, parts of which

could be seen sticking up from the ground, each in a different direction. The roots divided the arena equally into four parts. "It divides the arena, but it also divides all of Season." Brey met the tree and rubbed its golden trunk.

The girls stepped up beside Brey and placed a hand on the Tree of Season. His hand warmed with the tree underneath, diverting the chill of the air. He could feel the pulse of power as it surged from the girls into the tree and back. The Four gave Season its power, and Season gave its power to the girls. They shared a power much larger than even Brey could comprehend.

"Wow," Idalia whispered, staring down at her chest where her necklace laid. It was shining brightly. She took her hand off the Tree of Season, and the light from her necklace slowly inked away.

Brey dropped his hand as well. "The Showcase is made up of five trials. A trial for each of the four seasons. After the four trials for each season, you will compete in the last trial, the Finale. The Finale will lead to the Changing Ceremony, where one of you will be crowned. But we can get into all of that at a later time. Right now, we need to focus on the first trial. The Trial of Autumn." Brey stepped over a tree root.

The girls followed.

"If you were to ride that way," Brey pointed forward, "past hills that turn into mountains, you would reach Autumn." He paused, imagining a place he hadn't been to in years. "Orla, you were born of Autumn, and therefore, lay claim to Autumn and its people. You are queen. As each of you are queen of your own part of Season," Brey said, turning away from the scenery he could imagine and back to the girls.

"Who has been ruling the different parts of Season since we haven't been here?" Orla asked.

"King Quilo, your father, ruled over all of Season. But now that he has passed, the people are eagerly awaiting your return." Brey started walking away from the Tree of Season and out into Autumn. The girls followed without a sound. "You each have a power given to you by your season. We will work on honing that power, controlling it. So that you can use it to pass the trials."

"Okay, now we're talking," Eira said, rubbing her hands together.

"For the Trial of Autumn, you will compete with air." Brey told them. "Here, we can stop here," he said, finally coming to a halt. Sweat threatened to drip from his forehead, but he didn't reach to wipe it off.

"I want you to conjure up your elements," Brey said to the girls.

They stared at him, unmoving and unspeaking.

"How?" Aviva finally asked.

"I forget you are all very new to this," Brey said with a shake of his head. "But feeling the elements is something only the Four have the privilege of experiencing. Your father once tried explaining it to me, but it was lost on deaf ears."

The girls looked at one another, and then quickly looked away.

"I suggest you figure it out quickly. Autumn is coming for you," Brey said and walked away briskly, leaving the four girls staring after him.

His stomach dropped at the sight of their blank faces. He'd had many conversations with his king about the change that was to come with his decision to send his daughters away. Brey always believed the king was doing what he thought was right. What was best for the kingdom. They did not talk about just how hard it would be to prepare his daughters for absolutely everything, which came so easily to the previous Fours who were born and raised in Season.

Brey quickly trekked back to the castle. He quickened his pace and climbed the stairs to the very top. Queen Quinn was already there. He perched at the window beside her, placing a looking glass over his eyes.

Down below he could see the Four.

The sun dwindled. Sparkling lights came to life overhead, making it possible for Brey to see the girls. Leaves were swept up at the edge of the field, swirling in a tornado so fast the leaves crumbled and crunched.

The girls took off running in opposite directions, away from one another.

Orla's foot snagged on a fallen branch, and she went flying through the air. She landed face-first in the snow. She rolled over. She tried getting her feet under her, but a gust of wind knocked her down again and again.

She threw an arm out in defense. A loud whine exploded around her as a current met more wind and tumbled together. A tornado formed, picking up the snow and fallen branches. Orla stood, finally getting on her feet again. The tornado swept her up and spit her out. She landed many feet away, cracking her head on a rock.

Eira stopped running. She stooped down to the ground and placed her hands in the snow.

The tornado headed toward her. She turned toward the sound of the wind and shot out an arm. Spear-shaped icicles left her hand and flew into the darkness. Brey could hear the *whoosh* as the spears met the tornado and were shot back at Eira. She lifted her other hand, a wall of ice coming up from the ground, but not before a spear sliced its way along her arm.

Aviva had tears rolling down her face. The air was being sucked out around her, leaving her with no oxygen. She wrapped a hand around her throat and fell onto her knees in the snow. Dead leaves brushed by her, and she batted them away. But the more she fought, the more leaves came.

They were razor sharp and encircled her, cutting her face, arms, legs. She cried out in frustration and raised her hands over her head. Small twigs and larger branches made a shelter around her.

Idalia ran around the field. She waved her hand out in front of her. A tiny flame burst from her palm, illuminating a small patch of snow.

The swirling air around her snuffed out the fire, and she fought to bring it back, waving her hands furiously. But it wouldn't come. She dropped to her knees in the snow, unable to move.

Brey couldn't watch anymore. His chest hurt with worry. He turned away from the window and slowly walked out of the room and down the stairs. He took the pendant from his pocket and turned the dial. The Four were pulled to the castle by an invisible force.

Brey could barely look at the girls. They were battered and bleeding. "You cannot pass the trials alone. You must work together," Brey all but shouted at them. He turned away from them and rubbed his temples.

"If we have to work together," Eira said through shivering lips, "why does only one become queen?"

Brey whirled around, facing them again. "The trials test your power. The Finale tests your loyalty to Season. It will determine if you would do whatever it takes for the crown. And only one will." He shook his head. Sending them away had been a mistake. It must have been a mistake.

"Go home," Brey said with a wave of his pendant. They disappeared.

19

In the Land of Texas

Idalia shook her head and turned up the radio, trying desperately to drown out her sour thoughts. It was only Tuesday, her one day off a week, but she couldn't enjoy herself. Too many things were whirring in her mind. Too many unanswered questions. And she couldn't, for the life of her, figure out how to begin to answer them.

Her life had been relatively simple up until then. She had made it through her freshman year of college with little incident. All A's, perfect attendance, perfect record. And now, when she really needed to focus on what she was going to do after the next few years of college, her life exploded in all-out war. She didn't even know if there would be a time after college for her. All she knew was that she had time now. It was all that was guaranteed. And sometimes, even then, she could be whirled away to Season at a moment's notice.

Idalia shut her engine off and stepped out of her car. She walked up the driveway of a two-story brick home and knocked on the door.

A few moments passed. Idalia picked at her fingernails, waiting.

The door opened, and inside stood a petite redheaded woman. Her face lit up with a smile when she saw it was Idalia standing outside. "Oh, I didn't know you were coming," her mother said, grabbing Idalia and pulling her into a tight hug. "I didn't expect you until at least Christmas," she said in Idalia's ear.

"Thought I'd surprise you." Idalia shrugged.

"Oh, it's so nice to see you," her mother said. "Let me go get your father. He'll be so happy his daughter finally returned home," she said cheerfully. She skipped back into the house and went to get Idalia's father from the den.

Idalia closed the door behind her and made her way into the living room. She passed pictures of herself with her parents hanging on the walls. From age three to eighteen, her parents had family pictures made. Idalia smiled, looking at them. She loved her family. Even if they weren't her true parents. They were the best ones, and the only ones she needed. It was because of them and their undying love for her that she felt she didn't measure up to what they deserved.

"Idalia? Is that you?" her father asked, coming into the living room. "Your mother tells me you wanted to surprise us," he said, seizing her up into an embrace. "That's so sweet of you, my girl," he said with a twinkle in his eyes.

"Yes, Papa, it's really me," Idalia said with a laugh. "I needed some family time."

"Well, you've certainly come to the right place," her

mother said, bringing in a tray of tea and cookies. Being the ever gracious host.

Idalia sipped her tea and grabbed a cookie, relishing the feeling of home. The warm security it brought her. Nothing like how she'd felt only last night in the freezing cold of Season.

"How are your classes?" her father asked, sitting next to her on the couch.

"Interesting," Idalia said around a bite of cookie. "The semester has only just started. Still getting used to the new classes."

Her parents nodded in understanding, like they always did. Even if they didn't quite understand, they made Idalia feel like they did. And with the confusion hanging around Idalia, it was a nice sentiment.

"I have been wondering about something," Idalia started nervously. "But I don't want you to feel like I'm searching for something else. Y'all are my parents, and no one could ever take your place."

Her mother leaned forward in her nearby chair and placed a reassuring hand on Idalia's knee. "Honey, of course, we understand. What is it?"

"Well, I know y'all adopted me when I was three. But did you ever find out anything about my birth parents? Where were they from, and why did they give me up?"

Her father leaned back into the couch with a thoughtful look on his face. "No, unfortunately we never were able to find any information on them. And we searched and searched."

"We wanted you to know anything you wanted about them. But it was a closed adoption. Even the agency didn't know much about your parents." Her mother chimed in.

"I was just dropped off at a fire station, right?" Idalia asked, taking another sip of her tea. Trying desperately to rid herself of the swollen knot in her throat. It shouldn't matter to her. That she had been given up. Especially since she got a good set of parents out of it. But she did feel bad that she was well taken care of while Eira and Aviva had never known a family like she had. That if she had ended up anywhere else, these parents could have easily been someone else's, and she could've been left in the foster system.

"Yes," her father said. "When you were three years old. In the middle of summer, no less."

"I don't know what your parents were thinking," her mother said, shaking her head sadly. "Texas gets way too hot in the summer to leave a helpless child outside."

It was the first trial. King Quilo had wanted to know if she'd survive. Well, she had. And she'd do more than just survive. She would thrive. She had to.

"Thank you so much," Idalia said. "Y'all are seriously the best parents anyone could ask for."

"The best for the best," her father said with a wink, throwing an arm around her shoulders and pulling her into him.

"I should probably head back to school. Have some studying to do," Idalia said after a while of watching TV and talking with them.

"Of course, honey. Here, let me put some cookies in a tin," her mother said, jumping up from the chair and running into the kitchen. "You sure are lucky I made some fresh-baked cookies this morning," her mother called from the kitchen.

Idalia nodded. "That I am." She laughed.

Her parents walked her to the door a few minutes later. She had a tin full of cookies and a heart full of love for the two people who'd brought her in and taken such great care of her. She was eternally grateful to not have been raised by the harsh

Queen of Season. She could only imagine how different her life would've been and how different she would be.

"Visit soon," her mother said, hugging her again.

Idalia nodded. "Maybe even before Christmas," she said.

"Oh, my girl, don't get our hopes up," her father said with a laugh.

They let her walk out the door and get into her car. Idalia looked back at them, standing in the doorway, holding each other. That was love. A love she wouldn't have known, had her father, King Quilo, not given her up.

Idalia waved and drove away.

20

Eira bent behind a dumpster as beams of lights flooded the alley she was in. She held her breath.

Footsteps bounced between the alley hallways. "She's gotta be around here somewhere," a voice thick with anger rang out.

"It shouldn't be this hard to catch this girl," another voice said.

"Honestly."

Eira put a hand over her mouth to keep silent. She was struggling to breathe, but she had to hold on for a little while longer. She couldn't be caught again.

The cops sighed in frustration and ran back into the street. Eira let out a slow, shaky breath. But still she remained crouched down behind the dumpster. She didn't move a muscle, not for a long time. Not until the day turned to night.

She finally stood, her legs shaking and sore. Her stomach growled at her. She'd been running for days, starving and dirty.

She pulled the hood up over her head, hiding her face

despite it being ungodly hot. She needed to be hidden more than she needed to be cool.

Eira walked the streets, straying away from any source of light. Running across the road to get away from other pedestrians. Her face was recognizable, even covered in mud, due to it being plastered on every TV and phone. She was wanted for the first time in her life, and it wasn't a good feeling.

She needed a place to crash, but she couldn't go back to her bridge. She knew the cops would look there. They would look everywhere for her. And she couldn't leave town without getting her stuff from under the bridge. That was all she owned, all of her possessions, all of her money. She couldn't leave it behind if she was going to survive here.

Eira turned a corner, followed a chain link fence down another road, and kept walking. Her head pounded, and her stomach folded in on itself. She was going to faint. And then the cops would find her. She needed to disappear.

She barely made out a house in the darkness. The roof was sunken and charred black. The windows were broken. Curtains flew in and out in the hot breeze. The door had fallen on the broken porch, leaving it wide open. But no one was around. And Eira doubted anyone would be anytime soon.

She walked up concrete steps to get to the porch. She slipped, her foot falling through a broken board. She froze, waiting to hear if anyone would come for her.

But no one did.

Slowly, and as carefully as she could, she pulled her foot free. It was bleeding and already swollen. She limped inside and fell to the dusty ground. Her ankle throbbed.

A fit of coughs coursed through her. She threw a hand over her mouth to stop the coughs, but it just aggravated the dust even more. She dragged herself to a wall, her bloodied foot leaving a trail behind her.

Eira breathed a sigh of relief when she reached the wall. The angry wound on her arm from the spear of ice split open, pouring more of her blood on the floor of the abandoned house. Well, at least if the cops found her, she wouldn't be alive. The thought put a grim smile on her face.

The Tree of Season necklace she wore warmed on her chest. She grabbed at it beneath her shirt. It glowed a nice golden hue, letting her see a few feet in front of her.

Her arm looked bad. Her foot looked even worse.

"If only I could get this damn thing to work," she said aloud, frustration seeping out. Her words disappeared into the night air. "Take me to Season," she said, staring at the necklace, holding it tightly in her hands.

The glow of the necklace grew, as did the warmth.

Eira imagined Conformity Castle, its large gardens covered in snow. The spiral staircase inside the entrance hall. Her large and overly comfortable chambers. She imagined it all as if she were there enjoying it herself.

The necklace's light blinded her, and she was plunged into a wet, cold darkness that covered her every sense.

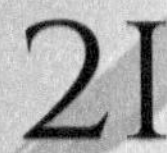

21

Aviva opened her eyes. Light came into her bedroom from the open window. She didn't want to move or get up. She didn't want to go to school for another day. But she forced herself to roll out of bed.

The torture she endured at school didn't compare to the torture she felt being home, she reminded herself.

She saw her reflection in the mirror as she brushed her teeth. Tiny scratches covered her face and body. Tiny, pointed, leaf marks. Luckily, she was a pro at makeup. She'd been covering scars for years. And no one could ever tell. Or they never bothered to question it.

Aviva slipped on a long-sleeved shirt and left her room. There was no breakfast waiting for her on the table. No money for lunch. Nothing. But at least Ted and Kathy weren't awake yet. Maybe today would be a good day after all.

She walked outside, immediately breaking into a sweat in the Texas sun. But she didn't roll up her sleeves. She couldn't. She had too many scars to hide.

The big, yellow school bus rolled up at the end of her street.

She met it and climbed in. She sat right behind the driver, where no one ever sat. They couldn't mess with her there, not that close to the driver.

She made herself comfortable in the seat, bouncing along. It was a long ride to school since she was one of the first pickups.

After a while, the bus pulled in front of the high school. Aviva let everyone get off before she moved from her seat. She threw her backpack over her shoulder and walked through the front courtyard where all the students waited for the first bell.

She walked through the crowd of students to get to the school doors. No one stopped her to laugh or ridicule. No one shoved someone into her. Maybe, just maybe, they had forgotten about her. Maybe they were going to finally give her a break.

"Orla?" Aviva's voice was small. Her hands shook by her sides. "Orla?" she said again, louder.

A brown-haired, brown-eyed beauty turned around to look at her. "Oh, hi," Orla said to her, a smile breaking out on her face.

"I've been looking for you all week." Aviva looked down toward the ground, toeing the dirt with her boot.

"Well, you finally found me," Orla said, stepping toward her.

The bell rang. Students streamed into school, pushing past their stalled group.

"I'll see you around?" Orla said when her friends pushed her away.

"Who was that?" Aviva heard one of Orla's friends ask as they walked into the school.

"She's new here." Orla turned back to give her a small wave.

Her friend pulled her hand down and leaned toward her. "I don't think you should be seen talking to her," the girl said, glancing back at Aviva.

Aviva gritted her teeth and squeezed her fists together tightly. She knew she didn't really know Orla that well. But she would've thought her friends would be friendlier. Orla had always seemed nice. Why would she be friends with girls like that?

The trees in the courtyard shook with the anger Aviva felt. It wasn't fair. She and all of her sisters had been given up, but Orla got adopted by a good family while Aviva barely could say she even had a family. It made her mad to see how different her life could have turned out. How carefree she could have been. How she could have had friends, good or not.

She felt eyes on her. Orla was staring at her as she entered the building.

Aviva let her hands flatten to her side, took a big calming breath, and stomped inside as the second bell rang out.

22

Orla sat on the bleachers with Samantha and Angela, waiting for the football game to start. The bleachers were packed full of students and teachers. Friday night football was back and in full swing.

Her phone buzzed in her hand with a text from her mom. She closed the message, ignoring the fifteenth message since she'd been at the game. A sigh escaped her mouth.

Angela leaned over toward her. "What's wrong with you?"

"My mom." She held up her phone. "She won't quit texting me."

Angela put two hands on her chest and swooned. "I love your mom. She's so sweet."

Orla nodded. "She is, but she's a lot. Dad, too."

Samantha swung an arm over her shoulders. "You think our parents will make a trade? Yours can adopt me, and you can have mine." She laughed.

Orla rolled her eyes. "No, they picked me."

"You're ungrateful," Samantha said, crossing her arms.

A few moments of silence passed as they stared at each

other with narrowed eyes. Then, fits of laughter erupted from them all. "I'm just saying. Mom doesn't have to keep bugging me," she said in time with another buzz of her phone. She typed a quick reply and slid her phone into her pocket.

The football team busted through a huge sign on the field. The cheerleaders ran after them, waving their pom poms furiously in the air.

"I'm so glad I don't have to do that anymore," Orla said, laughing at the cheerleaders as they got into formation for their first cheer of the night.

"Oh, hush. You know you miss it," Angela said, bumping Orla's shoulder with her own.

"Maybe just a little." Orla laughed.

She watched the cheerleaders move around, throw each other in the air, shout catchy cheers. She liked it enough, but cheerleading wasn't going to get her away from her parents. Good grades would. And now, without cheerleading taking away her time, she could devote all her extra time into making grades that would get her into a college far, far away from her doting parents.

"You miss being popular," Samantha said.

Orla's mouth dropped. "I'm still popular."

"You won't be if you keep taking in strays."

Orla raised an eyebrow. "Strays?"

"Yeah." Samantha nodded. "That girl you were talking to earlier. The new girl."

"Aviva?"

Samantha and Angela shrugged at the same time.

"Aviva isn't a stray," Orla said. She could feel the bubbles of annoyance rising. Her friends always had something to say about who she talked to. Especially once she'd ditched cheerleading. It was they who reaped the social popularity she had gained while cheering. Something Orla never cared for.

"Yes, she is. She looks it, too," Samantha said, looking out at the field.

Orla stood and looked down at them. Her head throbbed from where she'd cracked it on the rock. She let her vision settle before speaking. "You know, not everyone is afforded the same life we have. Not everyone gets an easy upbringing. Stop judging people on things they have no say in."

Her friends were too stunned to speak. Orla hardly ever raised her voice, let alone at them. But she couldn't shake the feeling she got when they talked about Aviva. The protectiveness that suffocated her. Aviva was her sister, she knew. But now the feelings coincided with the fact.

"And you were a stray once, too," she said, stomping away from them.

23

In the Land of Season

B rey walked out on the terrace overlooking the gardens of Conformity Castle. In the distance, he could see the gold shine from the Tree of Season. The tree used to illuminate the whole path from Conformity Castle to its trunk. But over the last few days, its glow had diminished.

Season was sick.

The snow was no longer sticking to the ground or falling from the sky. In a single instant, Conformity Castle would be surrounded with great winds, blistering heat, and then frigid air. Their beloved Season didn't know which season to remain.

King Quilo was dead. And with him, so was Winter. And now, Season fought to choose the next season. But it couldn't do that. Not with the Four fighting each other.

Brey went back inside, to his chambers, leaving the confusion of the seasons.

A knock sounded on his doors. He quickly crossed the room and opened it. Talia, Queen Quinn's servant girl, stood before him.

"Sir," she said meekly. "The queen requests your assistance with the people."

Brey nodded. "Very well," he said, throwing a cloak over his shoulders.

He followed Talia down the spiraling staircase to the bottom landing. Queen Quinn sat on a throne mounted high above the sea of people below her.

The people of Season crowded into the entrance hall, waiting to be heard. They pushed and they shoved until they reached the front.

"Winter is to be heard first," Quinn called out over the crowd's murmurs. "In recognition of King Quilo."

The people of Autumn, Summer, and Spring stepped back, allowing the Winter nation to move forward. A spokesperson stepped out of the crowd of blue. "My queen," the bearded man said with a bow. "Winter is dying. It is too hot; our shelters are melting. Our crops are burning. What are we to do?" the man cried out.

"My good sir," Quinn said, looking lazily at him. "There is nothing to be done. It is expected that Winter is dying as the king no longer lives."

"What about the princesses?" someone from the back of the crowd called.

"Unfortunately, the princesses are untrained in their powers. My dear husband did not think of the repercussions Season would face without its princesses," Queen Quinn said.

"But have faith," Brey said, looking sideways at Quinn. "The Four are training. The Trial of Autumn is coming upon us soon. And a new queen will be named within the new year. All is not lost."

"Your Majesty," a Spring folk cried out waving her hand crazily in the air.

"Yes?" Queen Quinn said, turning to look at the lady.

"Just the other day, a fire blazed through Spring, cutting down our gardens. Are we to do nothing?" the lady asked. Cheers erupted behind her.

"Do what you normally do. Rebuild," Quinn said with a dismissive wave of her hand. She stood from her throne and turned her back on the people.

The crowd exploded in cries and shouts.

Quinn looked at the chaos below her, a smile spreading across her face. "My children, what is done is done. All we can do from here is prepare. Prepare for hard times. Save what you can, store what you cannot. A new season will be here soon."

Quinn tossed her hair over her shoulder and followed the guards up the stairs. The screams of the people followed her all the way.

Brey raised his hand, calling for attention. The people quieted.

"With each passing of a king or queen, Season loses its power. We know this. We have lived this several times over."

"But never this long," a man said.

"Or this harsh," a girl spoke.

"That is true." Brey nodded in agreement. "But King Quilo paved a new way for us. He has ensured Season will be its strongest after the Changing."

"If we make it to the Changing," the Winter man said.

"The Four have only just learned of Season. Give it time. Give them your faith. As you did King Quilo. He will not let us down, and neither will his daughters," Brey said in a booming voice.

The people nodded and finally emptied the entrance hall. Brey had spared more time but not enough if Season continued attacking itself.

He hurried upstairs, back to his chambers. He went to his table where a piece of leather lay. He etched a message into its skin and folded it into a scroll.

Brey laid his pendant on top of the table, waved his hands over it. Light filled his room, blinding him. "I call on the Four."

Yellow, blue, green, and red stones lit up, opening the portal wide enough for Brey to drop the scroll into. He watched it disintegrate. Hopefully, the girls would get the message. If not, there might not be a home to come to.

24

In the Land of Texas

Aviva stared up at the ceiling of her dark bedroom. It was quiet in the house, too quiet. She wanted to leave her room, go to the living room, and maybe watch TV. But she knew she couldn't. She didn't want to wake up Ted and Kathy.

It had been a few weeks since she'd been beaten, and she'd like to keep it that way.

So, instead, Aviva lay awake for hours. Trying to force herself to sleep but failing. She hadn't seen her sisters in a while. Orla had tried seeking her out during school, but her friends or the tardy bells got in the way.

Aviva sat up and leaned against her headboard. She reached a hand out in front of her. A tree branch peeked through the open window. She twisted her arm in a circle and watched as the branch extended itself to meet her open palm.

Aviva laughed at the tickling sensation.

With all of her solitude, Aviva had gotten pretty good at wielding the earth. Trees were her favorite. They were friendly creatures. Way more friendly than anyone at school or home. Even more friendly than her absent sisters.

She heard movement down the hall. She threw her hand away from her body, repelling the tree branch back outside. She hurriedly threw her comforter over her shoulders and burrowed down into the bed.

The door to her room creaked open. She squeezed her eyes shut, faking sleep. Hoping whoever it was would go away.

Aviva felt the warmth of a body sit on the edge of her bed. A hand patted her leg. "Ah." Ted exhaled.

The stench of alcohol leaked into Aviva's room. She didn't move. Her body was frozen in a ball. She could feel her heart beating hard. She hoped Ted couldn't hear the pounding of blood rushing through her veins.

"I sure have missed you," Ted said. His words were slurred and almost unrecognizable in his drunken stupor. "Hey," Ted said, his voice rising. He shook her leg hard. "Wake up."

Aviva stayed still. She was squeezing her eyes together so hard she started seeing colors beneath her eyelids.

"Girl," Ted said, grabbing the comforter and ripping it from Aviva's grip. He shook her shoulder.

When she still wouldn't get up, he slung her onto the floor. Her forehead cracked against the nightstand. She raised a hand to her head. It was covered in blood.

"Get up," Ted said, pulling her to her feet.

She tried to pull away, but he was stronger than she was, even when he was drunk. He grabbed her chin and forced her to look at him. His beer breath suffocated her. "When I tell you to do something, do it," he seethed.

"Get off me," Aviva said, kicking and pushing at him. It was the first time she'd ever fought back. The first time she tried to stop him. She had always thought it was easier to give up. But she wasn't the same girl anymore. She was stronger.

"I let you live in my house, and this is how you treat me?" he asked, throwing her back against a wall.

Her head throbbed in pain. And her vision scattered. She tumbled to the ground.

A sparkling ribbon caught her attention from under her bed. She grabbed at it and shakily stood.

She threw her arms up in front of her face as he charged her. But he never made it to her.

Aviva opened her eyes to see Ted looking terrified. A wall of rocks floated in the air in front of Aviva, acting as a shield. She threw out her hands, and the rocks went flying toward him. He cowered, putting his hands over his head and falling to the ground.

Aviva took the chance to jump out the window and run away.

"Don't you ever step foot back in this house," Ted yelled into the night, poking his head out of her window. His voice echoed down the empty street.

Gladly.

25

Orla rubbed her eyes sleepily. She rolled over in bed, covered her ears to try to drown out the constant clinking noise.

"Orla," she heard her name whispered from outside her window.

She sat up quickly and looked around in the dark room. Outside her window was a dark figure. She couldn't see who it was. She raised her hand, and a whistling sound filled her room.

The figure threw up their hands. "It's me, Aviva," she said.

Orla dropped her hand. She went to the window and slid it open. "What are you doing here?" she asked with a furious whisper.

"My foster dad, Ted, he uh…" Aviva stumbled over her words. "I didn't know where else to go," she admitted.

Orla shined her phone's flashlight at her. A shiny, bright red strip of blood slid down the side of her face. A bruise was already forming beneath the gash. "Come on," Orla said, helping Aviva over the windowsill and inside her room.

"Thanks," Aviva said, awkwardly standing in the middle of Orla's room.

Orla closed the window and locked her bedroom door.

"What happened?" Orla asked, looking at Aviva's forehead again.

Aviva lifted her hand to cover the wound. Her fingers came away with blood. "Not everyone has a great home life." Aviva shrugged.

Orla didn't push it. Instead, she walked into the adjoined bathroom and wet a towel. She handed it to Aviva and sat on the bed while she cleaned her face. "You can take a shower if you want. And borrow some clothes since it doesn't look like you have any with you," Orla said with a shrug.

"Thanks," Aviva said, disappearing into the bathroom.

Orla lay on her bed, her eyes fluttering shut with the *splish splash* of the shower running. She was so tired. Mentally and physically. But it couldn't be any worse than Aviva felt, she tried telling herself. She didn't like the weird feeling in her gut, the one that squeezed her stomach so tight she felt she might puke all over herself. She had a good life. No, a great life. Aviva had to deal with things she couldn't even imagine. And Orla complained about her life. She rolled her eyes at herself.

Aviva came out of Orla's bathroom a few minutes later with something in her hand. "I found this in my room before I left. It's from Brey," she said, holding up the tied scroll.

Orla grabbed it from her. She slipped the knot free and unrolled the scroll. The soft leather held steady in her hand as she read.

The fate of Season lies in your hands, and Season is dying.
Brey

"Dying?" Orla asked aloud. "What does he mean by dying?"

Aviva shrugged, looking at the scroll over Orla's shoulder. As if something else would appear. "Hey, look," Aviva said, grabbing an identical tied scroll from the ground beside her bathroom door. She handed it to Orla.

Orla opened it and read the same words. *The fate of Season lies in your hands, and Season is dying.*

"If Season dies, what happens to us?" Aviva asked. Her voice shook in fear.

It was Orla's turn to shrug. "We'll figure this out in the morning," Orla said. "It's late, and we have school tomorrow."

"Will your parents mind?"

Orla was quiet. Her parents were wonderful. They were understanding. But they didn't know Aviva. She barely knew Aviva. Her parents had always told her to be wary of strangers, but Aviva wasn't a stranger. At least she wouldn't have been if they had grown up together in Season with their biological parents like they should have. Would they mind Aviva being here? "They shouldn't. I'll ask them if you can stay a while after school."

Aviva nodded. She looked around the room, searching for something.

"You can sleep on the bed, or I can get our blowup mattress."

"Yeah, okay."

It took a minute for Orla to find the mattress and extra bedding. She set it up on the floor next to her bed. Thirty minutes later, both of the girls were wide awake, staring into the darkness.

"Thank you," Aviva whispered.

"Of course, you are my sister after all."

26

Idalia's phone buzzed in her hand. She looked at the screen. One message from Orla. She clicked on it.

Hey, so I know it's been a while, but we need to talk. Can you meet at my house after school?

She texted a quick *sure* and went back to halfway listening to her professor explain a math equation. She hated math, but at least she was good at it. The class lasted another forty-five minutes. The whole time Idalia fought to keep her eyes open.

Idalia dropped her backpack off at her dorm before heading to Orla's house. Sitting on her pillow was a brown leather scroll tied with a golden ribbon. She pulled the ribbon and the scroll unfolded.

The fate of Season lies in your hands, and Season is dying.
Brey

Idalia stuffed it in her purse and went to the school's parking lot to get her car. She drove the five minutes to Orla's house.

"Hey," Orla said, answering the door.

"Hi," Idalia said uneasily.

"It's been a while," Orla said, letting her pass by her to go into the house.

"Yeah, I've been busy. Trying to maintain my grades and whatnot." Idalia headed into the living room.

"Same here." Orla said, walking in behind her.

She kept walking deeper into the house. Idalia followed her to her room. Aviva was sitting on a blowup mattress on the floor.

Idalia raised an eyebrow. "I wasn't invited to the slumber party?" Idalia laughed.

"Didn't have time to send out invites," Aviva said with a shrug.

Idalia reached into her purse and pulled out the scroll. "So, I'm guessing this all has to do with this?" she asked.

Orla and Aviva nodded, pulling their identical scrolls out. "What do you think it means?" Orla asked.

"Well, Brey did say we have to work together for the trials, right?" Idalia said.

Aviva nodded. "Until the end."

They grew quiet. Idalia didn't like the pit in her stomach at the thought of the end of the trials. If what Brey said was true, only one of them would survive it all. Only one of them would live. But they had to make it through the Trial of Autumn first. And to do that, they had to work together.

"What does he mean by that though?" Orla asked. "And where's Eira? She needs to be here, too, right?"

Idalia and Aviva looked at one another.

"I don't know," Idalia said.

"Eira's running from the cops. She's not going to be anywhere near here, probably," Aviva said. "So what should we do?"

"We have to get a handle on these powers. I'm not taking another beating like we did just practicing with Brey," Idalia said, balling her hand into a fist and concentrating. Her fist exploded in flames.

27

In the Land of Season

Eira landed on a bed of snow, looking up at Conformity Castle, barely able to see it as her eyes failed her. "Finally," she managed to call out before she succumbed to the darkness.

She didn't know how much time had passed before she was shaken out of her daze. She blinked several times, trying desperately to see something. But she couldn't. Her eyes were too weak, and she was too tired to focus on anything long enough to form an image.

"Guards." A vaguely familiar voice rang out around her.

Eira felt her body being lifted into the air and carried across the garden. She floated along, not able to tell which direction she was headed. Or whose presence she was in. All that mattered to her was that she was in Season. Finally.

It had taken her weeks and weeks to get the necklace to

work. Weeks of hiding. Weeks of starving. Weeks of losing feeling in her arm and foot.

But she'd made it. At last.

Eira felt the blanket under her as she was laid on a bed. "Get the mender," the same voice snapped.

She knew that voice from somewhere, she just couldn't put a finger on it. And it didn't really matter anyway. The darkness was coming back for her. And Eira thought it best to go with it.

Eira woke up hours later, feeling brand new. She exhaled, the weight of the world finally dropping off her shoulders. She could breathe easily being back in Season. She was home, the only home she had. The only place she could call home. The only place she was safe.

A tray of food was on the nightstand. She carefully reached over to grab it. There was no pain. In her arm or leg. She had gotten so used to feeling the pain, it was odd to be without it.

She stopped reaching for the food and took her arm in her other hand. A long, jagged scar ran the length of her upper arm. She touched it, expecting to feel something. But she didn't. It was as though her arm wasn't even there. She could see that she was touching it, but couldn't feel the pinprick of sensation.

She lifted the blankets off her body and lifted her leg close to her chest. Her foot was still attached. But it, too, felt like it had disappeared. If it weren't for the angry scar, Eira would've thought she lost it.

"It'll fade," the voice from Eira's dreams said, startling her.

Eira whipped her head around, searching for the owner of the voice.

Queen Quinn sat in a chair in a dark corner of Eira's chambers. Eira didn't speak; she could only stare at the queen. For the first time, Eira noticed the striking resemblance between them. They had the same white-blond hair, though Queen Quinn's was admittedly longer. They didn't share the same eye color, but Eira knew the look her eyes held very well. It was determination. It was the longing for power. She knew it because she felt it in herself.

"Eat," Queen Quinn instructed.

Eira reached over to the food, this time grabbing the tray and putting it on her lap. She ate ravenously. It had been so long since she had good food, a whole meal. She downed the juice in one full swig and wiped her mouth with the back of her hand.

"You've been here several days," Queen Quinn said, watching Eira with a careful eye. "It's time you go home now."

"What? No." Eira sat straight up, panic setting in. "I need to stay." A weight plummeted into her chest, making breathing hard.

"I'm sorry, Daughter. But it is against King Quilo's rules. He requested you only be here when necessary. No more," the queen said with little inflection.

She did not care for Eira, Eira could easily see that. But she had to let her stay.

"He's dead. His rules don't matter," Eira pleaded.

"Law is law."

"I can't go back. They'll catch me, and I'll go to jail." A tear threatened to fall from Eira's eye, but she sucked it back up and covered her emotion with a cough.

"It'll make you strong."

"I'll die," Eira said simply.

"I'm sorry, Daughter," the queen said again, "but you must return to your home."

Eira felt the warmth of her necklace on her chest. Heard the dripping of water. Felt the coldness of leftover snow.

Darkness pulled her under, but not until after she saw Brey step out of the shadows.

Eira fell and fell until she landed on the wooden floor of the abandoned house. Dust flew into the air. She winced and held her shoulder in pain.

She scowled at the sight of the house. The broken floorboards, the shattered windows. The cops would find her here. She'd already pressed her luck too many times. She couldn't evade them forever. Especially if she couldn't disappear.

She pulled herself to the wall and closed her eyes. At least she had eaten. She wasn't going to starve, yet.

A twinkle in the night caught her attention. Behind a collapsed chair, Eira found a scroll. She opened it, lifted it up into the moon's light, and read it.

The fate of Season lies in your hands, and Season is dying.
Brey

Yeah, well so was she. She tossed the scroll across the room. It hit the far wall and rolled against the floor, all the way back to Eira. She picked it up again, ready to throw it away. But holding it in her hand, she could feel the other girls' presence as if an invisible string pulled them together. It throbbed with power.

She would find them. But first, she would sleep.

She raised both hands in the air, moving them up and around her. A wall of ice surrounded her, keeping her cool from the heat. It was the best she could do. Tomorrow, she would do better. Tomorrow, she would find her sisters.

28

In the Land of Season

"It is time you practiced," Brey said to the girls when they appeared in the wide open arena near the Tree of Season.

The girls looked around, dazed and confused.

"Show me your elements," Brey instructed walking in front of them. They didn't have time to waste. He couldn't afford the minutes to let them get adjusted.

One by one, the girls focused. The swirl of air whooshed around Orla. A stream of water floated in the air in front of Eira. Snow-covered rocks piled on top of one another beside Aviva. And a ring of fire encircled Idalia.

"Very good," Brey said, nodding his head in approval. "I see you have been practicing."

"Just here and there," Idalia said with a shrug of her shoulders.

"Wasn't too hard," Eira said with a smug smile.

"Yes, conjuring your elements might be easy. But using them will be hard," Brey said. He finally stopped pacing in front of them. "Season is weak. And because of it, its sectors are in turmoil. We will use your powers to restore balance."

A man walked into the arena, four horses walking lazily behind him. "Kade will be your guide." Brey nodded at Kade. He'd known him for a long time. Kade was the best handler in Season, which was why King Quilo had requested he permanently reside in Conformity Castle and keep the stables.

Kade didn't speak as he walked up to the girls. Slowly, one by one, the four horses sauntered up to the girls. They blew air from their noses and nuzzled into the girls.

"Your horses have chosen," Kade said. Kade walked up to Orla and patted the huge gray horse. There were white spots splattered over its body, and it had a beautiful mane of white hair. "This is Samson," he said to Orla. He gave her the reins and helped Orla onto Samson's back. She wavered nervously.

"I've never done this before," Orla said, looking down at Kade.

"Samson will do all the work," Kade said. He went over to Aviva and a smaller, black horse. "Milo," he said to Aviva.

Aviva gracefully mounted Milo and sat on top of the horse's back confidently.

"Lady," Kade said to Idalia. He kissed the top of the chestnut horse's nose. Lady neighed happily.

Kade walked over to the last remaining horse. A stunning pure white horse stood close by Eira. "Willow." He offered his hands to help Eira up, but she declined, stepping into the stirrup and kicking herself over easily.

Kade nodded and walked back down the path he had come from.

"Remember, work together. And control," Brey called out after them as the horses followed Kade away from the arena. He watched them disappear, his chest tight. He did not like sending them into Season. Kade was great with the horses. But would he be able to handle the Four with newfound, uncontrolled powers?

Brey tore his gaze away and forced himself to walk away.

Idalia squeezed the reins in her hands as Lady followed Kade to the side of the castle. He jumped on the back of a horse, kicking his heels into its sides. The horse took off. Lady pulled her head forward, wanting to follow. Idalia gave her some slack, and she picked up her pace to get right behind Kade and his horse.

They rode past Conformity Castle, past hills and mountains, past a stream of half frozen water. They kept going and going. Until finally, they started seeing cabins. One by one, they popped up along the path. Little wooden cabins. Some were broken as if a huge wind had ripped through them. Some were sagging from the weight of a great snowfall. Some had been burned. And some were covered in vines. Uninhabitable. All of them.

Kade dismounted near a large white cathedral. Lady stopped, forming a circle around Kade with the other girl's horses. Idalia ungracefully slid off Lady's back and followed Kade into the cathedral. Her sisters did the same.

Inside, the cathedral was quiet. Eyes turned toward Idalia and the others as they made their way up the steps and into the building. People in shades of yellow were everywhere.

Laying on cots, standing along the walls, holding small children. They looked tired and hungry. But most of all, defeated.

"The princesses," someone whispered. Gradually, the whispers became louder. The deeper they walked into the cathedral, the louder the chant was.

"People of Autumn," Kade said with a stern voice. Everyone quieted. "We have come to help."

Claps and cheers rang out. "Finally," a few people murmured.

Idalia could feel the not so subtle hint of sarcasm seeping from the one word. How long had they been stuck like this? How long had their homes been destroyed? How long had they waited for help?

The people of Autumn ran out of the cathedral, pulling Idalia with them. The crowd stopped at the first row of cabins. They looked expectantly at her and her sisters.

"What are we supposed to do?" Aviva whispered to the other girls.

"Fix it?" she shrugged.

"Look," Orla said, pointing at a pile of wood at the end of the road. She moved an arm in the air in a come hither motion, and the pile of wood was lifted into the air. It floated down the street on a current of wind. The stack of wood landed at the girls' feet.

The people watching cheered.

Idalia balled her fists and pulled them down in front of her chest. Flames erupted in her palms. The rest of the girls conjured up their elements.

It took the rest of the day to make Autumn habitable. It wasn't perfect. Idalia could see mistakes, things that wouldn't hold forever, ways they should have done it better. But the looks of joy on the people's faces—they had done something right.

It was night when they finally mounted their horses and rode back toward Conformity Castle. The flickering flame from Idalia's hands led the way. The flame was smaller and smaller the longer they rode. Her energy drained, and with it, some of her power.

She could just barely make out Conformity Castle, torches surrounding the grounds. The horses galloped toward it.

A swishing sounded through the night. An arrow buried in the belly of Kade's horse. The horse toppled to the ground with Kade still firmly attached. Idalia screamed, pulling back on the reins. Lady screeched to a stop, kicking up snow and dirt. Her sisters' horses did the same. Trying desperately not to trample their trainer.

Idalia pushed out her flame even more, as far as she could. It burned higher and brighter so she could see better. She slid off Lady and ran to Kade, careful to not put the flame too close to him. He was lying face down in the snow, his horse halfway on top of him.

Blood from the horse's side swirled in a puddle around them. The other horses yelled, their calls disrupting what had been a peaceful night.

Orla and Eira came to Idalia's side. Orla bent down, putting a hand on Kade's exposed neck. "He's breathing. Barely," she whispered.

"We have to move him," Eira said, walking around to his other side, getting between him and the horse.

Idalia shot her flame out of her hand and into the snow. It burned, melting the snow around it. She shook the heat from her hand and helped Orla and Eira untangle Kade from the horse.

"Guys, look," Aviva said from behind them. She pointed to one of the rooms at the top of Conformity Castle.

Idalia looked. In the light of her flame, she could see Queen Quinn turn away from the open window and disappear.

"She had something to do with this. She must have," Aviva said.

"It doesn't matter right now," Idalia said, turning her back on Conformity Castle. "We have to hurry. We need to help him." She tugged Kade's leg from underneath the horse's body while Orla and Eira lifted its belly. Finally, he was free. But he was injured. Badly.

29

In the Land of Texas

A few days later, Brey sent word that Kade was dead. There was nothing that could have been done. He had been crushed by the weight of his own horse. And it was all Queen Quinn's fault. At least that's what Aviva believed.

Aviva and Orla sat at the kitchen table, slowly gnawing on breakfast. They were quiet. Aviva felt out of place in Orla's home. It was so nice and big. Bright and open. She had never lived somewhere like it before. And she was eternally grateful Orla's parents had let her stay with little discussion. They hadn't asked many questions, another thing that she was thankful for. But there was a sticky feeling in her stomach. One that meant she was out of place. This wasn't home, but it's what she had.

"Good morning," Orla's father said to Aviva when he

walked into the kitchen.

Aviva looked up from her plate to meet his smiling face. "Morning."

"Morning, Dad." Orla got up from the table to kiss him on the cheek.

"How did you sleep?" Orla's mother asked, joining them.

"Good," Aviva said, sipping the glass of juice Orla had poured for her.

"You know," Mrs. Fletcher started with a thumb and finger on her chin. "We have a guest room. You don't have to sleep on the mattress on Orla's floor."

"Oh. I don't mind." Aviva looked at Orla with a raised brow. "If you don't."

Orla shrugged. "I don't. I kind of like the company."

"Well, if you change your mind," Orla's mother said, trailing off into her coffee cup.

"Thank you," Aviva said.

"Hurry up, girls. You don't want to be late for school," Orla's father said, kissing Orla and her mother on the cheek before gathering up his briefcase and leaving for work. "Have a good day," he called behind him.

The door shut and Orla, her mother, and Aviva were left to finish their breakfast in the kitchen. "So, Aviva," Mrs. Fletcher said. "How long are your parents going to be gone for?"

"Mom," Orla said with a big sigh.

"I'm just curious, is all. We love having you here," she said, putting a hand on Aviva's arm.

Aviva fought the urge to flinch away. Orla's mother removed her hand and folded it into her lap.

"I'm not sure," Aviva lied.

"That's okay," Mrs. Fletcher said. "You can stay as long as

you need. I just want to make sure they don't mind," she said with a soft smile.

Aviva suspected Mrs. Fletcher knew more than she let on, more than what she or Orla told her. The way her eyes twinkled each time she looked at Aviva, a knowing look. Aviva shook off the thought.

"Oh, they don't mind," Aviva said. "Trust me," she whispered. As long as they still got a check for her, Aviva's foster parents could care less where she was.

Mrs. Fletcher smiled and put her cup and plate in the sink. "All right, girls, I'm heading out. You need to as well."

"Yes, Mom," Orla said, rolling her eyes. "We've only been going to school for years. I think by now we know when it starts."

"You better watch that mouth of yours," Mrs. Fletcher said, bumping her hip against Orla's with a small laugh. She threw an arm around Orla's shoulders and pulled her in for a tight hug. "Have a good day, girls. Make sure your phone is charged, Orla."

"Yes, Mom." Orla sighed.

Aviva waved to Mrs. Fletcher and watched her leave. "Your parents are great."

"Yeah, they are."

Aviva and Orla grabbed all their bags and left for school, riding together as they had been since she had snuck through Orla's window. Aviva liked riding with her. Finally, she felt like she had a sister. A true family. One that didn't take advantage of her. One that didn't hurt her. Even if sometimes she didn't feel like she deserved it.

"See you later, sis," Orla said to her when they parted ways in the hallway.

Aviva smiled. Happy, for once.

30

"We'll be back Sunday evening," Orla's father said to Orla. He had an arm wrapped around Orla's mother. "Don't do anything we wouldn't have done at your age." He winked.

"Well, Dad, that means we can do a lot," Orla said with a twinkle in her eye.

"No, it doesn't," her mother said, elbowing her father in the stomach.

He grimaced in fake pain.

"Call us if you need anything."

"But don't need anything." Her father laughed.

Orla gave them hugs.

They turned away from the door. "Maybe we should call the sitter," her mother said, starting to turn back around.

"Mom, no. We'll be fine."

Her father pushed her mother away from the door. "Let's go. The girls are old enough."

Her mother glanced back at her. "But—"

"We talked about this," her father said.

"Bye, guys," Orla said to them, pushing the door closed all the way. She turned to Aviva. "You ready?"

"For what?" Aviva asked wearily.

"The Halloween party we're throwing," Orla exclaimed, throwing up her hands.

"We're doing what now?" Aviva asked.

"We've been talking about it forever." Orla rolled her eyes. "Let's go, we have to get everything ready."

"Orla, I don't think this is a good idea."

"I know; it's a great idea." Orla said, pulling Aviva after her.

The doorbell rang. Orla went to the door and opened it wide. There was a group of kids from her school standing outside. They were dressed in various costumes, all ready to party. "Welcome," Orla said, her voice pitched in excitement. "Come in, come in." She ushered everyone into the already full house.

"There are way too many people here," Aviva said, coming up to Orla's side.

"Trust me, we're just getting started." Orla surveyed the living room. It was packed full of students jumping around to the beat of the music. Everything was dark except for the lights randomly strung from the ceiling.

More people piled into every crevice of her house.

Orla pulled Aviva along to find Idalia and Eira, who had arrived shortly after her parents left to help get things ready. She pulled them all to the middle of the living room. "Let's get this party started," she screamed over the music. She raised her hands, and a strong breeze ripped through the air.

"Orla," Idalia whispered harshly, grabbing her arm.

Orla winced and pulled away. "What? No one will be able to tell it's me." She sent another burst of air through her house.

"She's right," Eira said, shrugging. Eira called the water from the plants and vases around Orla's house. She bounced the water up and down over the vases.

Aviva laughed. She raised the plants up out of the pots and twirled them around the room. The branches made eerie shadows dance all over the walls.

"Come on, Idalia," Orla said, bumping into her.

Idalia rolled her eyes but lifted her hands. She shot the flames from the candles around the room high into the air.

People all around clapped and cheered. "Great effects," some girl said to Orla when she passed by them.

"Thanks," Orla said, smiling brightly.

The girls dropped their hands, and the house was blanketed in darkness again. "We're getting pretty good," Aviva said.

"Yeah, we are," Orla said, pumping her fists into the air.

"Now, all we have to do is figure out how to get Queen Quinn off our backs," Idalia said.

"I think I have an idea," Eira mentioned. She was interrupted by a guy sliding in between them.

He took Orla by the hands and pulled her from the group.

"Excuse me," Orla said, throwing his hands off her. Her heartbeat quickened. She didn't recognize him.

The guy blew out a frustrated breath. He opened his mouth to speak, but Idalia, Aviva, and Eira stepped up beside Orla. He pushed his way through the group without a word and stomped out of the house.

"Good riddance," Idalia said.

Orla slung an arm around Idalia and Aviva. They pulled

Eira into a big group hug. "Love you, guys," Orla said. "Glad to have my sisters."

31

Idalia sat in Professor Hendrix's class, avoiding eye contact. She hated being in his class, but at least the semester was more than half over. And she'd made sure she wasn't going to have to see him the next semester. Or really ever again since she was changing her major away from his field of study.

"Class dismissed," Professor Hendrix said. "Remember, final project proposals are due next week," he said while the students piled out of class.

Idalia waited behind. Her skin crawled as each student left, leaving her with less and less cover, but she had to talk to him as much as she hated it.

"Professor Hendrix," Idalia said, going up to his desk.

He didn't get up from his desk. Instead, he stayed seated looking up at her.

"Yes, Ms. Gallagher?"

"I had a question..." she trailed off.

"What is it?" he asked, his voice was hopeful as if he

thought she was finally going to take him up on his offer to bump her grade up.

"I was wondering if you had ever heard of a place called Season." Idalia bit at her lips and picked at her fingernails while she waited for his answer.

"Season?" he asked. He shook his head. "It doesn't ring a bell."

"Oh, okay."

"Why?"

"I just thought I saw it mentioned somewhere. Maybe not." Idalia shrugged. She pulled her backpack up on her shoulder and turned to leave his classroom.

"Wait," he said, standing and putting a hand around her arm.

Idalia felt heat rise to her skin.

He took his hand away and shook it in the air. "I can do some research and get back to you. What are you wanting to know?"

"Anything about it, really. I think I read somewhere that there was something called the Four. Season produces four heirs to their crown or whatever. They have to do some sort of tests, trials. The Trial of Autumn."

Professor Hendrix jotted down what she said on a notepad and nodded. "Is this what you're planning on doing your project on?"

"Yeah, if I can find some more information," Idalia lied.

"Interesting," he said, looking over the list he'd written. "I'll see if I can find something and get back to you."

"Okay, thank you," she said. She gave him a sweet smile despite her insides twisting and turning in disgust.

"Of course, Idalia. Anything for you."

Idalia turned away from him, rolled her eyes, and hurried out of the room. She hated the man, but maybe he could help. Maybe there would be something useful he could find about Season. Maybe he'd be able to figure out how to get through the first trial alive.

32

Eira snuck out of the abandoned house and onto the dark street. She stayed out of the lights from street lamps and front porches, pulling the hood of her jacket close over her head until she reached Idalia's dorm.

The other girls were already outside, sitting under a tree together. They were laughing when Eira walked up.

"Oh, hey, Eira," Idalia said.

"Hey," Eira said, sitting down next to them. "We're still practicing tonight?"

"Yeah, of course," Orla said.

"We're just waiting for everyone to clear out. Shouldn't be too much longer," Idalia said.

Eira looked around. There were only a few college students left outside. Some were hanging out under other trees with groups of friends. Some were sitting alone, eating or studying. All of them looked peaceful. Content. Something Eira couldn't feel. No matter how hard she tried. No matter what she did. Peace wasn't in the cards for her. Not after what she'd done. Not after everything that had happened in her life.

"How's the witch hunt going?" Aviva leaned over to ask Eira.

Eira shrugged. "They haven't found me yet, so good for me, I guess."

"What do they want you for anyway?" Idalia asked.

"Y'all haven't seen the news?" Eira asked.

"Of course we have," Orla said. "But what did you actually do?"

"I mean, you didn't really kill someone, right?" Aviva asked. A hiccup of laughter left her lips.

Eira shrugged and looked away. She didn't want to think about the cops trailing her. And she especially didn't want to think about why they were after her. "I'd rather not talk about it."

"Yeah, sure," Idalia said.

"Of course," Orla said at the same time as Idalia.

Silence filled the air. Eira was glad they didn't push the matter. They let her be. But she couldn't push past the feeling that they didn't care to know. That they didn't care about her. That she wasn't really one of them. She never would be. Jealousy hit her hard in her stomach as she looked at the three girls. The three that acted like sisters.

"Look, that's the last ones." Aviva pointed to the last couple to leave the courtyard.

Idalia looked down at her phone. "Yep, classes are over. Everyone should be in their dorms by now."

Eira rubbed her hands together as if she needed warmth. But she didn't. She just longed for the power she felt every time she let the water free. She loved that power. It felt like home.

Orla waved her arms above her head, and a small breeze fluttered around the circle. Aviva called the branches of the nearby trees down to where they sat. Idalia shot a flame into the middle of the group. Eira let the water flow through her and out, extinguishing the fire.

"Hey," Idalia called. She raised her flaming fists beside her. "Leave my fire alone," she said, her mouth set in a hard line.

Eira pushed the water out of her body and let it fill up in her hands. "Don't test me, little sister," she said, a wicked smile on her face.

Idalia threw a flame at Eira. Eira's ball of water met the fire in the middle of the circle. The water splashed everywhere. Orla and Aviva threw up their hands to protect their faces.

But they weren't fast enough. Everyone was soaked.

They all laughed and put out their elements. "We're ready," Orla said.

"I hope so," Aviva said, clenching her fists together.

"I think we are. We're working together just like Brey said. What's going to stop us now?" Idalia asked the group.

"Queen Quinn," Aviva said with a shrug.

"Don't worry about her," Eira said. All eyes turned on her. "What? I highly doubt she's going to try anything with the first trial coming up."

"You're right, Eira. We just need to focus on the Trial of Autumn. After that, we can deal with Quinn," Idalia said in finality.

Everyone nodded in agreement.

Hours went by as they manipulated their elements well into the night. They were having fun, growing stronger in their powers and their sisterly bond. Eira wished she could feel the bond between the others. Wished she didn't have a gate around her heart. Wished she didn't already have a sibling who had not had her back. A sibling who had let her down. Why would these sisters be any different?

"Come on, Aviva. We gotta go home," Orla said, pulling Aviva to a stand.

"See y'all later," Idalia said with a wave.

Orla and Aviva walked through the courtyard to the parking lot.

"I gotta get to sleep, too," Idalia said, standing. "Got class tomorrow."

"Okay," Eira said.

"See ya," Idalia said before turning and walking back into her dorm.

Eira was left all alone in the dark night. She pulled her hoodie tight around her and made her way back to the abandoned house. The only home she had.

She was glad Orla had taken Aviva in. She was far too young to be living the life she was living, but Eira had lived it. She was trying to get away from it, but still, her own sisters wouldn't give her a place to stay. Eira had never asked, but they never bothered to offer. They would betray her just like Samuel had. Just like everyone had.

33

In the Land of Season

Queen Quinn watched her daughters through the portal. She'd been watching for weeks, keeping tabs on them. But not for their own good, not as a mother who worried about her daughters' safety. No, she was watching as an enemy. And she didn't like what she saw.

The girls had grown too close to one another, getting stronger by the day. Brey, of course, was happy. But Queen Quinn couldn't have been more upset.

"Season will be strong again with its new queen," Brey said, watching the girls intently.

Quinn remained silent. She had nothing to say. And she wished she had nothing to fear. But she did. She feared her daughters. One of them would become Queen of Season after the Finale. And where would that leave her? In the same place everyone who came before her had gone. Into death.

"Brey, call Eira to Season." Quinn said. Her voice was strong despite the wavering she felt inside.

"Why only Eira?" Brey asked, his eyebrow lifted in confusion. "King Quilo wouldn't have wanted them here separately."

"I'm the queen, and you do as I say," she barked. She knew Brey was against her. He always had been. She had never been afforded the same loyalty as her husband. Brey was impatiently awaiting the trials and the crowning of the next Queen of Season. Most of Season was. But there would be no new queen if it were up to Quinn. She would be it. She wasn't letting Season go that easy. Not unless she was dead.

Brey did as instructed and called for Eira.

As the room exploded into light and a murky figure began to appear, Quinn said to Brey, "Now leave."

Brey nodded and left the room.

Eira appeared before her. Quinn waited, silent, while her daughter blinked her eyes quickly, trying to get them to focus on her surroundings.

"What am I doing here?" Eira asked. "Where are the others?" she asked, looking around the room.

"I wanted to speak to you," Quinn said. "Alone."

"Why?"

"Eira, my darling," Queen Quinn started. She tried to form her lips into a smile, but her cheeks were stiff.

"Don't start that *darling* stuff. You know we don't mean anything to you. You gave us up," Eira interrupted. She walked around the room, moving away from Quinn.

"It wasn't my choice," she said. A twinge of sadness and regret shadowed her words. A flash of a memory popped into her head. King Quilo sat on his throne, their daughters playing at his feet. She cried as she watched them play, laughing together. It would be the last time she was to see them.

"If I had only been able to keep one of you," Quinn said, "it would have been you."

Eira huffed. "Yeah, right. You didn't even let me stay last time I was here. I begged, and you sent me away." Eira crossed her arms over her chest.

"It would have. You reminded me most of myself," Quinn said.

Eira rolled her eyes, but Quinn ignored it and continued, "I had you for five years before King Quilo decided to change tradition. But even by then, you were independent. And strong, so very strong. You didn't let anyone tell you what to do. You were a terror to raise, even for that short time, but I knew you'd grow up to be queen."

"You know nothing about me," Eira said, turning away from Quinn.

"I know you need Season as much as it needs you. And more than your sisters."

Eira turned back around, facing Quinn. They locked eyes.

"Don't you want to be queen?" Quinn asked.

"I don't care about that," Eira whispered.

"You need a home, don't you?"

"Yes," Eira said.

"Then it's settled. Stay here, and I will teach you all you need to know to become Queen of Season. This will be your home, Eira. Stay with me, your mother. Your family."

Eira nodded slowly.

Quinn smiled. She would do it. She would make Eira the undisputed Queen of Season. She would make it impossible for the other girls to win. And then she would make it impossible for Eira to dethrone her.

34

In the Land of Texas

Orla's hand shot up into the air, stopping Mrs. Banks mid-sentence. "Yes, Ms. Fletcher," Mrs. Banks called on her.

Orla put her hand down.

"Can I go to the restroom?"

"You have five minutes," Mrs. Banks said, glancing over to the clock hanging above the door.

Orla stood and hurried out of the classroom. She made her way down the hallway to the closest restroom. She didn't really need a bathroom break, but she did need to get out of that boring lecture before she fell asleep and got into trouble.

She pushed the restroom door open. It swung easily on its hinges. She paused in front of the mirrors. Her reflection looked back at her. Her brown hair was tied up in a messy bun. Bags were beginning to erupt under her eyes. Late nights practicing her powers with her sisters were taking its toll. But they were getting better, stronger. They would survive.

She splashed water over her face and rubbed her eyes hard. It did little to wake her senses up. She turned around and leaned back against the countertop, crossing her arms over her chest. She closed her eyes for a moment.

Her head slipped forward, jolting her awake. She sighed, pushing away from the counter and making to exit the restroom.

A bright light twinkled in the mirror. Orla turned back and watched as the mirror faded away, engulfed by a small portal. She could see a piece of paper floating inside of the portal, swirling in circles. The paper drifted onto the countertop. Orla grabbed it and opened the letter.

Eira has aligned herself with Queen Quinn. I am not supposed to interfere, but I thought it best you all know.

Brey

Orla's eyes widened, finally wide awake. She stuffed the letter into her pocket and went to find Aviva.

35

"Hey, Aviva," Orla said, coming up behind her in the library. She pulled up a seat and sat next to Aviva.

"What are you doing here? Aren't you supposed to be in class?" Aviva asked in a hushed voice, looking toward her teacher, who sat a few tables away. Her teacher was reading a book and paid little attention to her.

Orla pulled a letter out from her pocket and placed it on the computer desk in between them. "We have far more important things to worry about than class."

Aviva glanced at Orla, confused. She recognized the parchment. It was the same type of paper Brey had sent his earlier note on. *What was going on with Season now?*

Orla smoothed the letter out with her hand. "Look what Brey just sent."

Aviva grabbed the letter and read over Brey's words. "Eira did what?" Aviva said in shock. Her beating heart quickened its pace. The breath in her lungs caught. "I thought she was on our side," she struggled to say.

"So did I," Orla whispered.

Aviva read it again. There was no way. Eira would never. She couldn't betray them like that. Right? "We gotta tell Idalia."

"I already texted her."

"Okay, good," Aviva said, turning back to her computer screen. News reports were plastered on it. Several different reports taking up the screen.

"What are you looking at?" Orla asked.

"I was trying to figure out why the police were after Eira. Trying to see if we could help her somehow." Aviva clicked through a few of the articles, scanning the headlines and details mentioned.

"Did you find anything?" Orla asked, leaning in close as if she couldn't see the screen from a normal distance.

"Yeah, I think so." Aviva clicked on an article. "Look at this," she said, scrolling through the words. She clicked on a link that brought her to a new page. The headline read:

FOSTER FAMILY: ONE DEAD, ONE MISSING.

Orla quickly read through the article. "You think Eira killed her foster brother?"

"I don't know, but I definitely think the police believe she did."

"Why don't you think she did it?" Orla asked.

"Because, look," Aviva said, pointing to a section of the article where it talked about the foster family. "Samuel was Eira's foster brother. What if it was self-defense?"

"Self-defense? It doesn't say anything about that."

Aviva nodded, clicking to another article that showed a picture of Eira and Samuel. They were laughing, their arms draped over one another. There was a look in Eira's eyes Aviva hadn't ever seen. A look of love. Family. Home. "Something just doesn't add up. One of them must have snapped."

"Does that really happen?" Orla asked, her eyes glued to the screen.

"More than you know," Aviva whispered.

"So after that, Eira just disappeared?"

"Yeah, I mean, wouldn't you? If the cops thought you killed someone?" Aviva asked.

Orla shrugged. "I guess, but why didn't they just ask the parents?"

Aviva clicked back to another article. "They did, but they weren't home when it happened, so they didn't know anything."

"Wow," Orla whispered. Orla's phone beeped. She looked down at it. "Idalia said we can meet at her place after school."

"Yeah, okay," Aviva said. "Sounds good." But she was barely paying attention to Orla as she continued clicking through different articles.

"I gotta go back to class," Orla said, standing. "See you after school."

Aviva nodded and went back to researching.

36

"Ms. Gallagher."

Idalia turned to see Professor Hendrix hurrying down the hallway trying to catch her as she left another class. "Yes?" she asked, slowing down.

"I did some research," he said, matching her pace when she picked up speed again.

Her skin crawled with their closeness, but she tried to ignore it.

"About Season," he added.

"Oh, right. Did you find anything?" Idalia asked, trying to keep her voice level.

"Not much. But if you want to come by my office, I jotted down some notes," he said, looking at her sideways.

"I'm actually on my way out," Idalia said. "Could you just tell me what you remember?"

"Sure," he said, the smile fading from his face. "So, I found a book where it talked about a place that had all four seasons year round. It was divided into four sections, each one taking on the essence of a particular season."

Idalia nodded. "Sounds about right."

"You asked about the Four. In the book it said there would be four descendants, one for each season. At the end of a test, one of the descendants would become the leader of the land. And the leader would decide what season the whole land would be."

"What does that mean?"

"I'm not sure, really," Professor Hendrix said, shaking his head in confusion. "It's interesting though. Where did you hear about it again?"

"I don't remember. Probably just popped up online somewhere."

Professor Hendrix shook his head. "It's definitely interesting. If you want to use it for your final project, I approve."

"Yeah, okay. Thanks," Idalia said. "I gotta go."

"See you in class," Professor Hendrix said, pushing open the door for her.

She walked under his arm, her body revolting in shivers, and headed to her dorm.

Orla and Aviva were already there when she arrived. "Hey," they said when she walked up.

"Hey," she said, unlocking her door and stepping inside. They followed her into the living room. "So what's going on?"

Orla pulled out the letter and showed it to Idalia.

Idalia nodded as she read. "Honestly, I kind of suspected it."

"Why?" Aviva asked with a snap.

"She just never seemed to fit with us. She has a lot in common with Quinn." Idalia shrugged. "I really think she has a personality disorder. I had a psychology class last semester that went over common disorders, and Eira definitely fits the symptoms."

"No she doesn't," Aviva said with her arms across her chest.

Idalia nodded. "For real, she was so quick to abandon us and start working with Quinn when we all know Quinn's not on our side. She's just doing whatever to survive in the moment. She has no loyalty." She shuffled through a few textbooks to try to find the page she had been rereading the other day about personality disorders.

Orla nudged Aviva. "Tell her what you found," Orla said.

"Oh, yeah. So I was trying to figure out why the cops are after Eira since the news never really said anything. I found some old articles talking about a foster situation. Apparently, a foster sister was thought to have killed her foster brother."

"Eira killed her brother?" Idalia asked, stopping her search through the books.

"That's what I think," Orla said.

Aviva shot a hard look at Orla. "It was self-defense."

"That's what you think," Orla said, looking at Aviva.

Aviva only shrugged.

"That's really not important right now. What's important is making it through the Trial of Autumn. And according to Brey, we aren't going to if we don't work together," Idalia said, frustration oozing from every word. She was less worried about Eira and her alliance and more worried about being alive at the end of their first trial. They needed to survive. They all needed to survive.

"We need to talk to her," Idalia finally said.

Aviva looked to Orla and then Idalia. "How? She's in Season."

"We've been called to Season. Why can't we call someone from Season?"

"Let's do it," Orla said.

They sat in a circle, their knees touching. They placed their necklaces in their hands. Each necklace began to glow, giving off a bright light that shot up onto Idalia's ceiling.

"We call Eira to us," Idalia said, looking up at the bright light. She tried to keep her voice monotone, free of emotion just as she imagined Brey did when calling them. Straight to the point, no feelings. Just direction.

Orla's and Aviva's laughter broke Idalia's concentration.

"What?" Idalia asked, breaking her stare from the ceiling, but they couldn't answer her. Idalia rolled her eyes. "I don't know what else to say. Just repeat it," she said.

Orla and Aviva breathed in a deep breath, calming their laughter. "We call Eira to us," they repeated.

The bright light got even brighter, blinding them. The ceiling eroded, piece by piece. A swirling portal ate at the plaster. Dust rained around the girls.

The portal opened, and Eira fell from it. She landed in the middle of the circle.

"What am I doing here?" Eira asked through gritted teeth.

"We need to talk," Idalia said.

37

Eira sneered at the other girls. She didn't want to be in Texas. She wanted to be in Season where she belonged.

"Talk about what?" She stepped between Idalia and Aviva to get outside of their circle.

Orla stood. "You're working with Quinn now?" she asked.

Eira only shrugged while walking around the room, surveying it as if she hadn't been there before. She kept her back to the girls, her gaze never meeting theirs.

"You know she's only using you, right?" Idalia asked.

"Using me for what?" she asked coolly, running her hand along Idalia's dresser.

Idalia threw her hands up in the air, frustration seeping all around. "To get the crown, obviously."

"She won't get the crown," Eira said simply, still refusing to meet their eyes.

"What makes you say that?" Aviva asked. "That's all she wants."

Eira rolled her eyes and finally looked back at the other three girls standing in a broken circle in the middle of Idalia's dorm room. "You of all people," Eira started with a glance toward Aviva, "should know that you don't get everything you want."

Idalia stepped toward Eira. "We have to work together to make it through the Trial of Autumn. Brey has said it a million times," she stressed.

"Well, what if he's wrong?" Eira said. "Quinn said that's how it used to be, but who knows about now. King Quilo changed everything when he sent us away."

"Of course she wants you to think that; she's trying to kill all of us," Orla exclaimed, raising her voice. A gust of air shot through the room.

"You better watch out, Orla," Eira said with a wink, "or you're going to kill all of us."

Orla clenched her hands and took a calming breath. "None of this makes sense."

"What doesn't?" Aviva asked, her voice small and withdrawn.

"Quinn. She can't even become queen, can she? So why is she trying to?"

"Like I said," Eira started with a roll of her eyes, "things changed. Anything can happen. But I'm not going to sit around and listen to y'all go back and forth. I'm going back to Season."

"So you're not going to help us?" Idalia asked.

"I'm going to do whatever I want to do," Eira said.

A portal opened in Idalia's room, a huge swirling mass in the middle of the room. Papers fluttered, books were thrown against the walls. Idalia's bed screeched against the wooden floor.

The girls looked to Eira. "I didn't do that," she said in a low voice.

The girls each felt the pull of the portal. Their feet slid across the floor. Eira grabbed hold of a dresser, but it was no use. The portal was too strong. And she went spiraling through it.

38

"It is time," Brey said to the crowd of people standing before him. The people of Autumn, Winter, Spring, and Summer huddled around him in the open field surrounding the Tree of Season.

The crowd shifted nervously, waiting for their princesses to arrive. They knew the future Queen of Season would be among them. And they would stand outside in the mix of seasons just to see the first test. To watch their princess pass or fail.

An eerie silence filled the air. Nothing was heard for miles. Nothing except for the soft hum of the portal Brey opened.

The Four landed in the muddy grass in front of the Tree of Season. They stood straight, shaking off the rough portal entrance.

"Welcome back," Brey said. The girls were no longer the unfamiliar girls he had brought home the first time. They didn't look confused or scared. They looked like they belonged. Like they were sure of themselves. Brey was proud.

"What's going on?" Idalia spoke up.

"It is time for the Showcase."

Orla, Aviva, and Idalia huddled closer together while Eira stayed to herself, off to the side. The clinking of metal turned the girls' attention away from Brey and to the outskirts of the crowd. The people of Season created a pathway, scooting hurriedly away from the center of the crowd. A horse-drawn carriage sauntered through the mass of people, stopping only when it reached the front of the crowd.

The golden carriage sparkled in the sunlight, blinding Brey and the Four. But it didn't compare to the shine that came off Queen Quinn as she stood in the carriage to overlook the crowd.

"The Showcase is a test of strength, survival, and skill," Queen Quinn said, her voice floating easily through the crowd. "My four daughters," she said, turning to smile at the girls. It was a proud smile, but it was fake. "King Quilo's daughters are here to show us their power. This is only the first trial, and it will not be their last. Only one will be Queen of Season. Let us watch as they take their first step on the journey to queendom."

The crowd erupted in deafening cheers. Their hands gathered in a thundering clap.

Queen Quinn sat back down in her carriage. Her horse galloped a few feet away and turned in a circle. She slowly stepped down from the carriage.

Brey faced the girls. "We," Brey said looking at Queen Quinn as she walked toward them, "cannot interfere or stop the trial. The trial stops only when you have passed or failed."

"How do we know if we pass or fail?" Orla asked, breaking the silence that had fallen on them.

"If you fail, you'll all be dead," Queen Quinn said with a flip of her hand. "I suggest not dying," she said.

"Do all that you can. Work together. Be strong. Find Autumn," Brey said.

The girls nodded in agreement. "We will," Orla said quietly.

"Now, go place your hands on the Tree of Season and stay alive." Brey motioned for them to go to the tree. He turned and held out an arm for Queen Quinn. She wound her arm through his.

The girls stood still for a moment, frozen.

Eira made the first step toward the tree. The others followed, leaving the people of Season behind and staring off into the distance as their princesses headed to battle.

Brey smiled sadly as he turned and led Queen Quinn away.

39

Orla stepped up to the Tree of Season. She placed her hand on the trunk. The tree was warm under her touch. And the necklace that hung around her neck glowed with heat. She saw the other girls place their hands on the tree. A blinding light shot out from the trunk, but none of the girls let go.

Orla shielded her eyes with her other arm and turned away from the smoldering tree. Leaves fell around them in spirals, turning from a luscious green to a dead brown. Through the haze of leaves, Orla could see the people of Season on the outskirts of the arena.

A wall of glass erupted from the ground separating the girls from the crowd of onlookers. The tree quivered. Its roots burst from the soil and snaked away from the tree, going and going for what seemed like forever. Orla couldn't take her eyes off the roots as they slithered in the grass across the arena. They didn't stop when they hit the glass wall. Instead, the roots pushed the wall farther and farther away until the people of Season disappeared.

"What's happening?" Aviva screamed from the other side of the tree. Orla could barely hear her through the falling leaves.

Before anyone could answer, the tree began to spin. The earth gave way, and Orla's feet came off the ground. The only thing stopping her from being thrown around was her hand connected to the tree. It was as if there was glue holding her hand to the trunk. She was thankful for it.

"Hold on," Orla heard Idalia yell. But the roar of the wind kept her from being able to respond.

Orla closed her eyes and held her other hand to her mouth. She was going to be sick. But then the tree stopped, and the glue holding her hand steady disappeared. She was launched into the air. She couldn't stop the scream coming from her mouth. Couldn't keep the ground underneath her and the sky above as she toppled across the arena.

She covered her face with her arms and fell toward the grass. Her arms and legs burned as she slid onto the ground. She rolled over on all fours to catch her breath. Her stomach revolted from the sudden stillness. "Ew," she whispered, wiping her mouth and moving away from the foul-smelling vomit.

Orla stood on shaky legs, no longer used to being upright. She turned in circles. The forest surrounded her on all sides. And she didn't see her sisters.

"Idalia?" she called, her hand cupped around her mouth. "Aviva?"

She waited for a beat but heard nothing.

She felt a tickle on her leg and looked down to see a gaping hole in her jeans. She brushed off her knees and winced in pain. Underneath the dirt was a nasty skid mark on her knee. Blood dripped down her leg, soaking her torn jeans.

"Idalia? Aviva?" she called again. "Eira?" she yelled. But no answer.

A blinking light in the sky caught Orla's attention. She looked up, holding her hand above her head to block out the shining sun. The light blinked on and off, beckoning her. She started walking, hoping it was in the right direction.

40

Eira was prepared for the launch. She landed gracefully on the ground. It was as though she spent the majority of her time being catapulted across arenas. Her boots slid across the grass, kicking dirt up around her. Her eyes welled with tears, and a fit of coughing wracked her body. She waved her hands in front of her to clear the air of dirt.

Eira knew she had to find Autumn, a helpful tip from her mother. So she took off in the direction of the blinking light overhead, heading deeper into the woods.

Despite the cool air flowing around her, Eira broke out in a sweat. She didn't know how long she had been walking, but her feet ached, and her face was drenched. She was used to it, though, from all of her time walking around in the Texas heat.

She waved her hands in front of her, conjuring up a gust of snow. The snow drizzled on her skin, and she breathed a sigh of relief. A puddle of clear, sparkling water formed in her palm. She brought her palm to her mouth. She gulped the water down and wiped a hand across her forehead.

She was getting closer to the blinking light in the sky. It

was almost directly overhead, and through a gate of trees, Eira could make out the beginnings of Autumn.

She picked up her pace, her aching feet pounding against the ground one after the other. By the time she reached the town's center, she was out of breath. She bent down with her hands on her knees, trying desperately to steady her breathing. But she didn't have the luxury of time. She knew the other girls were going to be coming soon. She didn't want to encounter her sisters, but Quinn had said they all had to be in Autumn for the trial to end. So she was here, and she needed to hide.

41

Aviva rolled against the ground, her shoulder slamming into a fallen tree. She couldn't get up. She was breathless. Her stomach was lurching in all kinds of directions. Her vision was black with pain. She knew this pain well, having felt it several times before. She was broken, but she had to get up.

She crawled to her feet, her arm useless at her side. She clutched at it with her other hand and pulled it across her chest. She summoned the earth. Vines spread beneath her feet, slithering up her body until it secured her arm in a brace. She shook her body, her shoulder remaining in its fixed position. The pain and dizziness subsided minimally.

Faintly, she heard her name. She turned in circles, trying to figure out which way it came from. But the forest was dense, and her name seemed to echo between the trees.

"Orla? Idalia?" she yelled, hoping one of her sisters was near.

There was no answer.

A twinkling light in the sky caught her attention, and she

took off in the direction of it. Her pace was slow but steady. Every now and then, she heard her name. She tried to respond, but her answer was lost in the wind.

"Aviva?" she heard from behind her.

She whipped around to look.

Idalia staggered up to her. "Finally," she whispered.

Aviva could barely hear her despite being an arm's length away. The wind had picked up. It roared all around them, lifting and shaking the leaves into a frenzy.

"Are you okay?" Aviva asked Idalia, stepping up closer to her.

Idalia nodded. "For the most part." Idalia looked Aviva over. "Are you?"

"I had a bit of a rough landing." Aviva shrugged her one uninjured shoulder.

"You're telling me," Idalia said with a shake of her head. "It would've been nice to know we were gonna be thrown from a tree." Idalia rolled her eyes.

They huddled together against the onslaught of the wind. Idalia lifted a flaming hand, warming them up instantly. Aviva hadn't noticed how cold it had gotten or that she could barely feel her hands and face. But with Idalia's flame, she began to thaw out. To get the feeling back. But with it came the beginning of pain.

"Have you seen Orla?" Aviva asked.

Idalia shook her head.

"What about Eira?"

"No, I haven't seen anyone."

"What do you think we're supposed to do here?"

"Who knows?" Idalia said. "I guess find Autumn like Brey said. Whatever that means."

Aviva nodded in agreement. They hadn't been prepared.

Not really. Not for any of it. Not the powers, not the trials. Nothing. But now they were stuck. And they had to survive.

"We need to find Orla. She's probably freezing," Idalia said.

Aviva only nodded. She started off in the direction of the light in the sky. It shone brightly against the darkening night.

42

Idalia was thankful for her flame, the warmth she was able to bring at a moment's notice. Without it, she was sure she and Aviva would've frozen to death. And gotten lost.

As they walked, the forest grew darker. So dark they could only see a few feet in front of them. Even with Idalia's bright flame shining around them.

"Orla," Aviva called.

"Orla," Idalia repeated. Her voice grew hoarse from yelling over and over. There was no sign of Orla. Idalia could only hope Orla was following the light in the sky just as they were. They were getting closer to the light, finally, after what felt like forever. Idalia's legs were numb. And she didn't know if it was from the cold or from the miles of walking they'd done.

"Look," Aviva said, pointing straight ahead.

Through a break in the tree line, Idalia could just make out buildings. She looked from the buildings to Aviva and back again. "Where do you think we are?"

"Let's find out," Aviva said. She took off running toward

the buildings. Idalia had no choice but to run after her.

Just as she was about to reach Aviva and the edge of the forest, Idalia tripped. She went plummeting into the earth. Her flame died, and blackness surrounded her. She sat up, angrily wiping muddy snow and leaves from her face. She stretched out her hand, feeling the familiar warmth return. She looked behind her, expecting to see a tree branch or root.

"Orla?" she called, reaching her hand out into the night. She climbed across the wet grass to an outstretched leg. "Orla," she said again, lifting onto her knees and shaking her sister's shoulders. She shined her flame at Orla's face. Her eyes were closed, but Idalia could see her chest rising and falling.

"Aviva, come here," she yelled. She kept shaking Orla waiting for her to respond, but she didn't.

Aviva slid next to them. She grabbed a handful of half-melted snow and threw it at Orla's face. Orla jumped alive, sputtering and spitting. She wiped her face furiously. "Aviva?" Orla said looking at her. "Idalia?"

"It's us," Aviva said. She winced as her arm moved.

Orla jumped up, wrapping them in a hug. Idalia closed her fist just in time to not burn them. They were plunged in darkness. "I've been looking for y'all." Orla squeezed them.

"Seems like you were taking a nap," Idalia said with a small laugh, fighting the tears threatening her eyes.

"Ow," Aviva muttered.

Orla leaned back against the tree, and Idalia lit her hand up again.

"I guess I did. I don't really remember how I got here," Orla said while scratching her head.

"There's a town that way." Aviva pointed toward the buildings. "Let's go find somewhere to sleep."

"And something to eat. I'm starving," Orla said.

Idalia's stomach growled. She hadn't thought about food until now, and she realized just how long it had been since she'd last eaten.

Aviva and Idalia helped Orla to her feet, and they all hobbled to the town.

They passed the tree line, but there was no movement in the town. The only light came from a few dimly lit lanterns hanging outside buildings. There was no one.

"This is weird," Aviva whispered.

Idalia nodded.

"We're in Autumn," Orla said. "Look," she said, pointing toward the town's center. The white cathedral of Autumn sat proudly in the middle of the town.

"This is so strange," Idalia said, her voice barely above a whisper.

No one said anything for a long moment.

Aviva turned away, opening the door to a wooden cabin they had restored not too long ago. She stepped inside. "Guys, come on," she called to her sisters.

Idalia turned away from the cathedral and followed Aviva into the cabin.

"We should stay here," Aviva said, melting into a chair.

"I agree," Orla said, falling down onto a couch with a sigh. She rubbed at her knee.

Idalia rummaged through the kitchen and found a few snacks and drinks. She brought them to the living room and placed them on the floor in front of the couch. She lit the fireplace with a flick of her wrist.

"We'll figure out what's next tomorrow," Idalia said. For now, they had food, drinks, and somewhere safe to sleep. That was better than she could have hoped for. They were together. And so far, alive.

43

Knocking woke Orla the next morning. "What is that?" Her voice was covered in a thick layer of sleep. Despite being in a poorly repaired cabin with little food and uncomfortable sleeping arrangements, Orla had gotten more than enough rest. She felt refreshed, albeit a little hungry and sore, but her eyes opened easily.

"Someone's at the door," Idalia said, wiping her hand across her eyes.

Aviva rolled off the mattress they had all shared through the night, wincing. "I'll get it," she said after standing up slowly. She padded over to the door. The loud knocking masked her footsteps.

Orla stood and stretched, rolling her shoulders and bending her knees. One knee was a bit more stiff and burned with the movement, but other than that, she felt good. She turned toward the door.

Aviva opened the front door, her head disappearing for a moment. "No one's here," she called back to her sisters.

Orla made her way to meet Aviva at the door, pulling a

yawning Idalia behind her. They were knocked back by a hard wind. It whipped their clothes around. Their hair swirled around them, lashing them in the face.

Orla's knees threatened to buckle underneath her, but she fought against the wind. It slowly faded away until they could walk back toward the door and step outside. A nearby tree blew fiercely in the wind, its branches hitting the side of the cabin.

"Look," Aviva said, pointing to the top of the largest building in Autumn.

Orla followed her finger to the white cathedral overlooking the whole town. Sitting at the very top of the building was Brey and Queen Quinn.

"Guess they want a front row seat," Orla said. Her voice was hard. She stood rigid. On edge. She could feel their eyes on her. Judging. Watching. Knowing what was going to happen but not helping.

The air took on a chill. Aviva and Orla hugged themselves to warm up. Idalia lit a flame in her hand. It faltered in the chilly wind but held steady enough to give off a little heat to the group as they inched closer together.

"So," Aviva started, turning in circles searching for something. "What do we do?"

Orla stood up straight. "There's something coming." She looked past the cathedral to the edge of Autumn. A vibration swept through her, again and again. She could feel the power around her, the power surging through her town. She walked toward the power she felt. "The air—there's something different about it."

Autumn darkened, a black cloud forming over the town. Orla turned her face to the sky. As she looked up, the clouds fell, heavy water droplets pounding onto the streets of Autumn.

Idalia's flame sizzled out. She shook her hand out, shaking pounds of water off her. "What's happening?"

"Who knows? We are in some fantasy land we never knew about," Aviva said in what sounded like a whisper.

A great *whoosh* swept through the town as the wind became harder, faster, more formed together.

Orla stopped moving, standing in a puddle of rainwater. Her face was covered with droplets. Her cheeks stung each time a new droplet fell from the sky and landed on her skin. The thrum of magic coursed through her. Her element was strong here, as strong as it had ever been. "There." Orla pointed.

At the edge of town, debris flew in every direction. Tornadoes ripped through buildings, getting closer and closer to the girls as if drawn to them. The rain picked up, along with the wind. Slowly, the massive storm ate its way toward them.

"Is this what I think it is?" Aviva asked.

Orla dug her feet into the sopping earth, trying to remain steady. "If you think it's the beginning of a hurricane."

"We're dead," Idalia said. "There's no telling what this thing can do. What Season can do. It just made a hurricane out of nothing, for crying out loud." She beat the air with her fist.

"What do we do?" Aviva cried through the storm.

"We have to stop it," Orla said. Her voice filled with desperation as the hurricane blew through the town. Her town. The town they had just repaired for her people. Why would Season ruin Autumn again?

Orla threw a hand in front of her face. A large piece of wood, from a now demolished house, stopped in midair and dropped to the ground.

Idalia grabbed Orla's shoulder. "We gotta move," Idalia yelled.

Orla let her lead her in the opposite direction of the storm.

Orla and Aviva followed Idalia, close on her heels. They made it inside a building just as a tree tore from its trunk and landed across the building's entrance. Orla jumped out of the way of the huge splash of water grating up the sides of the building.

They ran deeper into the building. Orla wasn't sure the structure would hold against the onslaught coming from outside. The wind and rain increased; she could feel it in her pulse. With each beat of her heart, the storm strengthened.

The hurricane closed in. Orla ducked against a wall in the innermost hallway of the building, placing her forehead against the cold frame. She covered her ears with her hands to block out the shattering of glass in the rooms all around them and waited with her eyes squeezed tight.

A black figure ran through the back of the building. "Eira?" Aviva said, running after it.

"Aviva," Idalia yelled. "Forget about her." Her words died in the wind.

Aviva didn't stop. She disappeared around a corner.

Idalia shook Orla's arm. Orla looked up at her with wide eyes.

"Let's go."

"Let's go? We should be sheltering in place," Orla exclaimed.

Idalia shook her head and pointed to where Aviva had gone. "Aviva took off. We have to find her, now."

Orla huffed but untangled herself from the wall. They ran after Aviva.

They found Aviva in a room far in the back of the building. Eira was on the opposite wall. Both of them had their hands raised. Water pooled around Eira, and broken branches were in the air next to Aviva.

"Quinn doesn't want to help you," Aviva cried over the wind and rain. "She just wants us all dead."

Eira ignored her.

Idalia slid into the room, pulling Orla with her until they stood right next to Aviva. Fire erupted in the air in front of them, ready for an attack from Eira.

"We're supposed to be working together," Orla said.

"Brey said it was the only way we'd survive." Idalia stared down Eira and pushed her feet into the ruined floorboards. She was going to survive, no matter what. She had to.

Eira only shrugged. "Quinn told me another way."

"Oh yeah?" Idalia said. "What's that?" She stepped forward.

"I kill all of you now, and I become Queen of Season," Eira said matter-of-factly.

"And then she'll just kill you," Aviva said. Her voice was raised, her mouth set in anger.

The roof shook, knocking dirt and dust from the ceiling onto the girls. Idalia covered her eyes, momentarily letting her flame go. A beam fell from the ceiling, landing in the middle of the room. A section of the roof was torn from its rafters and thrown to the side easily. A scream echoed around her.

"You really think I can't kill her first?" Eira laughed. She shot out her hand, a wave of water following it.

Idalia blew her flame out from her fists and into the middle of the room. It connected with the water, and a mist covered the room. Orla threw a ball of air at Eira, hitting her square in the chest and catapulting her backward into the wall. Eira sent more daggers of water through the room, striking the huge log Aviva had called over.

"We have bigger problems than each other," Aviva shouted, looking up into the sky.

Idalia followed her gaze. It was pitch black above them.

Idalia tried bracing herself, but she was thrown back against a wall. She looked for something to hold on to, but everything was being sucked up and spit back out by the hurricane.

Idalia watched Orla's mouth move but couldn't hear anything besides the roar of the wind.

Orla grabbed hold of the wall, using it to propel herself forward across the room. She was heading toward Eira. Idalia looked at Aviva, pointed toward Orla moving across the room slowly, nodded, and followed Orla.

They made it to Eira minutes later. Her arms hurt from pulling so hard, and her legs felt like Jell-O. She didn't know how Aviva had managed to follow her with an injured shoulder wrapped in branches. It was hard enough with two working arms and legs. The wind was strong. But she had to be stronger.

Eira lifted her hands up, water swirling around her.

"Stop," Orla said when she was close enough, putting her hands up in defeat. "We're giving it power," she said, looking up at the open sky.

The hurricane was still brewing. Rain pattered down through the opening in the roof. It hadn't died down even though it had been on land for what seemed like forever.

"What do we do?" Aviva asked, coming around the other side of Eira, blocking her in between them all.

"Stop using our powers," Orla said.

"What?" Eira said, "That's the dumbest thing I've ever heard."

"She's right," Idalia said, taking her place to corner Eira. "The hurricane will stop if we do." She wiped the rain from her eyes quickly, making sure to keep one eye on Eira at all times. She slipped as the wind whipped around them. She went down, her knee splashing into the water as she lost her footing. She bared her teeth and stood back up.

"It needs warm water and low air pressure. With y'all fighting each other," Orla said, looking between Eira and Idalia, "it's getting just that."

"We can't just ride it out," Eira said. "We're supposed to destroy it."

"We destroy it by knowing when to stop." Idalia dropped her hands. She couldn't win this fight. Not like this. Eira was her sister. She couldn't battle her. Not in the middle of a hurricane. Not now. Not if they were going to pass this trial.

"I need cold water," Orla said after a few tense beats of working the air around them.

Eira put her hands into the water. Slowly, inch by inch, the water froze.

Idalia jumped up when the water turned to ice under her. "What do you need me to do?" Idalia asked, stepping closer to Orla, partially shielding her from Eira.

"Nothing, yet," Orla said, still concentrating and looking up into the sky.

Moments passed with little change.

"It's not working," Eira huffed.

"Give it a second," Orla said.

The rain kept coming down hard. It turned to ice when it touched the cold floor. Idalia could only hear the *pitter-patter* of rain droplets. No more wind. No flying buildings or crashing trees. The black clouds had lightened to a calm gray.

Orla dropped her hands.

"How'd you know to do that?" Aviva asked, her voice booming in the now still air.

"School. They went over hurricanes after Harvey. Glad I paid attention now," Orla said. She wiped the sweat off her forehead and shook off the excess water.

"You can stop that now," Idalia said to Eira. She was still turning the water droplets to ice.

"I don't have to do anything you say," she shot back.

"If you hadn't listened to us, we'd all be sucked up in a storm by now," Idalia retorted. "What do you not understand about us having to work together?" She took a half step forward, the flame itching to come out of her palms. Eira grated her nerves. Left her on edge. She squeezed her fists tight.

"Oh, I don't know," Eira said sarcastically with a roll of her eyes. "Probably the fact that there will only be one Queen of Season. Not four. One. Which means one, two, three," she said pointing to Idalia, Orla, and then Aviva, "will be dead."

"Let's just go see Brey, tell him we're done," Orla said, rolling her own eyes.

Idalia followed Orla to the front of the building, through the maze of fallen walls and broken furniture.

The town was destroyed. There were trees and parts of buildings thrown all around. Water was standing in roofless houses and on the streets. Idalia waded through the mess, holding onto a branch she had managed to grab.

"How do we get Brey's attention?" Aviva asked, looking up at the cathedral.

"Send a signal," Idalia said, pulling herself close to her younger sisters. They searched the area for something, anything to use.

Aviva moved dead trees with a flick of her wrist, piling them high on top of each other until they poked through the water. Orla blew the pile with a large wind, drying the wood. Idalia shot a fireball to the center, and despite the water-damaged wood, the pile lit. Smoke filled the air.

Idalia looked up at Brey and Queen Quinn. The cathedral had been untouched by the storm. It looked picture perfect to her.

Orla raised her hand in the air, waving to Brey and Queen Quinn. They didn't respond, no matter how much she waved her arms about. "They're not paying attention," she said.

"Because it's not over," Idalia said, looking down one of the streets of Autumn. A huge wave rolled toward them.

Aviva raised her arm, calling the fallen trees. She pushed her good arm out in front of her. Trees, branches, rocks went flying from all around. They stacked up in between the houses, making a dam. "Eira," Aviva called behind her.

Eira huffed, but shot her hands out toward the dam. It froze solid.

The huge wave rolled through the street, gathering up the debris from the hurricane. It crashed against the makeshift dam, sending shards of ice water all around. Idalia and the others ducked behind a wall, shielding their heads with their hands.

The water died down and slowly disappeared from Autumn. The town was destroyed by both the hurricane and the flood. It would have to be fixed all over again, from top to bottom. But they were alive, and that was all that mattered.

Orla waved her arms again, but Brey and Queen Quinn didn't move.

"It's not really them," Idalia said. She pointed to the top of the cathedral. The air twinkled in front of Brey and Quinn. "It's like a hologram or something."

"So how do we get back?" Aviva asked.

Idalia lost her footing. A strong force pulled her back, back through the town, back through the forest, and back to the Tree of Season.

44

"Excellent work," Brey said when he reached the girls at the Tree of Season. His face lit up with joy. He was proud. They had done remarkably well, considering the circumstances King Quilo and he had laid out for them. They had surpassed his expectations. They had survived. "The Trial of Autumn is complete."

Out of the corner of Brey's eye, he saw Eira's hand lift into the air.

A sharpened spear of ice landed squarely in Queen Quinn's chest. Her hands went to the spear, holding it delicately in place. She tried to talk but only gurgles came out. Blood poured down her chin as she coughed.

"That's for Kade," Eira said, going up to Queen Quinn. Eira pushed Quinn's shoulder, and she fell onto the muddy ground.

Brey couldn't bring himself to say anything. No one could. His jaw dropped. It was true that he had waited to see Quinn lifeless. She didn't deserve to be queen, in any fashion. But for one of the Four to dole out such an execution? Unbelievable.

Eira turned from them all and stormed away from the Tree of Season and through the silent crowd, all alone.

"What in the—" Orla said, breaking the silence. The other two stood motionless, staring at their mother's body in the grass. It was stained with red.

Brey gulped. His brain unfroze, the wires beginning to fire again. "You must leave," Brey said, gathering up the girls and pushing them away from the dying Queen of Season.

"What about Quinn?" Idalia asked, looking back at their mother with her hand over her mouth. Her eyes were wide.

"I'll take care of it," Brey said, propelling the girls through the crowd. "All you need to worry about is the next trial."

Brey quickly ushered the girls inside Conformity Castle, away from the people who had gathered to watch the Trial of Autumn.

"Go home now," Brey said, pulling out the pendant and opening the portal. "Don't worry about Season; I'll take care of it."

45

In the Land of Texas

The Four appeared back in Idalia's dorm with a burst of light, a swish of air, the dripping sound of water, the smell of fresh grass, and the warmth of the sun.

Eira stood and dusted her pants off. The others wouldn't quit staring at her. Her skin crawled, but she rolled her shoulders and held her head high.

"Well, I'm gonna go." She walked toward the door.

"Wait," Idalia said, jumping up and taking a step toward her.

Eira stopped.

"Was this your plan all along?" Idalia asked.

Eira laughed. "My plan?" She rolled her eyes.

"Quinn," she said in a whisper. "I can't believe it…"

"Why would you do that?" Aviva asked, pulling herself up with the help of the nightstand.

Orla stood, too. "Why would you kill her?"

Eira looked at them. Really looked at them. Idalia's face was clenched, her jaw tight. A small twitch overcame her eye. There was sadness behind Aviva's eyes. For what, Eira didn't understand. Orla looked as though she might cry. "She needed to die."

"No one *needs* to die," Aviva stressed.

Eira turned away from them. Her sisters were too much. They cared too much. They worried too much. They would never have what it took to win. She opened the door to Idalia's dorm. Before walking out, she called over her shoulder, "No one's standing in my way to be queen. Not even our mother."

Eira disappeared, leaving Aviva, Orla, and Idalia in a stunned silence.

"What does that mean?" Orla asked, rubbing at her eyes.

"I think it means she's the next Queen Quinn," Aviva said, sadness creeping into each syllable.

"And she has powers," Idalia said, staring at the open door. She walked a few steps to close it and turned back to the girls. "Brey is going to take care of it. Whatever that means. We're safe. We made it out."

Orla nodded. "You're right."

"I didn't like her, that's for sure," Aviva said, barely glancing Idalia's way. "But that doesn't mean she should've died. Eira killed her."

Idalia stepped up to Aviva. "Hey," she whispered.

"Eira killed her. She killed Quinn. She probably killed her

foster siblings. She's going to kill us." Aviva looked up at Idalia, a tear gliding down her cheek.

Idalia put her arms around her, pulling her in for a hug. Orla wrapped her arms around them. "It's okay. We're safe. We made it out," she repeated.

"We'll take care of one another, Aviva. No one is going to hurt you," Orla said against Aviva's shoulder.

Aviva took a shaky breath.

Idalia dropped her arms and stepped back, wiping at the tear that had escaped her own eye. "But let's try not to worry about this right now. It's Thanksgiving," she said, looking down at her phone. "Well, almost anyway."

"Yeah, I should get home," Orla said. "Let's go, Aviva." They put their arms around one another and walked to the door. There was a weird feel to the air around them. Something was off.

"We made it through the Trial of Autumn," Idalia said. "Let's be happy about it."

"Yeah, okay," Orla said, faking a smile.

"See you soon," Aviva said with a small wave.

Idalia watched them leave her dorm. She was alone in what felt like forever. She breathed a sigh of relief. They had passed the first test. And Queen Quinn was dead. She agreed with Aviva. Eira shouldn't have killed her, but what else could they have done? Quinn was set on becoming queen. She was set on killing all of them. Deep down, Idalia was glad to know that Quinn was gone. One less thing to worry about.

She left her dorm, headed to her car, and went to see her family, escaping the mix of emotion that boiled in her.

"Oh, my girl, I thought you weren't coming until tomorrow," Idalia's father said when he opened the door to see her standing outside under the porch light.

"Wanted to surprise you, Papa." Idalia winked.

Her father opened his arms, and she stepped inside them, feeling the warmth of having a true family.

Orla stopped in front of her house. Red and blue sirens lit up their street. "Uh oh," she whispered.

"Maybe I should go?" Aviva asked, uncertain in the array of lights.

"No, come on," she said, pulling Aviva behind her.

They walked into Orla's house, passed a storm of cops, and to Orla's parents, who sat on the couch. Her mom had tears streaming down her face.

"Orla," her mom called, jumping up from the couch and hugging Orla hard. "Where have you been?" she asked, holding Orla out at arms' length.

"We were just at Idalia's." Orla shrugged sheepishly.

"It's been two days," her mom yelled. "You should've called." Her mom pulled her in for another hug. "I was so worried," she cried, grabbing Aviva and hugging them together.

"I'm sorry, Mom," Orla said, wrapping her arms around her mom and Aviva. "It won't happen again."

"Of course it won't," she said, wiping tears from her face. She set her mouth in a firm line. "You're grounded. Now go to your room."

Orla bowed her head and walked toward her bedroom. The cops began filing out of her house, leaving her parents and Aviva in the living room. "Come on, Aviva," Orla said, motioning for Aviva to follow her.

But Orla's mother held her back. She stopped just before getting to the hallway.

Orla's mother looked over Aviva. "What happened to your arm?" she asked, holding Aviva carefully away from her body.

"I, uh, fell," Aviva said, her voice low and her eyes down.

Orla's mother nodded and took a big breath. "I have some news. The cops called your parents. You have to go home."

"What? No, Mom, she can't go home." Orla stomped back into the living room.

"It's not our choice. It's the law."

"But Mom," Orla started. "It's not safe there," she whispered.

A cop came up behind Aviva. "Are you ready to go home?" the cop asked.

Orla met Aviva's eyes. She opened her mouth to speak, but Aviva stopped her.

"I'll be fine," she whispered to Orla with a small wave.

The cop led her out of the house.

"Ma'am," her mother said, intercepting a cop on her way out of the house. The cop stopped. "I need to report suspected abuse."

The cops eyes widened, and she pulled out her walkie.

"Mom," Orla said, looking up at her mother.

"I know, honey. I know," she said, wrapping an arm around Orla.

Her father hugged the pair of them, and they watched the cop drive Aviva away.

The other cop came back to them. Orla stepped back and let her mother answer the cop's questions.

Eira sat alone in the empty and abandoned house. She held her necklace in the palm of her hand, squeezing and squeezing. "Take me to Season," she said over and over again.

No matter how or what she tried, the necklace wouldn't open the portal. She was stuck.

She threw the necklace across the room and crossed her arms over her chest. She huffed out a huge irritated breath.

She leaned back against the wall and closed her eyes. She dreamed of Conformity Castle and Season, wishing she could go back and stay forever.

46

In the Land of Season

Brey stood at the edge of Conformity Castle, watching as the sea of people finally disappeared into the beginning of night. Finally, he was all alone. Only the castle remained beside him, silent. Its spiral towers lifted high into the night sky, as if beckoning the heavens to open.

Other things plagued Brey's mind besides the churning sky and crushing wind. He turned away from the rolling hills, the distant horses, and lit carriages. Brey traced his steps back through the garden, the same journey he had made not even an hour prior.

The Tree of Season spread out before Brey. Golden leaves fell around him, swirling in the wind. Four roots snaked away from the center of the tree, dividing Season into four sections. Brey trudged through the mud as he came upon the tree. There were several sets of footsteps leading up to the Tree of Season.

A tightening filled Brey's chest. He wanted to close his eyes, but he refused. He needed to see what was before him. He needed to see the body of his dead queen.

Five pairs of footsteps were etched into the dirt around the tree. He recalled the scene from earlier.

The Four faded into view in front of the Tree of Season. They were stained with mud, covered with leaves, holding bruised and injured limbs. But their faces were bright. They had completed their first trial. Survived the hurricane and flash flood Autumn threw at them. It was over. Only three trials and the Finale were left. A warmth spread into Brey's chest as he remembered the pride he had felt.

Queen Quinn had stood beside Brey, frozen and unemotional as he congratulated her four daughters. And before Brey knew it, an ice spear catapulted through the air and struck his queen in the chest. She had fallen, blood pouring from her chest.

Brey knelt down to a puddle. He dipped his finger into the mud, rubbing it between two fingers. It was tinged with blood, but it was no longer fresh. He wiped his hand on the side of his pants. He stood, surveying the area. The only footpaths were to and from the castle. There were no imprints besides the five that he could account for. No one had disturbed the landscape.

There was blood but no body. His queen had disappeared. Vanished into thin air.

He ran from the tree back to Conformity Castle. He had to tell the Four.

47

In the Land of Texas

Eira banged her head against the dirty wall. A puff of dirt surrounded her, and she coughed through it. Her eyes welled with tears. She couldn't tell if it was from the dust or the suffocating feeling inside her chest. She didn't like the tremble of her hands or the quiver of her lips. She wasn't used to the emotion erupting from her, and she tried to brush it aside.

Eira let out a frustrated scream.

Slowly, she rose to her feet. Her legs throbbed. Electricity raced through them as they woke up. She had been sitting for a long time. She didn't know for how long, just that night had turned to day.

She walked a few steps across the wooden floor to the opposite wall. She bent down, weaving her hand around dust bunnies. She covered her mouth as dust rose.

A bright light burst from underneath her hand. A shocking warmth flooded into her cold body. She picked up the glowing necklace and looked at it.

The diamond-studded gold circle encased a golden tree. Four roots spread out in different directions, each with a small stone on a root. Her favorite stone, the blue sapphire, shone brightly up into the dark room. It illuminated the entirety of the room in a blue hue. It reminded Eira of her sapphire-covered room back in Season.

"Take me to Season," she said through gritted teeth as she glared down at the necklace. "Please," she begged.

A tear fell from her eye and dropped onto the necklace. She closed her fist around the necklace and contemplated throwing it again. Maybe even breaking it. But then she'd never make it to Season. And that was all she wanted. To go back to Season, the only place she felt like she belonged.

Her stomach rumbled. She groaned at the hunger pains beginning to creep up on her. How long had it been since she ate?

She crossed the room and peeked outside. Bright, blinding light flowed into her eyes. She shot a hand up to cover her eyes from the onslaught of sunlight. Once her eyes adjusted, she saw people walking the streets too close to the abandoned house for comfort. She couldn't leave in the daylight, so she'd have to starve. But Eira was used to starving. Her days of living on the streets prepared her.

She pushed the hunger from her mind and went back into the cool darkness of what she guessed used to be a living room. She had spent quite a few nights in the abandoned house.

She had definitely lucked into finding this place just when she needed it most. Surprisingly, the cops hadn't found her.

They were probably still canvassing the streets, looking into every homeless person. *Good.* She closed her eyes and leaned against the wall.

Eira nodded off, sleeping the day away. Hoping to make it to the night so she could sneak out and find some food.

A *whoosh* woke Eira out of her light sleep.

She opened her eyes with a groan. Her head throbbed. She was starving, but she ignored the grumbling of her stomach. Instead, she searched for the source of the sound, looking out into the middle of the living room.

She scrambled to stand and took a few steps to the center of the room. There was a wavering in the air around her. And a strong breeze of ice cold wind threatened to push her down, but she stood her ground. She reached her hands out in front of her, into what looked like empty space.

An electric shock wracked her body. She shook her head and widened her hands out in front of her, pulling at the air.

In between her outstretched hands, the air changed. It was no longer the dark, dusty room of the abandoned house in front of her. Instead, a great castle stood at the back of luscious green hills speckled with the beginning of snow.

She stepped through the portal, her shoes landing on soft, mushy grass.

"Season," she whispered as she took in the beautiful castle in front of her. Its tall towers reached up into the glistening twilight.

"I'm home." Eira pushed her feet to a run.

She catapulted forward, down a rolling hill. Her foot slipped on the wet grass, and she went flying through the air. She tumbled down the hill, kicking up slick snow and wet mud. She put her arms out, trying to stop herself, but she kept rolling until she landed at the base of the hill.

Eira shook herself off, dusted her pants clean of the ice, and walked the rest of the way to the castle. Lanterns were lit along the stairs, lighting her path. She started up the stairs, walking toward voices.

But she froze.

She couldn't be here. She had killed the queen. Brey would have questions she couldn't answer. She had to get away.

Eira ducked behind a bush, hiding from a few of the cooking staff. She watched through the bush as a big, burly woman with a tight bun dumped a bucket of soup off the steps. Her stomach screamed in protest. She clutched at it, bending down even more to remain invisible.

The burly woman and an assistant went back into the castle. Eira waited a few beats before standing and sprinting away from the castle.

Eira tiptoed around the stables waiting to see someone, but no one was there. She slowly opened the barn door and walked inside. A blast of warm air hit her face, and she welcomed the change of temperature. She walked through the barn, all the way to the end. She poked her head over the gate to see a pure white horse laying in the middle of a pile of hay.

Eira opened the gate and stepped inside. Willow's eyes opened, and she stood, towering over Eira. Eira stepped closer, reaching out a hand to pet the horse's neck. Willow nuzzled its nose into Eira's hand and neighed softly.

"Want to go for a ride?" Eira threw a blanket and saddle over the horse's back.

Eira led Willow outside into the cold wind. She put a leg in the stirrup and pulled herself onto the horse's back. She leaned down, throwing an extra blanket around her shoulders.

"Willow," Eira called over the wind. "Take me to Winter."

48

In the Land of Texas

Aviva was frozen in the back seat of the cop car. She looked forward, straight out at the road, not daring to glance at the house to her right.

In her peripheral vision, she could see the uniformed cop saunter up the sandy driveway. He made his way up the porch steps and stopped at the blue door, lifting a hand to knock. He quickly rapped on the door twice with his fist. He put his hands on his hips, turning to look back at Aviva and his partner with a shrug.

After what felt like eternity for Aviva, the door opened.

She closed her eyes so tight colorful dots popped behind her eyelids. She wanted to run away, to go back to Orla's house where it was safe. Where she had felt loved.

"Let's go," the partner said, opening Aviva's door and moving to the side.

Aviva slid against the leather seat, touched her feet to the ground, and froze. A chill ran down her spine as she looked at Ted and Kathy standing at the top of the porch. She could feel their anger. Sense their hate for her.

The partner placed a warm hand on Aviva's back, careful not to touch her battered arm and led her toward the house.

It was a house Aviva never liked. One that never felt like home. Where she was scolded, hit, grounded, abused. Where she was a prisoner and her captors were master manipulators. Ted and Kathy were the one of the worst things to ever happen to her. But she knew she couldn't tell anyone. She'd tried that already. And her caseworker hadn't done anything. She looked up at the cop, opened her mouth to say something. But then shook her head and thought better of it. She wouldn't do anything. No one did.

"It'll be okay," the partner said, leaning down to whisper into Aviva's ear. She slipped a card into Aviva's hand. "Please call if you ever need help. And we'll be in touch with your caseworker."

Aviva knew better than to get her hopes up.

"Oh, Aviva," Kathy cried, embracing her. She hugged too tightly around Aviva's injured arm.

Aviva bit down on her lip to stop the quiver of pain.

"My baby, are you okay? We've been worried sick," Kathy exclaimed looking back at Ted, who remained still and emotionless.

Ted wasn't as good of an actor as Kathy. But he was angrier. And when he was mad, Aviva got hurt.

Kathy held Aviva out at arms' length, looking her over, faking worry. Aviva kept quiet, gritting her teeth and clenching her jaw. Kathy's sharp fingernails dug into Aviva's shoulders. Aviva wanted to shake her off, but she knew it was best not to move. Best to let Kathy pretend to be a loving and doting mother.

"Mr. and Mrs. Johnson, sorry for all the trouble—"

"Oh, it's no trouble," Kathy said, interrupting the cop. "We're just so glad to have Aviva home and safe. We were so sick with worry," she said.

The cop nodded. "Stay out of trouble, kid," the cop said to Aviva, tipping his head and leading his partner back to the car. The partner paused at her door before getting into the passenger's seat. She turned and looked back at Aviva sandwiched between Kathy and Ted. She shook her head sadly and slid into the car, leaving Aviva all alone with her foster parents.

Ted's hand dug into Aviva's shoulder. She held her breath, not letting the pain show. She had to keep a happy face until the cop car pulled away. When the car disappeared from sight, Ted whipped Aviva around to face him. He leaned down, face to face. Aviva was assaulted by a breath of alcohol.

She wanted to cover her mouth, to stave off the gagging she could feel building in the pit of her stomach. But she didn't dare move.

"Now you listen here," Ted said through gritted teeth, "if you ever try to pull a stunt like this again, we'll send you back to where you came from." His eyes were shining with hatred and his fingers burrowed into Aviva's skin. "Is that what you want?"

Aviva shook her head even though a part of her wouldn't mind being rid of Kathy and Ted. She would do almost anything to get away from them, but she wouldn't go back into the system. Not when she was this close to being out.

She took a big, deep breath. Two more years. That's all she had left with the Johnsons. Two years until she could run away and never look back. But for now, she was stuck.

"Get inside," Ted said, pulling away from Aviva and pushing her toward the door.

Slowly, Aviva took a step forward. She waited for the blow to the back of her head that she just knew was coming. But it didn't.

She walked inside. "Go to your room," Kathy said, closing the front door. "And don't you think about coming out," she said, wagging her finger in the air.

Aviva wouldn't dream of it.

49

Idalia sat by herself in a dark house. Her extended family had come and gone for Thanksgiving. Only her parents remained in the house. But they were asleep, tucked away in the back corner. And she was finally all alone.

It had been days since she'd been alone. Days since she'd been able to think straight. Days since she and her three sisters had to fight their way through an enchanted town. Days since one of her sisters killed their biological mother.

She laid her head in her hands, and a sob escaped her mouth.

Her head snapped up as footsteps sounded down the hall. "Are you okay, honey?" her mother's soft voice asked as she walked into the living room.

"Yeah, Mom, I'm fine."

"Are you sure? You've seemed down lately," Idalia's mother said, walking past her to get to the kitchen. Idalia heard as she opened a cabinet and pulled down a glass. She waited for the faucet to turn off before talking again. "What's been going on?"

"You wouldn't believe me if I told you," Idalia said, not meeting her mother's eyes as she walked back into the living room.

Her mother sat on the couch next to her and pulled her close.

"Try me," she said.

Idalia wanted so badly to tell her mother everything. About finding an enchanted necklace that sent her to a world far away. About the three sisters she had found. About her biological father, the king of Season, dying and leaving her mother in charge. About having powers and having to use those powers to fight her sisters or die. But she couldn't talk about any of those things. Her mother wouldn't believe her. Who would? What sane person would believe that a fantasy land existed? Or that she was in the running to be its queen?

"It's really nothing, Mom. Just a lot going on with school and everything."

Her mother shook her head and took a sip of her water. "Okay, honey. If you ever want to talk about things, you know where to find me," she said while standing up from the couch. "I'm going back to bed."

"Okay, night." Idalia settled back into the couch.

"Oh, honey," her mother said, stopping on the way out of the living room. "Don't classes start back up soon?"

Idalia nodded. "Yeah, I'm heading back to campus tomorrow."

She nodded, turned, and walked into the back of the house. Idalia heard the bedroom door close and closed her eyes with it. She was tired. Mentally. Physically. Maybe even emotionally.

Idalia opened her eyes, rubbing them vigorously to stop the burning from the onslaught of light. She stumbled to her feet, keeping one hand in front of her eyes and the other outstretched in front of her.

"Well, look who finally decided to wake up," Idalia's father said when she entered the kitchen. He was sitting at the table, a cup of coffee in his hand and the newspaper laid out before him.

"Hard not to when it's so bright in here." She rolled her eyes.

Her father stood, came around the side of the table, and kissed her on the cheek. "I'm going to work. Are you going back to campus?"

"Yeah, in a little bit."

"All right." He brought her to his side for a hug. "I hope to see you soon, my girl."

"You will, Papa," Idalia said with a smile.

Her father smiled and dumped his coffee into the kitchen sink. He kissed Idalia's mother and walked out of the door. Her mother looked lovingly after him as the door shut.

"I have to get ready, too," her mother said. "Text me when you get back to campus?"

Idalia nodded. "Of course."

"I love you."

"I love you, too." Her mother gave her a quick hug and scurried off to her room to get dressed.

Idalia went to the guest room where she'd been staying over the Thanksgiving holiday. She showered and packed up all of her things. About an hour later, she plopped into her car and drove away from her parents' house.

She wasn't ready to go back to campus. Wasn't ready to focus on school. And definitely wasn't ready to face her sisters and Season again.

50

Orla stared at her bedroom door, or rather where it was before her parents had taken it down. She had forgotten what it was like to have any sense of privacy. It had only been a week since her parents grounded her, but it felt like an eternity.

She could hear her parents rummaging around in the living room, and she wanted to join them but she was mad. Mad that they would punish her for disappearing the week of Thanksgiving when it wasn't her fault. She'd had no say in being pulled into Season for the Trial of Autumn, and if it were up to her, she wouldn't have gone.

But it wasn't up to her, and she couldn't leave her sisters to fight for Season alone.

A knock sounded on the side of the doorframe. Orla's father poked his head into her room. "Hey, what are you doing, kiddo?"

"Not much, Dad. The same thing I've been doing for the last week. Which is nothing, especially since I was fired from missing work so much," Orla said with a roll of her eyes.

He sauntered into her room and took a seat next to her on the bed. Her mother followed him. "We've been thinking," he said, looking up at her mother.

Her mother nodded, urging him to go on.

"With school starting back up again, we're going to give you your phone back."

Orla's eyes grew in size as she watched her father pull her phone from his pocket.

"But," her mother chimed in with a stern look, "you only get it while at school. Once you get home, you have to put it up."

Orla nodded vigorously, her gaze never leaving her phone.

"And," her father said, holding the phone just out of reach, "you're still grounded. So what does that mean?"

"No going out, no after school activities, come home straight after school," Orla rattled off with a roll of her eyes.

"You know, if you keep rolling your eyes, they're going to get stuck up there," her father said. He finally placed Orla's phone in her hand. "We love you," he said.

"Love you, too, Dad," she said, not looking up as she scrolled through her messages.

He stood, looking down at her, and shook his head. "I hope you think twice before disappearing again."

"You really scared us," her mother said softly. She pulled Orla into a hug, squeezing her shoulder tight.

Orla tried swallowing through the lump in her throat. She couldn't say anything as her parents left her room. She had felt terrible when she had finally made it home after the Trial of Autumn. There had been a mountain of police in and outside her house. And her mother and father had looked so worried. And all she could do was lie about where she'd been. No one would have believed her if she'd told the truth.

51

In the Land of Season

Bright light shone straight into Eira's eyes. She rolled away from the light, across the padded floor, and covered her face. She didn't want to get up. She was too tired.

Willow nuzzled her side, making it impossible for Eira to doze off. "What do you want, Willow?" Eira asked the horse, turning to look at her. The sunlight hit the horse's mane perfectly, glistening off her pure white hair.

Willow stood, stomping her feet against the wooden floor.

"Okay, okay. I'm up," Eira muttered, rolling her eyes. Eira crawled over to a pail of water and splashed cold water on her face. Her eyes widened, and her cheeks flushed with the sudden onslaught of temperature.

Willow pranced to the door, begging to go outside. "I guess today's the day," Eira said, standing up. She straightened her shoulders, dusted the hay off her pants, and met Willow at the door.

Eira poked her head outside. The streets were filled with people going from one place to another. Kids ran freely with smiles on their faces. They bundled up snowballs and threw them at each other. Their laughter filled the town.

"Let's get this over with," she said, pushing open the barn door and walking out into the street.

Eira kept her head held high, despite the sinking feeling in her stomach.

The children stopped their games, snowballs falling from their hands. Townspeople froze in their places. And then the whispers started.

"It's Lady Eira," some woman said, motioning to her friends.

"Princess of Water," someone whispered when Eira passed by.

Eira kept walking, not sure where she was going but making sure everyone saw her. This was her town. She belonged here. She had to belong here.

A group of men stood in the center of town. Eira led Willow right up to them. The men stopped their chattering.

One met Eira's cold blue eyes. He dropped to a knee and bowed his head. "Princess of Winter," he said loudly. His companions kneeled beside him. "What have we done to deserve the honor of your presence?"

Eira turned away, making a circle. The townspeople had followed her. Eira's heart beat hard. She was sure it would break free. She swallowed through the thick lump in her throat. "I'm looking for a place to stay," she said, her voice wavering. She wasn't used to people looking at her and actually seeing her.

"Of course, my princess. We will set up the manor for you," the man said, still kneeling at her feet.

Eira nodded. "Make it quick. I'm starving," she said. Her voice was stronger, harder.

The man bowed even farther, his nose almost touching the snow. "Anything else we may do for you?"

Eira took a moment to think. She had a group of men stooping at her feet and a whole town waiting to do her bidding.

"No, that is all."

"Yes, my queen," the man said. He stood, raising a hand in the air. "The Future Queen of Season is here," he yelled, his voice echoing all around the town. He placed a hand over his heart and bent his head.

A loud ruffle was all Eira could hear as the townspeople fell to their knees. "Our queen is here," they chanted. Their voices filled every crevice of Winter.

Eira's chest tightened. She had never been named queen of anything. Never had power over anything. Over anyone. Not even herself. She rolled the sick feeling from her shoulders. Being queen would take some getting used to.

The man stepped up beside Eira, offering his arm. Eira wrapped a hand around it wearily.

"Right this way," he said, walking away from the kneeling townspeople. "Welcome to Winter."

52

In the Land of Texas

Aviva sat in the library, in front of a computer screen, scrolling through articles as her teacher walked around monitoring. It was only a computer class, so Aviva didn't know what the teacher was actually monitoring. But it was fine with Aviva, she had uninterrupted time to herself.

No one talked to her, or even bothered to glance her way. There were whispers all around. Whispers of the fun things her classmates had done over Thanksgiving break and their plans for Christmas break. Aviva tried to ignore them. She didn't have the luxury of fun. Especially now being back with her foster parents.

The teacher walked behind Aviva, eyeing her screen. But even the teacher didn't talk to her. She was all alone. And she wondered when that would ever change.

A crinkling in the air drew Aviva's attention down to the computer desk and away from the screen. A small gap opened, leaving nothing but empty space. She couldn't see the table below the opening, only a black hole.

She quickly covered the hole with her hand and looked around. *Good. No one's paying any attention.* She reached her hand inside the black hole, digging around the portal until she felt the soft leather of a cloth. She pulled it out, and the portal closed behind her hand.

There is no body. The queen is missing.
Brey

Aviva couldn't take her eyes off the beautiful script. This couldn't be right. The queen was dead. She had to be. She'd seen her fall into the mud with the spear in her chest as blood covered the earth. She had felt it as the blood seeped into the earth, her earth.

"Ms. Fletcher, what are you doing in here?" Aviva's teacher yelled from across the library. "You're interrupting my class."

"I'm sorry, Mr. Barens, but I need to borrow Aviva," Orla said, coming up behind Aviva and pulling her to her feet. "It's urgent," she said, hauling Aviva out of the library and into the quiet hallway.

"Sure it is," Mr. Barens said with a dismissive wave of his hand.

Orla pulled out an identical letter from Brey. "Did you get one?" she asked Aviva.

Aviva nodded, holding hers out for Orla to inspect.

"How is this possible? We all saw what Eira did," Orla said, her eyes wide. Aviva couldn't discern if it was fear or excitement that glued Orla's eyes to her eyebrows.

"I don't know," Aviva whispered. She was still in shock herself. Eira had stabbed their mother with a spear of ice. There was no way she had survived. She couldn't have.

Orla pulled out her phone, scrolled through the contacts, and hit the dial button. She waited, tapping her foot against the tiled hallway.

"Who are you calling?" Aviva asked, swinging her head back and forth to make sure no one was coming down the hallway.

"Idalia," Orla said shortly. "We need to meet."

Idalia was going to regret skipping classes again, but she had to. Her sisters needed her. And Season needed her. And for some reason, she couldn't stop running when they called. There was some kind of magical pull to Season. One she hadn't felt before finding the necklace that changed her life.

She paced her dorm room, waiting for Orla and Aviva to pull up. They needed to hurry.

She looked down at the message from Brey. She couldn't believe it. They'd fought through Autumn, making it out of the hurricane and barely escaping the flood. She couldn't handle another obstacle. They still had three more trials and the Finale to survive. She couldn't handle another person trying to kill her.

A knock sounded on her door. Idalia quickly padded over

and opened it. Her sisters filled the frame. She hadn't seen them since the Trial of Autumn. It felt like so long ago when it had only been a week.

Orla and Aviva stepped inside. An awkward silence fell around them as Idalia closed the door.

Aviva looked around. "I'm guessing no one has heard from Eira?"

They shook their heads.

"No," said Idalia. "And I don't have any way to contact her."

"Maybe she's already in Season," Orla suggested.

"Yeah, probably," Aviva said. "She is the one who killed Quinn. She'll probably want to know what's going on."

"Let's do this," Idalia said, moving into the living room. She sat cross-legged on the floor and placed her necklace into the palm of her hand. Aviva and Orla followed suit.

Their knees touched in a wonky triangle form. They held their necklaces in their palms, facing up at the ceiling. The three identical necklaces burst into light, brightening Idalia's living room, flowing onto the ceiling and walls.

"Think about Conformity Castle," Idalia instructed.

Aviva and Orla nodded.

Idalia closed her eyes, envisioning Conformity Castle. The spiraling grand staircase that filled the entrance hall. The hills upon hills of green grass that made up the gardens. The tall towers that housed their rooms. It was beautiful. It was her other home. It was her birthright.

The space in between the girls sparked. The air separated, and the room filled with electricity. A portal opened, and through it, she could see the castle.

Idalia stood. She stepped through the portal, leaving one life behind and stepping into another. She looked behind her, through the portal, and back into her living room. Papers were flying everywhere. The furniture was scraping across the floor. Clothes were thrown around.

"Why do we always have to do this at my place?" she asked with a sigh.

The portal closed, leaving pristine air in its wake.

She turned and looked up. Conformity Castle lay before her, just as beautiful as when they'd left it.

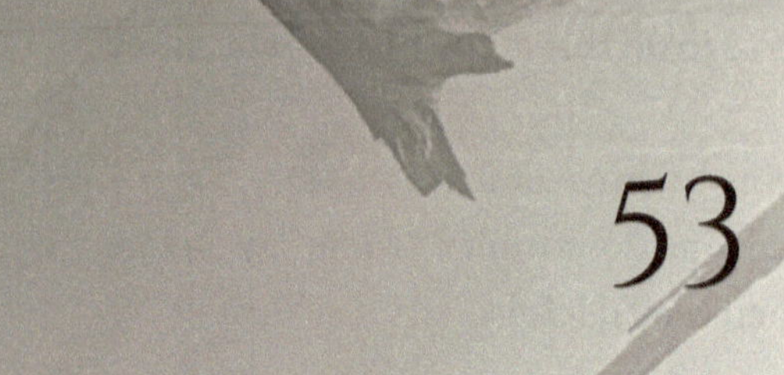

53

In the Land of Season

Orla trudged through the muddy snow, following the path through the courtyard. She could see the golden archway high in the sky above the steps that led up to Conformity Castle.

There was no one around. No noise except for her and her sisters' footsteps as they climbed the steps of the castle. They pushed open the large door and entered the antechamber. The marble floor was as immaculate as ever, as if it had been untouched for some time.

"This is odd," Idalia said, coming up to Orla's side.

Orla could only nod.

"Maybe I should go look for Eira, see if she's here somewhere," Aviva said. Her voice bounced off the walls, echoing.

"I think we should stay together," Orla said. She didn't wait to see if they agreed. Instead, she started climbing the winding staircase in the middle of the entrance hall. She was careful not to disturb the rug that ran along the middle of the stairs, just as Brey had done a few months ago the first time they had visited Conformity Castle.

Her hand grazed the wool that was wrapped around the railing. It was soft, a hard contrast to the harshness in the air.

The girls climbed stair after stair, stopping at each landing, waiting to hear signs of life. They were nearing the top before they heard anything.

"Coming from the bedrooms." Orla motioned toward the row of rooms that filled the hallway.

She stepped off the landing and headed down the hall. The voices grew louder the closer they got. Orla passed the door with a small water insignia etched into it. She didn't stop; she kept walking down the hall, but she heard Aviva stop and peek inside Eira's room.

They passed their own rooms, each designated with a specific drawing. Fire for Idalia, a feather for Orla, and a boulder for Aviva. But they didn't stop. Orla kept walking, farther than they had ever ventured before. Somewhere she wasn't sure they were allowed to go. But they were princesses, and this was their home. At least it was supposed to be.

They passed more doorways, turned down another hall, and then stopped at four doors. The doors were each painted a different bold color. Blue, red, yellow, and green.

Orla hesitated, her hand just above the doorknob. She turned to look at her sisters. Idalia shrugged. Aviva peered forward, trying to see what was behind the closed door. Orla pushed the yellow door open.

Four older women were huddled together in the middle of the bland room. There was nothing adorning the walls. There was no window overlooking the garden. The room was the complete opposite of the girls' rooms.

"Lady Orla," a burly woman said, sauntering over to the girls.

Orla outstretched her arms and hugged the huge woman. "Pete," she said with a smile. Warmth flooded through her.

"It's so nice to see you again. I'm so glad you're back," Pete said in Orla's ear.

Orla didn't say anything; she couldn't with the tight squeeze of Pete's arms. Pete let go and held her at arm's length, checking her over. Orla had missed Pete even though it hadn't been that long. In the short amount of time Pete spent dressing Orla, they had grown close.

A woman clad in blue padded across the room. "Where is Eira?" she asked the girls.

Orla shrugged.

"We were hoping she was here," Aviva said.

The woman shook her head. "No, she hasn't been here."

"Where is she then?" Aviva asked, but no one had an answer.

"What brings you ladies back?" A small voice asked from the back of the room.

Idalia stepped closer to the voice.

"Candace," Idalia said, reaching out a hand to the petite woman.

Candace placed her hand in Idalia's, and they firmly shook in greeting.

"We received a letter from Brey. We need to talk to him."

"Ah," Candace said with a nod of her little head. "Right this way," she said, leading the group out of the room.

Orla and the others followed Candace down the hall, turned a corner, and kept walking.

"Where is everyone?" Aviva asked.

"Gone," the woman in blue said shortly.

"Harriet, don't be so harsh," Pete said.

Harriet huffed. "It's true."

"Why?" Idalia asked.

There was silence.

"After the Trial of Autumn," the lady in green started, "after Queen Quinn's disappearance, Brey sent them all away."

"Now, Lace, that isn't true," Candace said from the front of the herd. "Brey sent them to their homes for the holidays. They'll all be back well in time for the next trial," she said.

"Right," Lace said with a disbelieving shake of her head.

"Here we are," Candace said, stopping in front of the last door in the hall.

A small hand had been carved into the wood. And underneath the picture were four words: *The Hand of Season.*

Candace turned and headed back down the hallway. Pete, Harriet, and Lace followed her, leaving the girls standing in front of a closed door. Orla stood still for a moment, waiting for their ladies to disappear down the hall before raising her hand to knock.

There was rustling behind the closed door. Loud thuds as books fell off tabletops. Footsteps stomped across the room, and Brey swung the door open. "Girls," he exclaimed, throwing his hands up into the air. His face was plastered with a smile.

"Brey," Orla said slowly, her eyebrow inching up.

"Orla, dear," Brey said, ushering them inside. He peeked his head outside, looking down the hall, and closed the door quickly behind them. He leaned back against the door with a sigh. "You got my letter, I suppose?" he asked, finally pushing off the door and walking into his chambers.

The walls were bare; no decorations flooded the room. But

there were tables upon tables filled with books taking up every nook and cranny.

"Yes, we did," Orla said.

Idalia slowly stepped farther into the room, tiptoeing around fallen stacks of books. She ran her fingers over the leather-bound covers. "What are you up to, Brey?"

"Oh, just some research," he said, following Idalia to the center of the room where a circular table stood. He spun the top, looking for a certain book that lined the edge of the table.

"What for?"

"To see how someone could survive a spear to the heart. See where a runaway queen could hide. Or why she would be hiding. Lots of things," he said counting on his fingers. His eyes were crazed as he spun the table round and round.

Orla watched him closely. He seemed so different than he had been when Quinn was around. His words were different, less guarded. He was a different man without a king or queen to lead him.

"Where's Eira?" Brey asked, suddenly stopping at the table. He didn't look up as he slid a finger inside a book and opened it.

"That's what we were wondering," Aviva said, finally speaking.

"She's not here," Brey said, "if that's what you thought." He closed the book, dust rising in the air. "But then again, maybe she is."

"Can you tell us about Queen Quinn? What happened to her body?" Idalia asked carefully, enunciating every syllable as if Brey was deaf.

Brey shrugged and went back to spinning the table. "I went to look. There was blood. No body. No trail. She disappeared." He was talking fast. Too fast for Orla to follow.

"There was no sign of her?" Aviva asked, stepping forward. Brey shook his head.

"How is that possible?" Orla asked. Her voice was barely above a whisper.

Brey shrugged again and turned away from the girls. "Who knows? I don't," he said. He picked up a book, thumbed through it, and dropped it on the floor with a loud *thud*. He stepped over it and walked to the open window. A light breeze flowed through the room. Brey shivered.

"It's getting dark," Idalia said, noting the sky turning a deep purple.

Orla nodded in agreement. "We should probably go."

"We can't leave him here like that," Aviva said, pointing toward Brey.

"We can't stay here," Idalia said.

"Yeah," Orla said, grabbing Aviva's arm. "You know how much trouble we got into last time we disappeared," she said with a roll of her eyes.

"We'll be back soon, Brey," Idalia said, walking backward to the door.

Brey didn't move.

The girls closed the door behind them. The hall was quiet. Only a few lamps lit the corridor, casting eerie shadows on the walls. They joined hands, their necklaces shining on their necks, and closed their eyes.

In a blink, they were back home.

54

Eira sat up in bed. A light tapping on the door had woken her from the best sleep she had gotten in ages. Her bones were no longer sore from sleeping on the wooden floor of the old building with her horse. She stretched out her arms, high over her head, and took a deep breath.

Her bedroom door opened. A small girl in a large white apron rolled a silver cart into the room. She looked at the floor as she pushed the cart over to Eira's bedside. She took the lid off the plate, steam floating up into the air. "Your breakfast, my queen," the girl whispered. She curtsied, barely bending her knees and quickly walking out of the room, shutting the door behind her.

Eira's stomach growled as she looked at the spread. It was everything she wanted and more. Eggs, muffins, bacon, juice. She shoveled the food into her mouth as if it would disappear if she took too long. Finally, she was full.

Another knock sounded on the door, but it didn't open. Eira let her legs dangle off the high bed and slowly dropped to the cold floor. She padded over to the door and opened it.

"Good morning, my queen," the man from yesterday said, bowing in front of her. "Would you care for a tour of Winter?"

Eira looked down at herself. She was still wearing a T-shirt and shorts for bed. "Uh, yes, I would. Let me get ready."

"Of course," he said, stepping back and allowing Eira to close the door behind her.

A few minutes later, Eira emerged from the room with clean clothes, brushed teeth, and her short hair pulled back away from her face. The man leaned on the wall next to her door.

He snapped to attention the moment Eira's foot stepped over the doorway. "Right this way," he said, holding out an arm for her.

Eira took his arm and was led through the manor. They stepped outside, into a beautiful snowy day. The man placed a large fur coat on Eira's shoulders and slapped a fur pelt around himself.

"Thank you, uh..." Eira said, eyeing the man.

"The name is Donovan, my queen."

Eira nodded. "Thank you, Donovan."

Donovan led Eira down the steps of the manor out into a large garden. Shrubs lined a cobbled walkway. The snow falling from the sky covered most of the ground, growing thicker and thicker with every one of Eira's steps.

"I believe Winter is happy to see you have returned," Donovan said, leaning over to be closer to Eira.

"Why do you think that?"

"It hasn't snowed like this in quite some time. Years."

Eira looked out at Winter. Out in the distance she could see rolling hills to one side and a forest on the other. It was wide open. Ran on and on as far as Eira could see.

And in the middle of the great expanse of land was the

hustle and bustle of Winter. Eira's little town was quaint but busy. Small shops lined the streets. Children ran freely from one house to the next, meeting with friends. Townspeople milled around outside, some heading to open their shops while others went home to their small stone buildings and fireplaces. Eira loved all of the noises Winter brought. Laughter, trees blowing in the wind, cats and dogs shaking off snow. It was a much needed change from cars running down streets, train horns blaring in the middle of the night, people yelling at each other.

"I'm glad to be here," Eira said, finally turning back to Donovan.

Donovan didn't talk. He let Eira take in her town as he walked into the center of it, where they had met the day prior.

A large stone gazebo sat in the middle of the town. There was a firepit, a few cold benches, and a family sitting on the steps. Donovan led Eira up the steps and to the fireplace. He rubbed his hands together collecting warmth from the embers. "I suppose you're accustomed to the cold?"

Eira nodded. "Comes with the territory," she said. She took her hand out of her pocket and hovered it over the fire. A sheet of ice materialized, covering the fire. "I hardly feel the temperature anymore," she said, waving her hand away and letting the ice melt.

"What a blessing. Winter has been known for its harsh weather," Donovan said, stepping toward the firepit. The light from the flame reflected off him.

Eira turned away from him, looking out into Winter. She crossed the floor of the gazebo, standing at its edge, and squinted her eyes. A large object was barreling toward them. She watched and waited as the object got closer and closer, slowly becoming clear.

"We have a visitor," Donovan said, returning to Eira's side.

A carriage skidded to a stop in front of the gazebo. The driver hopped off the carriage and went to the side, lifting the curtain for the passenger. A large woman, clad in blue from head to toe, stepped out. Her feet made large indents in the snow. "Ah, just who I was looking for," she said walking up the steps of the gazebo. She took Donovan's hands in hers and leaned forward, giving him a kiss on each cheek.

"Harriet?" Eira asked. "What are you doing here?"

"I could ask you the same question," Harriet said, turning to face Eira. She bowed her head for a millisecond. "My lady," she added.

"I thought you stayed in Conformity Castle?" Eira asked.

"I go wherever my princess goes," Harriet said. "And we have things to discuss. Come, come," she said waving a hand and turning abruptly to head back to the manor.

Eira watched her leave. When she was just out of earshot, Eira turned to Donovan. "So anyone can come into Winter whenever they want?"

"Why, yes, of course."

"We're going to have to fix that," Eira said, stepping down the gazebo stairs and following Harriet to the manor.

When Eira stepped inside, Harriet came around and slipped the coat from her shoulders. She handed it to the doorman, who ran off with it. Eira waited for Harriet to speak, but she didn't. Instead, she walked around the room, running her fingers over the furniture. She lifted it up into the air and shook her head with disgust when it came away with dirt on it.

"You need to talk or something?" Eira asked.

"Ah, yes," Harriet said, rubbing her hand against her thick blue skirt. "It's regarding your sisters."

"My sisters?"

Harriet nodded, walking away from a table in the corner of the room. "They're looking for you."

"Looking for me? How do you know that?"

Harriet waved Eira over to the small sitting couch. Eira sat down beside her. "They paid Brey a visit yesterday."

"What for?"

"He sent a note."

"A note?" Eira said, trying to speed up the conversation. But Harriet was more focused on the dust between her fingers than the story she was telling.

"Brey sent a letter about Queen Quinn."

Eira swallowed against a lump in her throat. "How do you know?"

Harriet laughed. "Girl, we know everything that goes in and out of Conformity Castle. We like to stay informed," she winked.

"What about Queen Quinn? She's dead, isn't she?"

Harriet shrugged her big shoulders, the heavy material of her skirt rising and falling against the marbled floor. "There was no body when Brey went back to the Tree of Season. No body. No trail. He doesn't know what happened to her."

Eira nodded slowly. Quinn's body hadn't been found. That wasn't a good sign. Something needed to be done. "What did my sisters want with Brey?"

"An explanation. And Aviva wanted to know where you were. She seemed concerned." Harriet glanced at Eira, finally taking her eyes away from the dust.

"I haven't seen or spoken with her since the Trial of Autumn. I'm not that close to them."

"It's probably for the best," Harriet said. "Three of you will die for one to become queen. No need to grow an attachment to someone who might not be around for long."

Eira couldn't speak. She still wasn't sure how they were going to get through the next three trials and the Finale, but that was a thought for another time.

"How long are you going to be around?" Harriet asked.

"For a while," Eira said. "I'm not welcome in Texas. I'll be staying here in Winter."

Harriet nodded. "Well then, let's get this place in proper order. Run along now," she said, taking Eira's hand and pulling her to a stand. "Your manor will be ready shortly."

55

In the Land of Texas

"We're going to be in so much trouble," Orla said, looking out the window of her car. Aviva nodded but remained silent. They rolled to a stop on the sidewalk next to Aviva's driveway. Ted was sitting outside on the porch.

A tight band wound around Aviva's neck, making it hard to breathe. She couldn't move, didn't want to get out of the car and face whatever was coming for her.

Orla placed a hand on Aviva's shoulder. She jumped away. "Sorry," Orla muttered. "Do you want to see if you can stay at my house again?"

Aviva shook her head. She was glad Orla had never asked about the situation with her parents. She knew it was probably fairly easy to guess. But still. Orla had never made Aviva admit that her foster parents were abusive. And for that, she was going to keep Orla and her family out of the line of fire.

She could feel Ted's eyes on her, boring through her soul. Her skin prickled, but she opened the car door anyway. "It's okay," Aviva said, sliding out of the car. "I'll see you tomorrow at school."

"Yeah, okay," Orla said, staring after her as she closed the door and walked up the driveway.

"And where have you been?" Ted asked, a strong slur to his words. There was a case of beer next to his rocking chair, and several empty cans littered on the porch.

"Had a school project," Aviva said, averting her gaze from the beer cans. She knew bringing attention to them would make things worse.

"Mhmm," Ted said, tilting his head to the side. "Sure you did."

Aviva stepped over a can and opened the door. Ted grabbed her arm before she could step inside. He pulled her back, forcing her shoulder to scream in anguish. She needed to get it looked at but couldn't. She'd tried holding it together, but without her branches to keep it secure, it hadn't felt right since the trial. But wearing a sling of branches would only draw attention to an injury she couldn't explain.

"Next time you lie, there will be consequences," he said. His eyes were glazed over. He could barely maintain eye contact with her.

Aviva nodded, tugged her arm away from Ted's grip, and walked inside. She heard him fall back against the rocking chair, another beer can clinking against the ground.

She hated him. Hated him more than anyone else. But he was never going to let her go again. She'd had one chance to get away, and the cops brought her back. She needed to get away from Ted and Kathy. She needed to finally be free.

Season was her only option. But she couldn't leave Idalia and Orla, could she? She couldn't just disappear. And to leave Texas. The only place she'd ever lived. The place she had grown up in. Could she leave it all behind?

Aviva sighed and sat on her bed. She pulled her head into her hands, her shoulders shaking. Her arm hurt, but her heart was in more pain. Why couldn't she have been as lucky as Orla and Idalia? Why couldn't she have gotten good adoptive parents?

The front door shut, a loud *thud* rang through the house. Ted stomped around, running into things as he made his way through the house.

"Hey," he called out.

Aviva didn't answer. She waited with her one good hand raised in front of her body. Tree branches licked at her window, asking to be let in. She could protect herself. At least now she could protect herself.

Ted's fist slammed against her door. "Open up," he said, leaning heavily on the door.

Aviva shot her hand forward. The tree branches crawled through the room, stretching from the tree outside to the doorknob. A branch wrapped around the handle, keeping it steady and locked as Ted tried to shove the door open. Another branch ran along the bottom of the door, strengthening the wooden structure.

Ted finally realized it wasn't going to budge. Ted slurred words Aviva couldn't comprehend. He gave one final jab to the door before turning and leaving Aviva alone.

For once, Aviva had taken control. Her powers kept her safe when no one else would.

The tree branches slithered back outside, leaving the door and Aviva vulnerable. But Aviva knew they could be called back in an instant. She relished in the power she felt in her hands.

One of the tree branches wrapped around Aviva's shoulders lightly, as if it were hugging her. Warmth spread through her. The fear and pain were gone. Aviva finally felt safe.

56

Orla slowly turned the key in the doorknob, waiting for the *click*. The lights in the house were off. It was pitch black all around her. She was hoping that meant her parents were fast asleep.

She shined her phone down at her feet, carefully stepping into the house. She turned around to shut the door behind her and locked it. Turning back around, Orla started toward the living room. She didn't dare turn on any lights.

"And where have you been, young lady?" her father's voice bellowed through the dark house.

Orla jumped back, her hand flying to her chest. It took a minute for her to be able to breathe again. "Dad, you scared me."

"Good," he said. He sat on the edge of the couch with his arms crossed in front of his chest. Her mother reached up to turn the lights on, and fluorescent bulbs showed how mad Orla's father was. He had a deep scowl across his face. His eyes were piercing, and his cheeks were red with anger. "Answer the question."

"Oh," Orla said, running a hand nervously through her hair. "Work?"

Orla's mother stood and paced across the living room. "Are you sure that's what you want to go with?"

"I mean, I had a school project I had to finish," Orla said. Her legs were shaking, and beads of sweat welled on her forehead. "And then, I went by to see Lizzy at the coffee shop."

"That's interesting," her father said with one eyebrow raised. "Especially seeing as you no longer have a job at the coffee shop."

Orla licked her lips and swallowed, but there was something stuck in her throat, and she couldn't get rid of it. She coughed, sweat dripping down her face. She wiped it away. "That's what I had to talk to Lizzy about," Orla mumbled.

"Sweetheart, stop lying." Her mother sighed.

Her father reached out his hand. "Give me your phone."

"What?" Orla said, holding her phone to her chest. "Why?"

"Because it's apparent we still can't trust you," he said shortly. He jabbed his hand forward, waiting for Orla to place her phone in his palm.

But she clutched it, not willing to give it up. "Look, do you want to know the truth?"

"No," her father said, rolling his eyes, "we want to continue to be lied to."

Her mother let out a small laugh.

"I was hanging out with Aviva after school. She didn't want to go home," Orla said. It wasn't the truth, at least not completely. But it was all Orla had.

"How is she?" her mother asked, her face softening.

"I don't know, Mom. I just know there's something terrible going on over there."

Silence fell around them.

"I felt so sick having to send her back. It was obvious she didn't want to go," her mother sniffled.

Her father placed a comforting hand on her shoulder.

"She wasn't lucky enough to be adopted by great parents like I was," Orla said, hoping the change of subject would make her parents back off.

"Nice try," her father said. "Give me your phone and go to your room."

Orla huffed. She stomped over to her father and slammed her phone down into his palm. "So not fair," she mumbled, marching off to her room. She walked straight through the open doorway, her door still missing from its hinges. She fell face-first onto her bed, banging her fists angrily against her comforter.

57

Idalia rolled out of bed, rubbing sleep from her eyes. Her alarm was blaring. *Beep, beep.* Over and over, but she couldn't find her phone to turn it off. She wanted to stay in bed, let the alarm keep beeping, and forget the rest of the day. She had already missed her first class of the day. But she couldn't miss her next one. She really needed to focus on school again. She had to get through the semester with all A's. Had to.

She pulled on some sweatpants and a T-shirt, bundled up her wavy red hair, and slipped on tennis shoes. She threw the pillows off her bed and finally found her phone nestled between her headboard and mattress. She clicked the alarm off and hurried outside.

It was December, but the sticky air felt like summer. *Texas sure has things mixed up*, Idalia thought as she ran through campus to make it to class.

She slid into a chair just as Professor Hendrix walked into the classroom. His eyes searched the room until they landed on hers. A small smile spread across his lips. Idalia's body revolted in shivers.

She quickly looked down at her desk, refusing to meet his eyes again.

Idalia tried taking notes, following along with the slideshow, but she couldn't. Her mind was too far away, back in Season, to pay any attention to the creepy professor who kept trying to meet her glance.

"Okay, class," Professor Hendrix said as he packed up his desk. "The final presentations begin next week. I will email the presentation order before then."

The class erupted in movement as all of the students around Idalia put their things away and left. Idalia was left behind.

"We've missed you around here," Professor Hendrix said as Idalia tried leaving the classroom. "Where have you been?"

"I've been busy. Dealing with stuff," she said shortly. She tried stepping around him, but he blocked her way. Heat rose in the pit of her stomach. She felt the familiar flicker of flames at the tips of her finger.

"That's a shame," he said, not noticing how red her hands had become. "You never turned in your final project for approval."

"Yeah, I know."

"You can't pass my class without the presentation," he said. He took a step back and looked at her from head to toe. "Well, you can if you've decided on that extra credit." A lopsided grin stretched across his face.

"I guess I failed then," Idalia said.

Professor Hendrix grabbed her arm and pulled her to him. "Oh, come on," he whispered. His hot breath washed over her.

"I said no," she said. She couldn't stop the anger rising inside her chest. Couldn't stop the heat that built up.

She yanked her arm back. Sparks flew from her fingertips and landed on his desk. Papers burst into flames.

Professor Hendrix jumped away from Idalia. A look of terror washed over his features. He was too stunned to speak, let alone move. Idalia turned on her heel and walked out of the room leaving the professor to deal with the aftermath of his proposal.

A smile crossed her lips.

58

In the Land of Season

Eira sat on a throne in the middle of the gazebo, overlooking the town of Winter. The ground was icy, snow piling up around her. The wind was harsh as it licked her face. She was so used to the numbness the air garnered she barely felt the cold. She closed her eyes for a moment.

She was glad to finally be back in Season. She didn't have to run from cops here or hide away in damaged houses. She didn't have to be in the same places she had been with Samuel. She didn't have to relive his betrayal. Instead, she had a whole town of people willing to do her bidding and a luxurious house all to herself. She took a breath, breathing in the wintry air. She loved the feeling of the cool air going into her lungs. She loved everything about Winter.

A loud crash sounded off to Eira's side. Her eyes snapped

open. She turned to stare at the man who had plummeted into buckets of water, spilling them all over the ground.

Eira gritted her teeth and stood. She clenched her fist at her side as she looked at the mess the man had made.

The man looked up at Eira as she neared. He was shaking. Eira didn't know if it was the cold that was making him shake uncontrollably. He should be used to the cold by now, like she was. Or possibly it was fear he felt. The fear Eira stirred in him. Eira wanted to smile at the thought. But she didn't. She maintained her hard expression.

"Get up," Eira said, blowing an irritated breath through her teeth.

"Y-yes, my queen." The man shivered. He tried standing, but his feet couldn't grip the snow-covered ground. His face turned red. He kept trying, his arms and legs flailing underneath him.

"I said get up." Eira's voice grew louder. She brought a clenched fist into the air. A pile of snow rose, mimicking the movement of her fist. The man wriggled as the pile of snow moved across the ground, collecting more of the frozen ice. The pile grew in size until it was larger than the man.

Eira watched as the pile of snow ate up everything around it. It was hungry, just like her. Hungry for power. She paid no attention to the crowd of people gathering. Her eyes remained on the squirming man.

She shot her hand up into the air. The pile of snow gobbled the man up, standing him upright. The snow held him in place, making it impossible for him to move. Just his head poked out of the snow. Eira walked up to the snowman, face to face. "When I give you an order, you follow it," she seethed.

The man tried to nod, but snow crept up his neck and around his face.

Eira turned to look at the crowd. Her people wore different shades of blue representing Winter and her power over water. Some of them refused to look at the man covered in snow. Others couldn't take their eyes away.

"That goes for everyone," Eira shouted. "You listen to me, or you face the consequences." She squeezed her fist together tightly, so tight it turned white.

Her nails cut into her palm with the strength of her grip, but she didn't let go. No, she wasn't going to let these people see her weak. She wasn't going to let these people think they could betray her. She wasn't going to play nice like she had with Samuel. Samuel had been her best friend. Not again. She would never let someone that close again. She would never let someone hurt her the way Samuel had.

The man's screams echoed around her as she walked back up to her throne and took her seat overlooking her town. She relaxed her hand.

"My queen," Donavan said, coming up to Eira's side.

Eira looked at him sideways.

He bowed his head respectfully. "It may be best to leave the townspeople alive."

"That is your opinion, Donovan," Eira said with a flick of her wrist.

Donovan nodded. "Yes, my queen." His voice was rough, stone on sandpaper. But Eira enjoyed hearing it. "I only suggest as your loyal servant and advisor, if you want to keep the people of Winter on your side, you make a point to protect them."

"Do their loyalties break that easily?" Eira asked, looking up at Donovan. The pelts of fur flapped in the wind. Glimpses of his bronze skin peeked from beneath them. Eira couldn't tear her eyes away.

"No, my queen, of course not."

She nodded, still looking at his waist. "Then I will do as I please."

"Yes, my queen," Donovan said with a nod. If he noticed Eira's stares, he didn't show it. But then again, no one questioned the queen. She wouldn't allow it.

Eira blinked, finally breaking her gaze. She stood from the throne, stretching out her back. The thick coat was heavy on her shoulders. She rolled them, loosening her muscles. She had been sitting for too long. Staring out at the town and her people diligently working. Fortifying it.

"It's coming along nicely," Donovan said, stepping to her side.

Eira looked to her right, past the blood-splattered snow. Trees had been cut to make logs, and the logs had been stacked to create a border.

Eira shook her head. "My sisters could tear that down in a second. Make it stronger."

"Yes, my queen." Donovan walked away from Eira, down the steps.

"Donovan," Eira said.

Donovan turned to look back.

"Send Jedrek to me."

Donovan nodded.

Eira didn't wait to watch Donovan disappear into Winter. Instead, she turned and walked into her house. It resembled Conformity Castle. A large staircase sat in the middle of the antechamber. Eira shrugged off her coat, leaving it hanging on the stair railing, and climbed to the second floor.

She stepped off the landing and followed the hallway to the back of the house. There was a single blue door in the middle of a large white wall. She opened it and stepped into her chambers.

The walls were dark blue like the midnight sky. The large window on the far wall let in just enough light. Eira liked the dark room. She liked the huge bed covered in a tan fur blanket, liked the sitting chair next to the bed, and liked the adjoining bathroom. She liked everything about her room. But what she liked the most, was that it was all hers.

She didn't have to share with someone. She didn't have to adhere to someone else's rules. She was the owner. She was the leader. And she loved it.

A knock on her door broke her train of thought. "Come in," she called.

A tall man in a blue uniform walked through the door. He bowed. "My queen," he said.

"Jedrek," Eira said with a nod. She sat in the chair next to the bed, making herself comfortable. "Do you have any updates?"

"Yes, my queen," Jedrek said.

"Well, go on." Eira motioned with her hand.

Jedrek nodded. "We have four thousand men readily available."

"Four thousand, that's it?"

He was silent.

"Are they trained at least?"

"Yes, and I'm sure we can get more volunteers. It will take time to train them," Jedrek said. He paced back and forth in front of Eira.

"Do that," she said, watching him as he easily strode across her floor.

"Of course, my queen." He paused his march, turned on his heel, and headed to the door. His hand stopped on the doorknob. "May I ask a question, my queen?" he said, turning back around to face Eira.

Eira nodded.

"Why do you need an army? In past years, only the five trials were needed to prove who would rule Season."

Eira's hand twitched. The freezing cold of ice spread to her fingertips. But she took a breath and pulled it back in. "I do not plan on completing the five trials, Jedrek."

"Then how will you become Queen of Season?"

She looked at him and smiled. "I'm going to kill my sisters."

59

In the Land of Texas

"Hey, Idalia," Katie called from the bottom of the stairs.

Idalia looked down over the railing and waved.

Katie jogged up the stairs and met Idalia at her door. "I haven't seen you in a while," Katie said following Idalia inside her dorm.

"I know, I've been busy." Idalia packed up boxes while Katie stood in the doorway.

"Same. Finals were tough this semester."

Idalia nodded, focusing more on packing up her dorm room than her friend.

"What are you doing for winter break?" Katie asked.

Idalia shrugged. "Just going home for now. What about you?"

"Brittany and I are planning a vacation. We just don't know where yet." Katie laughed. "You can come, too, if you want."

"I'll let you know," Idalia said while walking past Katie to bring another box of stuff downstairs to her car.

"Okay, well, text me?" Katie asked, following her.

"Sure," she said, pushing her box into the back seat of her car. "I'll see you soon," Idalia said, going back upstairs for another box.

Katie did a half-wave, got in her car, and drove off.

Idalia felt bad watching her leave. But she had too much on her mind to focus on friends. Eira was still nowhere to be found. Brey was focused on finding Quinn's body. And in just a few short months, the second of five trials was going to pull her and her sisters back to Season to fight to the death.

She had control over her element, that much became clear when she set fire to Professor Hendrix's desk. But she didn't know if Orla and Aviva were practicing theirs. And she had no clue what Eira was doing, or if she was even still alive. Or where she was.

She didn't know a lot.

Idalia blew out a frustrated breath and shook out her tight hands. She hated not knowing things. Hated not having the answers.

She shook her head clear of thoughts of Season and her sisters. She locked her dorm room behind her and went to turn in the key.

"My girl," Idalia's father said after opening the door. He opened his arms and pulled her in for a hug.

Warmth flooded Idalia. A warmth deep inside her, one that wasn't controlled by fire.

"Hey, Papa," she said.

"Come in, come in." He let her go and moved out of the way to let her step inside. "How were finals?" he asked.

"Good, I passed all my classes. Got all A's." Idalia beamed.

"That's wonderful," he said, a smile breaking out on his lips. "My smart girl." He kissed her forehead.

Idalia nodded. It was a miracle she had passed. Especially since she'd skipped so many classes the last few weeks. Professor Hendrix even gave her an A for the final. A final she didn't even turn in. Idalia guessed her fire show was good enough for him. She smiled thinking about the look on his face the last time she saw him. He'd looked terrified. Maybe now he wouldn't try hitting on her. If she ever saw him again.

"Your mother is cleaning up the guest room for you," her father said, sitting down on the couch. "I'm sure she'll be right out."

"Okay," Idalia said, sitting opposite him.

A few minutes later, her mother came into the living room. Idalia stood to hug her. "It's so good to see you, honey," Idalia's mother said.

Idalia laughed. "I was just here a month ago for Thanksgiving."

"Oh, I know," she said, waving her hand in front of her, "but it's never enough time with you."

"So, what's the plan for tonight?"

Idalia shrugged. "I don't have any."

"Ooo," her mother said, rubbing her hands together excitedly. "Let's do a movie night."

Idalia smiled, happy to be back home. The stress she had been feeling melted off, and she sank back into the couch. "Sounds great."

60

A knock sounded on Orla's doorframe. She ignored it, laying completely still on her bed.

"Sweetheart?" her mother said, poking her head in the room.

Orla blew her brown wavy hair out of her eyes. She was facing her wall, back turned away from her mother. So, she didn't see her mother step into the room. But she heard the creak of the floor as she padded over to the bed. She sat on the bed next to Orla and placed a hand on her back.

"Are you going to stay in here all day?"

"There's nothing else for me to do," Orla said with a roll of her eyes. "I'm grounded, remember?"

"You could help put up the Christmas decorations like you do every year," her mother said, jiggling her shoulders.

"No thanks."

"Fine," her mother said with a sigh. "Have fun being held up in your room for the next week and a half."

"I will."

Orla's mother got off the bed and walked out of the room.

Orla could tell she was upset by the heaviness of her steps, but she didn't care. She was stuck in her room with nothing to do for two weeks. No phone, no friends, no fun.

She wished she had her bedroom door back, but her parents hadn't budged on that yet. Not after she'd gotten her phone taken again.

She rolled over and looked up at her ceiling, blowing a frustrated breath out of her mouth. She closed her eyes and tried to fall asleep, but she couldn't. She'd already been asleep for the majority of the day, and now her mind couldn't rest. She needed to get out of her house. But her parents would never let her leave their sight.

She looked over at her window. A small smile crept onto her face.

She quickly got off the bed; pulled on jeans, a jacket, and shoes; and creeped over to her window. She slowly pushed it open, making sure it didn't creak. She swung a leg outside her window and dropped down to the ground.

Orla pushed the window back into place and took off down the street. She didn't know where she was headed, but at least she was outside.

She walked the street, passed streetlights and neighbors she'd known for years. It reminded her of when she'd snuck out for her birthday. She'd had a getaway car then, and her parents never found out.

Her stomach turned in circles the farther away from her house she got. "Ugh," she said, turning around and stomping her feet against the pavement. She traced her steps back to her house, across her yard, and through the window back to her bedroom. She went into the living room where tons of boxes of decorations were laying around. Her mother stood in front of the Christmas tree, eyeing it thoughtfully. She turned when Orla walked in. A smile broke out on her face.

Orla's father came into the room with two steaming cups of hot chocolate. He handed her a cup. "Glad you could join us," he said with a smile.

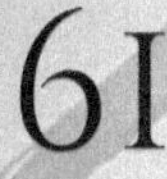

viva stared at the small box wrapped in glittery red paper. Ted and Kathy were looking at her, waiting with smiles on their faces. She slowly unwrapped the box, balling-up the wrapping paper and putting it beside her on the leather couch.

Aviva looked up at Ted and Kathy. They nodded, encouraging her to take the tape off the top and open it. So she did.

She dropped the lid to her side and pulled out a piece of coal. It rested in the palm of her hand.

Her parents burst out in laughter. "You really thought we were going to get you a present?" Kathy asked, covering her mouth while squealing.

"After all the trouble you've caused," Ted said, shaking his head with a sly smile on his crusty lips.

Aviva didn't react. She put the piece of coal back in the box, closed the lid, and sat with it on her lap. Her face was blank, void of any emotion. She waited what seemed like hours for them to stifle their glee. Her hand tightened around the box, almost crushing it. She blew out a slow breath, relaxing her fingers. She could feel the trees outside trying to reach her, draw her in. But she let them go, not ready to use their power.

"Go to your room," Ted said with a wave of his hand.

Aviva stood, left the present behind, and walked to her room. She could still hear their laughter as she closed the door.

Aviva's stomach growled. She crossed her arms over her stomach and folded in on herself. She'd been in her room for hours. She could hear Ted and Kathy moving around the house, cooking, opening gifts, eating, laughing. Having a great Christmas day without her.

She looked out her window. It was dark, but small twinkly stars blinked in the night. She wanted to slip out of the window, down the street, and into oblivion. But running away didn't seem to work out too well for her. She had just been brought back to the house. Back to the people who didn't even want her. Hardly even took care of her.

A knock on the door made her straighten up. Ted stumbled in.

"How was your Christmas?" he asked, leaning heavily on the bedroom door. "I said," Ted yelled when she didn't answer, "how was your Christmas?"

Aviva still didn't answer.

Ted took a step into the room and swung the door shut behind him. It made a loud noise, but Aviva was sure Kathy would pay no attention.

Aviva's hand balled into a fist. She focused on her breathing, trying to remain calm. But with each step Ted took toward her, Aviva was growing angrier. The tree branches spanked against her window asking to be let in. Ted glanced at the window, watching as the branches swayed back and forth with no wind under them.

"You think I'm scared of you?" he asked.

"No," Aviva said. "But you should be."

Ted paused, and a look of confusion crossed his face. And then it was swept away by red hot anger. He lunged forward, hands outstretched. They collapsed around Aviva's neck, squeezing until she couldn't breathe.

Aviva kicked her legs, clawed at his hands. But he was strong. Her vision grew blurry, and sparkly dots filled her vision. It reminded her of the night sky she'd just been looking at. She stopped fighting him, her arms and legs limp at her sides. She couldn't feel his hands crushing her throat anymore. Maybe he had stopped.

Glass shattered into the room, and she fell to the floor. She clutched at her throat, making sure it was still there as she gasped for breath. She coughed, covering her mouth. She wiped her mouth and looked up from the floor.

A tree had plummeted into the room, branches spiraling around them. One branch wrapped around Ted's own neck, holding him against the far wall, far away from Aviva. He was blue, his eyes wildly searching the room for someone to help him. But then he went limp. The branch didn't let up. Aviva could only watch as all of the air was suffocated from Ted's lungs.

Blood pounded in her ears. She could barely hear the thump from Ted's body being dropped onto the floor, lifeless.

She pulled herself up, using her bed as support. She

grabbed her backpack, filled it with clothes and her toothbrush, and hopped out of the broken window, weaving around the tree branches snaking in. She followed a trail of leaves as it led her far away from her house and her dead foster dad.

62

Eira stood at her window. Out in the garden, she watched as lines and lines of her soldiers marched back and forth in formation. They looked good, like a real army. Not that Eira had ever seen an army up close. But she knew it was better than what her sisters had. It had to be.

Jedrek stood beside her, his mouth shut firmly in a grim line. He had been cold to her ever since she told him she was going to kill her sisters. But he was still loyal and that was all Eira cared about.

"How many do we have now?" Eira asked, trying to count the lines of soldiers. They moved around in circles, intertwining with one another, and she couldn't keep up.

"Almost five thousand," Jedrek said.

"Very well." Eira stepped away from the window. "How many soldiers do my sisters have in their towns?"

"I'm not sure, my queen. We don't have access to their records."

"If you had to guess," she said with a wave of her hand and a roll of her eyes.

Jedrek thought for a moment, still glancing out the window. "Summer has the largest number of residents. A good thousand or so more than Winter."

Eira nodded. "Of course Idalia would have access to more soldiers."

"They aren't trained," Jedrek said. "None are. Season isn't accustomed to war. We're accustomed to protocol. The five trials."

Eira stomped her foot on the ground. Jedrek turned to look at her. "I know you are against my plan," Eira said, crossing her arms in front of her. "But I am queen. And I will be Queen of Season in a few months' time. Things are changing. If you have a problem with it, you should have taken it up with my father while he was alive."

"Rest in peace, King Quilo," Jedrek muttered under his breath.

"Yes, rest in peace, father who abandoned his daughters to be blindsided with Season and its protocol."

"My apologies, my queen," Jedrek said, bowing his head.

"No need for apologies, Jedrek," Eira said, sweetening her voice. "Just action."

"What is it you would have me do?"

"We need more soldiers. There can't be any chance of failure."

"We do not have any more men."

Eira paused, looking out of her chamber window. Past the five thousand marching soldiers, past the snowy mountains of Winter. What was it that Quinn had kept telling her before the

Trial of Autumn in all her lessons? An iron fist makes for an easier reign. So that's what she'd do. She'd become her mother. No matter who hated her for it.

"I will call on my sister. I will use her own men to end them all."

Eira's Tree of Season necklace burned in her hand. She squeezed it tightly. Her eyes shut while she focused. She envisioned her sister. Black hair, the same striking blue eyes Eira saw every time she looked in a mirror, hunched shoulders, a scared gaze on her face.

A ripping sound filled her ears as the space in front of her opened up into a portal. Wind cascaded around her, threatening to topple her over. But she held her ground, her feet planted firmly on the wooden floor of her bedroom.

Eira snapped her eyes open as her sister fell through the portal, crashing into her. Eira's necklace flew from her hand, and the portal closed with a loud *clap*.

Eira picked her necklace up from the floor and turned to face her sister. Wide, blue eyes stared back at her from the ground.

"What am I doing here?" Aviva asked, looking around. She wiped sweat from her brow and stood.

"I wanted to see you, little sister," Eira said. "It's been a while."

"Yeah, you disappeared on us." Aviva turned in circles, taking in the unfamiliar room. "Where are we?"

"In Season, of course," Eira said with a laugh. She took a slow breath, trying to remain calm. If her plan was to work, she needed Aviva to need her. She needed Aviva to like her. At least for a bit.

"Well, duh. Where in Season?"

"Winter."

Aviva nodded. "So this is where you've been all this time?"

"Yes," Eira said, walking to her bed and sitting down. She patted the spot next to her, but Aviva didn't join her. "I couldn't stay in Texas. Cops are still after me. Might as well make this my new home. It's a lot better than what I had in Texas, anyway." Eira shook her head. Thoughts of sleeping under bridges and going days without food tried flooding back in, but she cast them aside.

Aviva nodded. "I can relate," she said.

"I thought you'd be able to."

Aviva crossed the room, going toward the big window and sitting in the blue chair. She turned her head to look out the window.

"What's that?" Eira asked, lifting a finger to point at Aviva's neck. A speckling of red peeked over her collar.

Aviva lifted her hand to cover her throat. "Oh, this?" A small cough escaped her lips. "It's nothing really."

Eira stood, moving closer to Aviva. She pried Aviva's hand from her neck. A deep, red ring ran around her neck. "That doesn't look like nothing," Eira said.

Aviva looked at her, her blue eyes rimmed with redness.

"That looks like a hand," she said, noting the fingertips beginning to form on Aviva's neck.

Aviva shrugged. "It happens."

"To us, yes," Eira said, stepping back. "But not to everyone." She closed her eyes tight. An image of her own neck, bright red with a similar handprint, taking over her mind. She pushed it away. She needed to focus. She needed to get Aviva on her side. She did not need a reminder of Samuel or the night everything changed for both of them.

Aviva turned away.

Eira cleared her throat. "You know, we're a lot alike." She returned to her spot on her bed.

Aviva nodded.

"It may just be our circumstances. How we grew up. But I don't think Orla or Idalia can really understand us, you know? They live these perfect lives, not a care in the world, while we're bounced from place to place, having to put up with things like that," Eira said, gesturing to Aviva.

"It's fine. It won't happen again," Aviva said, finally meeting Eira's gaze.

"Oh, it won't?" Eira asked, eyeing her carefully.

Aviva shook her head slowly.

Eira saw something behind her eyes. A feeling of relief. And fear. Something she was very used to feeling. "That's good," she said. "You protected yourself, that's all."

Aviva nodded, sniffling.

"Trust me, I get it," Eira said. "More than you know."

Aviva covered her swollen neck with her hand and nodded again. "Yeah, they don't understand us," she said. "But it's not their fault."

"Oh, no, of course not," Eira said, shaking her hands in front of her chest furiously, as if the thought of putting blame on her sisters was absurd. "It's just the luck of the draw."

"I can't go back," Aviva whispered after a few moments of nothing.

"You're more than welcome to stay here with me." She scooted to the edge of the bed, placing her hands out in front of her, as if calling Aviva to her.

"Are you sure? I can go somewhere else. Spring, maybe."

"No, no. I would love to have you here. Being around a sister is just what you need right now," Eira said, smiling sweetly. She jumped up and padded over to her bedroom door and poked her head outside. "Harriet," Eira called down the hallway.

Harriet met Eira at the door. "Yes, my queen?"

"Could you show Aviva to a guest room? She'll be staying with us for a while."

"Yes, my queen," Harriet said with a small tilt of her head.

Eira motioned for Aviva to follow Harriet down the hallway. Aviva did, leaving Eira standing in the doorway with a smile playing at her lips. Things were working perfectly for her. Aviva was going to welcome her with open arms, and Eira was going to use the extra soldiers to rid Season of her sisters.

63

"Good morning, Aviva," Eira said, standing at Aviva's bedroom door.

Aviva rubbed the sleep from her eyes and pushed back her hair.

"How'd you sleep?"

"Fine," Aviva said, erupting into a yawn. She covered her mouth and turned to head back into the room. She crawled on the bed, wanting to lie down and go back to sleep, but Eira was watching her every little move. "Do you need something?"

"No, not particularly," Eira said, stepping into the room. "But I thought we might get outside today. It might make you feel better," she said, sitting down beside her.

"I'm fine," Aviva said, turning away from her. She wanted to curl up in a ball. She needed to process what had happened. What she'd done.

"No, you're not. I can tell."

Aviva shrugged. She opened her mouth to say something, but the words escaped her.

"It's okay to not be okay. You've had a rough couple of days," Eira said, placing a hand on her shoulder softly.

Aviva jumped at her touch. "Yeah, I know," she said. Her skin prickled.

"Your neck looks a little better," Eira said, looking down to see the ring around Aviva's throat. It was no longer a harsh red handprint. It was now a splotchy blue and purple bruise.

Aviva lifted a hand to touch her throat. She swallowed back the pain. "Doesn't feel much better."

"It just takes time," Eira said. She stood, leaving Aviva sitting alone on the bed. "Get dressed. I think fresh air will do you some good," she said.

Aviva nodded and waited for her to leave. The door clicked shut behind Eira, and Aviva fell back against the wool sheets. She closed her eyes, almost drifting off to sleep when someone knocked on her door.

"Breakfast," a voice said through the wooden door.

Aviva heard small footsteps skip away. She rolled over and left the warm bed to go back to the door. A tray of food was sitting at the door. She bent down to pick it up, kicked the door closed behind her, and brought it to her bed.

"Took you long enough," Eira said, glancing sideways at Aviva when she finally met her downstairs.

"Sorry." Aviva shrugged.

"I have a surprise for you," Eira said.

The doorman slipped on Eira's coat and handed Aviva an identical one.

"Right this way," Eira said, stepping out into the cold morning.

A man covered in fur led two horses from the gazebo to the manor. One horse was pure white. The other was much smaller and completely black.

Aviva smiled, her cheeks burning from the unusual expression on her face. "Milo," she called, running out to meet the small, black horse. "How did you get here?"

"Apparently our horses are linked to us or something. They can always find us. And Donovan saw him hanging around outside the wall," Eira said.

Milo buried his head against Aviva's shoulder. "So good to see you again, buddy," Aviva whispered into his ear.

Milo bobbed his head up and down.

"Thank you for delivering the horses, Donovan," Eira said, taking Willow's reins from him.

"Of course, my queen," Donovan said. He bowed low and stepped away.

"Let's go for a ride," Eira said to Aviva.

Aviva nodded, and they both mounted their horses. Eira kicked Willow with her heels, and she took off through the center of town and into the forest. Milo galloped to follow her.

Aviva dodged low-hanging branches as they trotted through the forest. Her hair whipped around her, getting caught in her mouth. Her eyes watered from the cold wind. But she loved every minute of being on Milo, escaping her thoughts and being in nature. Eira was right, she did need to get fresh air.

Eira pulled Willow's reins, and the horse planted her feet, coming to an abrupt stop. Eira slid off the horse's back and landed in the thickening snow.

Aviva followed her and tied Milo around a tree next to Willow. She walked up a small hill to meet Eira at the top.

"I just love it here," Eira said when Aviva joined her.

Aviva nodded. "It's beautiful." There were rolling, snow-covered hills as far as she could see. Trees were scattered everywhere, no paths disrupting them. A great pond opened up at the bottom of the hill, ice covering every inch. "A lot better than Texas."

"I'm never going back," Eira said, making her way down the hill.

Aviva followed her, trying her best not to slip against the snow.

"And you don't have to, either."

"But Orla and Idalia are there."

"They can come here. We can all live here in Season, like we were meant to." Eira smiled.

"It would be nice to have Idalia's fire right about now." Aviva laughed, rubbing her hands against the fur of her jacket.

Eira rolled her eyes. "Here," she said, slipping off her coat and handing it to Aviva.

Aviva took it cautiously.

"You don't need it?"

Eira shook her head. "No, I'm used to the cold. Can hardly feel a thing."

Aviva wrapped the coat around her, glad it was big enough to go over her other jacket. She hugged herself, waiting for the warmth to rise. "I don't think they would leave Texas," Aviva finally said.

"You're probably right," Eira said. She stepped onto the frozen pond. "Why would they when they have everything you could possibly want?" Eira's voice hardened slightly.

Aviva's gaze lifted. "You say that like it's their fault," Aviva called from the edge of the pond. She didn't follow Eira onto the ice.

Eira turned to face her, a bright smile plastered on her lips. "Of course not. It just would've been nice if our father would have made sure we all grew up in nice families. Then we wouldn't have had to go through foster care and everything that came with it."

"At least you got out," Aviva said, her voice low and her gaze on the ground.

Eira walked back over to the edge. She put a comforting hand on Aviva's shoulder. "You can, too. Stay here with me. There's nothing for you in Texas."

"I'm thinking about it," Aviva said, her shoulders sagging in defeat. "If I go back, it would just cause more problems. I'd end up in jail for killing Ted." She paused. "My caseworker has never helped me out. I don't know how many times I've tried telling her about them. But she won't do anything. I don't know why." Her voice cracked, and she looked away from Eira.

"Stay for as long as you'd like," Eira told her. "I like having you around, little sister."

Aviva's throat closed with emotion.

"Let's head back; you look cold," Eira said, leading Aviva up the hill and back to the horses.

They rode back to town in silence. Aviva saw Donovan waiting for them in the gazebo. Eira slid off Willow and handed the reins to Donovan. He took Milo's reins as Aviva dismounted.

"Take them back to the barn, and make sure to give them a treat," Eira said to Donovan.

"Yes, my queen," he said, leading the horses away from town.

Eira took Aviva's hand and guided her back to the manor.

"Eira?" Aviva asked.

"Yes?" Eira said, looking down at Aviva.

"Why do they call you *queen*?"

Eira shrugged. "They just do. I'm sure the people of Spring would call you queen, too," she said. "But don't you think about leaving me for Spring." She hugged Aviva into her side. "Winter hasn't had enough of you yet."

64

In the Land of Texas

Orla lay on her bed, looking up at the white ceiling, trying to count the number of times the fan spun around and around. She rolled her eyes and sighed, giving up and turning over to lay her head on her arms. *This is the worst Christmas break ever.*

A quick knock sounded on her door, one of many presents her parents had given her. They had put a big bow on it and hung it back on its hinges Christmas Eve. The highlight of her break so far.

The door flew open, and Orla's father walked in. He tossed a wrapped box onto her bed. "We forgot this one last present," he said with a twinkle in his eyes.

Orla sat up quickly and tore the wrapping off the box. Her phone sat nicely in the padded box. She looked up from her phone. "I'm ungrounded?"

"For now," he said.

"Thank you." She scurried from her bed and wrapped her arms around his neck, jumping up and down.

He laughed and pulled away from her. He kissed the top of her head. "Anything for my favorite daughter."

"I'm your only daughter." Orla rolled her eyes but laughed.

He turned on his heel and left Orla to her phone.

She turned away and hopped back onto her bed. She scrolled through the notifications. Idalia hadn't stopped calling or texting in days.

Orla pressed Idalia's missed call and waited as it rang. The line beeped, and Orla could hear Idalia's breath coming from the speaker.

"Hey, hey," Idalia said.

"Hey, what's up?"

"I'm just out for a run. Bored." There was a pause as Idalia took a few deep breaths. "What have you been up to? You haven't been answering my calls."

"My parents took my phone," Orla said, rolling her eyes. She fell back against the bed, the covers poofing up around her.

"Oh, what for?" Idalia asked.

Orla heard a door shut behind Idalia.

"For disappearing again."

"But that's not really your fault," Idalia said.

Orla laughed. "Yeah, I know. But I can't tell them why I keep disappearing. Then I'd be more than grounded. They'd probably send me to the crazy house," Orla said, covering her mouth. She tried to stop the laughter from escaping, but she couldn't. She could just imagine the looks on her parents' faces if she were to tell them about Season.

"But anyway," Orla said, finally getting a hold of herself. "They just ungrounded me, so it's whatever."

"Mhmm," Idalia mumbled. "So I'm guessing Aviva is grounded, too?"

"Oh, I don't know," Orla said, lowering her voice. "I dropped her off when we got back from your dorm. Her foster dad is scary."

"What do you mean?"

"I don't know, I just don't get a very good vibe. And Aviva really didn't want to go back. I felt bad leaving her there. I know they don't treat her right."

"Hmm," Idalia said. Orla could imagine Idalia lifting her thumb and forefinger to her chin to think. "Maybe we should go check on her?"

"I wish. I doubt my parents will let me leave, even if I am ungrounded."

"Doesn't hurt to ask."

Orla shrugged and stood from the bed. "I guess so. Hold on," she said, pulling the phone down away from her ear. She walked through the house and back to the living room where her parents were sitting on the couch.

"Yes?" her father asked, muting the sound on the TV.

Orla covered the phone with her palm. "Idalia was wondering if we could go see Aviva. We're worried about her," she said.

Orla's parents looked at each other. "I've been concerned about her, too," Orla's mother said. She looked away from Orla's father and turned toward Orla. "You can go check on Aviva." She nodded.

Orla raised the phone to her ear.

"Yep, I heard," Idalia said. "Let me shower real quick, and I'll come pick you up."

"Okay," Orla said and hung up the phone. "Thanks, Mom and Dad," she said.

"Come sit with us while you wait," her mother said, patting the spot next to her on the couch.

Orla sat down next to her parents.

Her mother draped an arm around her shoulders and pulled her in for a hug. "Love you, honey," she said.

Orla smiled. "Love you too, Mom."

Idalia pulled up outside Orla's house and honked the horn. She waited a few minutes, growing impatient as the minutes ticked by on the dash. She placed her hand over the horn, about to press down again, when Orla finally walked through the door. Orla waved behind her and quickly made her way down the driveway to Idalia's car.

"What took so long?" Idalia asked when Orla slid into the passenger's seat.

"Sorry. It was a whole production trying to leave," Orla said, rolling her eyes.

"Your parents are a little much," Idalia said, switching gears and pulling away from the curb. She turned at the stop sign and headed away from Orla's neighborhood.

"You're telling me," Orla said, leaning back into her seat. "This way," she said, pointing down another street.

Orla directed Idalia through town, across railroad tracks, and into another neighborhood. "It's down this street," Orla said, leaning forward.

"I don't think I can get in here," Idalia said. Cars were piled up along the street, making it impossible for Idalia to drive through.

"We could walk," Orla shrugged. "It's not very far down there."

"Okay," Idalia said. She turned her car around and parked at the end of the street, next to a stop sign.

They both got out, looking around.

Idalia walked around the side of her car to meet Orla and clicked the lock on her key. "You can never be too safe," she said when Orla looked over at her with one eyebrow raised.

They walked down the street, weaving around cars. "What is going on?" Idalia asked as they got closer and closer to Aviva's house.

Blue and red lights flickered, bouncing off surrounding cars and houses.

"Come on," Orla said, grabbing Idalia's arm and pulling her down the street.

Orla dropped Idalia's arm. She pushed through a crowd of people filling the street. "Orla, wait," Idalia called, but Orla kept pushing through the crowd.

"I'm sorry, excuse me," Idalia said as she managed her way through the crowd. She found Orla peering over a roadblock sign.

"Look," Orla said, pointing toward a house.

There were swarms of policemen walking in and out of the house. An ambulance sat outside the house, right next to the curb, the back open and waiting for someone. Cop cars surrounded the house, keeping people away.

"Who lives there?" Idalia asked, trying to see if she recognized someone standing beside the house.

"Aviva," Orla whispered harshly. "What if they hurt her?"

Idalia placed a hand on Orla's arm. She wasn't sure if it was meant for reassurance or to keep Orla from running over to the house.

Two men in uniforms pushed a gurney out of the house. A white sheet covered the slopes and curves of a body. A gasp swept through the crowd. Orla covered her mouth, and her eyes watered.

"You don't know if that's her," Idalia said, her voice shaking.

Orla waved her hand through the air, and a gust of wind followed it. The white sheet fell away, revealing a face. "Oh, thank goodness," Orla said, turning away from the scene.

"But where's Aviva?" Idalia asked, searching through the crowd.

Orla shrugged. "Maybe she's still inside," she said after not finding her outside. "This way," she said, pulling Idalia to the side of the house.

They crept around the house, away from the cops and onlookers. "I don't think we should be over here," Idalia said, looking back at the front of the house.

"Look," Orla said, pointing to the back of the house. A tree had fallen and shattered a window. She pulled Idalia into the backyard. They peeked through the broken window. The room was full of tree branches and vines. Dirt covered the dresser and door.

"She's not here," Idalia said.

"We have to find her," Orla said, backing away from the house. They ran down the street and slipped into Idalia's car.

Idalia looked at Orla. "We will. We will find her."

65

In the Land of Season

Aviva tossed and turned, trying to find sleep again. But sleep wouldn't come to her, not without bad dreams. Every time she closed her eyes, Aviva saw the life drain out of Ted's eyes and heard the *thud* of his body crashing to the floor. Aviva gagged at the image.

She opened her eyes, staring at the canopy above her. It wasn't her style to have drapes hanging from the ceiling around her bed frame, but she wouldn't complain. Eira had given her a place to stay, saved her from going back to Texas and probably going to jail for murder. Saved her from being alone. The least she could do was be happy with whatever room she was offered. At least it didn't smell like Ted or his alcohol.

Aviva kept her eyes open for hours. They burned, tears

threatening to run down her cheeks. But she rubbed at them and stayed awake.

A knock sounded on her door. Aviva jumped out of bed. "Lady Aviva," a woman called through the wooden door.

Aviva opened the door. A woman clad in blue stood in the doorway. Aviva had seen her before when her, Idalia, and Orla had visited Brey. She was cold, her face hardened into a scowl. But then again, most of Winter had frozen scowls on their lips.

"Breakfast is served," Harriet said, pushing a cart of food into Aviva's room. She lifted the lid off the pans to reveal eggs, biscuits, and strips of bacon. "Eat," Harriet said gruffly. "Lady Eira would like to see you shortly."

Aviva nodded while loading up a plate full of food. She carried it back to the bed and began eating it, savoring every bite. She was starving. Aviva looked up from her plate. "Are you just going to stand there the whole time I'm eating?"

Harriet nodded. "I was told to escort you to Lady Eira once you're finished."

Aviva shoveled a few bites into her mouth, downed some juice, and followed Harriet to Eira. They walked the same path Aviva walked several times a day. Aviva had memorized the way from her room to Eira's. Up the stairs, turn left, left again, then right. But every day, she was escorted by someone. Never having a second alone, apart from when she was supposed to be sleeping. It was odd, but Aviva pushed the prickly feeling away.

"Ah, good morning, little sister," Eira said when they walked into her room.

"Morning, Eira," Aviva said, waiting for Harriet to leave her side.

She finally did, and Aviva crossed the room and stood by

Eira in front of the large window. Eira was watching men in fur march back and forth.

"Could I ask you something?"

"Sure," Eira said, her gaze not leaving the mass of people down below.

"What happened with your foster brother? Samuel?" Aviva asked.

Eira took a breath, her shoulders moving up and down slowly. She placed her hand on the window; ice crawled from her fingertips to the glass.

"You don't have to answer," Aviva said quickly. "I've just been wondering ever since I looked up those articles, trying to figure out what you were running from."

"No," Eira said, taking another huge breath. "It's okay."

Aviva waited, her heart pounding. She wanted Eira to be innocent. Or at least justified in her actions.

"I did what I had to do," Eira said. "Just like you did. Samuel was my best friend. The best sibling anyone could ask for." Eira took a big breath. "I loved him. He was the absolute best. Until one day he just snapped. He lost it. He came after me, so I did what I had to do."

"You killed him?" Aviva whispered.

"Yes." Eira nodded.

Aviva tried speaking, but she couldn't find any words.

"It's okay," Eira said, putting a hand on Aviva's shoulder. "It gets easier to live with, especially if there's a good reason for killing them. And you had a good reason."

Aviva swallowed the bitter knot in her throat. Tears stung her eyes. She looked away. "What are they doing?" Aviva asked, pointing to the men outside, changing the subject. Eira's hand dropped from her shoulder.

"Training."

"For what?"

"War, Aviva," Eira said with a roll of her eyes.

Aviva's throat was dry. "What war?"

"Look, I know this may come as a shock to you, but I don't plan on dying in Season. Or anywhere for that matter." Her tone was harsh, words were rushed. "I'm building an army. I'd like you to join me."

"What about Orla and Idalia?"

"What about them?" Eira said, turning to face Aviva. "They aren't like us. They will never understand us."

"So what are you planning? You're just going to have your army kill them?" Aviva's voice rose, blood pumping furiously through her. She could barely hear over the thumping in her ears.

"Better them than me." Eira shrugged. "They had a good life in Texas. They're not taking mine in Season."

Aviva stepped back, putting distance between her and Eira.

"Will you join me?" she asked.

Aviva shook her head. "What? No," she cried. "I'm not going to kill my sisters."

Eira laughed. "Oh, Aviva, you're going to have to one way or another." Eira waved her hand.

Aviva felt hands lock around her arms.

"Or you die. Your choice," Eira said.

She turned her back on Aviva. Strong hands pulled Aviva from Eira's room. They drug her down the hallway, down the stairs, and back into her room.

She was pushed into her room so hard she fell to the floor. The bedroom door shut with a *bang*, and a lock clicked into place.

66

Aviva sat on the bed, her legs crossed, and her necklace in her palm. "Orla, Idalia," she repeated over and over, chanting their names. Imagining where they could be in Texas.

"I'm not strong enough," she said to herself. She furrowed her brow and kept trying to open a portal. Sweat pooled at the top of her forehead, and her hands were white from closing them so hard. "Come on," she whispered, her voice cracking.

Her throat was sore, and her eyes hurt. But she put the pain out of her mind and focused on her sisters. The ones she could count on. The ones who weren't going to try to kill them all.

"Aviva?" Orla's voice crossed her mind.

"Orla?" Aviva said aloud. "Orla, are you there?"

A murky image of Orla appeared in the middle of the room. "I'm here," she said. "Kind of." Orla's image looked around the room. "Where are you?"

"I'm in Winter. I need your help," Aviva said. She lowered her voice. "Eira's gone bad. Real bad."

"Okay, hang tight. We're coming."

Orla's image disappeared, and Aviva was all alone again in the cold, dark room.

Orla pulled Idalia behind her, running up the stairs in the entrance hall of Conformity Castle.

"Ow, you're hurting me," Idalia said, snatching her arm back.

"Sorry, but we need to hurry. Eira has Aviva."

"I know, I know," Idalia huffed.

Orla sprinted up the steps and turned corner after corner until she came to the door with a hand on it. She didn't even bother knocking. She just barged in.

Brey stood with his arm resting on the wall. He didn't turn to look at the girls when they opened the door. He only stared out the window, watching as the light from the sun filled the entire room.

"Brey," Orla said, stepping up to him. "We need your help."

He sighed, his shoulders rolling backward. He stood tall and did a quick shake to loosen his joints. "What can I help you with?" he asked, walking to the middle of the room.

Orla glanced at Idalia, who only shrugged. "We need a map, or something. We need to get to Winter."

"Winter? What for?" Brey asked. He rifled through stacks of papers on his desk, quickly pulling a few off to the side.

"Eira has Aviva," Orla said.

"We need to find her," Idalia added.

Brey nodded, a look of concern etched on his face. "I see," he said, his voice barely rising above a whisper. He licked his thumb and continued searching through the stacks. Minutes were filled with only the sound of papers scraping against one another.

"Eira has changed," he said.

"We know," Orla agreed. Her foot tapped impatiently on the floor. They needed to hurry. They needed to get out of there, get to Winter, and get to Aviva.

He shuffled through a stack of books on another table. "She takes after her mother, that one. Creating an army," he scoffed. "That's something Queen Quinn would do."

"An army?" Idalia asked, catching Orla's eyes.

Orla shrugged. Eira with an army. Of course she had an army. Of course she was trying to break the rules. Not go through the trials. She was trying to change the game. One they had only just started playing.

He placed a book to the side. "What are the protocols good for, anyway?" he asked himself.

His back straightened as he lifted a large piece of parchment from underneath the stacks of books. "Here it is," he said, whipping around and shoving the paper into the middle of the three of them. "The map," Brey said, shaking it.

Idalia grabbed it from him and unrolled the edges. Conformity Castle was in the center of the map. The Tree of Season was just behind the castle to the north. The rest of the map was divided into four sections. Each section was a different color.

"Here," Brey said, reaching around Idalia to point to the blue part of the map. "That's Winter. That's where you'll find Eira, and hopefully save Aviva. The bloodshed must be saved for the trials." Brey turned and walked across the room to the window.

"Go now," he said. "Tell the horses to go east. Just go east, and you'll reach Winter."

Idalia nodded and rolled up the map, then slipped it into the calf of her boot.

"Thank you, Brey," Orla said.

"Don't bother with pleasantries. Hurry," Brey said, waving them out of the room.

Orla closed the door behind them and led the way through the castle, out into the garden and to the stables. They passed several stewards, handmaidens, and stable hands. Brey must be letting them back in.

She mounted Samson and bent down to whisper in the horse's ear, "Go east."

Samson neighed and galloped away from the stables. Orla looked behind her to see Idalia's horse catching up to them. She leaned down, staying steady on Samson's back, letting him lead them to Winter.

67

Idalia slipped off Lady's large back and landed on the ground, snow seeping into her boots. She tied Lady's reins around a tree and waited for Orla to do the same. "Wait here," Idalia whispered to Lady, rubbing her hand across her long face.

The horse shook out its mane and bobbed its head as if agreeing with her.

"Let's go," Idalia said, walking up beside Orla.

"How are we going to know where to go?" Orla asked.

Idalia shrugged. "There's not much on the map." She pulled out the map and looked over Winter. The east section of the map was stained blue. There was only one building drawn in the middle of the section. "I guess we start here," she said, pointing to the building.

Orla nodded. "What if we get recognized? Don't we need to stay hidden?"

Idalia readjusted her blanket, covering her head and pulling it taut around her. "Good thing we grabbed the blue ones." She laughed nervously.

She had never done something like this. She'd never had to save anyone before. Never had to disguise herself, sneak in, and rescue someone. But she'd do it. She'd do it a million times to save her littlest sister from Eira.

Orla fixed her blanket over her head. She walked away from Samson, heading toward the light coming from the town. Idalia followed her.

They trudged through the snow quietly, not bothering to speak to one another. Both focused on other things. Idalia swiveled around, checking their surroundings, making sure no one was coming for them. That no one was going to give them away. Or snatch them up, too.

"Eira's really trying to start something here," Idalia said, looking up at a tall border of tree trunks. It was a good six feet taller than the girls. "You go that way," she said, pointing in the opposite direction, "and I'll go this way. See if there's a way in somewhere close."

Orla nodded and took off away from Idalia. Idalia kept a hand on the tree trunks as she followed them along. There was no break in the wall. She turned and headed back the way she'd come.

"No luck," Orla said, meeting her in the middle.

"Me either." Idalia looked up at the wall. She placed her hands on the tree trunks. They were smooth and too wet in the icy wind. She put a foot on a low trunk and tried climbing up, but her foot slipped out from under her, and she landed hard on her back.

"You can't climb it. It's too high," Orla said, holding back a laugh at Idalia rolling around in the snow.

"I see that," Idalia said, rolling her eyes and standing back up. She dusted off the snow and shivered. She rubbed her hands together to try to bring warmth back into them. Slowly, her body filled with a burning fire. The snow melted off her and into a puddle at her feet. "Much better," she said.

"That's so not fair," Orla said, her lips quivering in the cold wind.

Idalia shrugged, a small smile creeping onto her face. "So, what are we going to do?" Idalia asked, looking back at the border. "I could burn them down," she said, bringing a ball of fire to her palm.

Orla reached out and covered her hand. "People are going to see us," she whispered harshly. "You can't do that."

Idalia let the flame go and ran a hand through her hair. "Then how are we going to get through?"

Orla lifted a hand into the air. Her forehead furrowed in concentration. A swirl of wind rose over the border and wrapped around the top log. It picked it up, separating the log from the rest of the wall, and dropped it gently to the side. "This might take a minute," Orla said, moving her hand to send the wind to another log.

Idalia waited, watching as the wall disappeared and the pile of tree trunks grew. Orla stopped. She wiped her brow and took a deep breath.

"You okay?" Idalia asked.

Orla nodded, dropping her arm. "Tired. Takes a lot out of you," she said. Orla climbed over the rest of the wall and dropped to the other side.

Idalia followed.

"Leave it," Idalia said, placing a hand on Orla's arm. "We're gonna need a quick getaway."

"But what if someone notices?"

"Hopefully it doesn't take that long to find Aviva." Idalia took off into the town.

Footsteps pounded against the ground, harsh breathing

flowed through the windy night. Idalia put a hand out to stop Orla. "Look," she whispered.

Men marched back and forth through a field of snow. Their boots kicked up ice, sending it into the air and onto pant legs. The men's faces were blank, expressionless.

"Must be the army," Orla said.

Idalia nodded. "They look just like Eira," she said. The cold, emotionless countenances made Idalia shiver. She didn't understand how someone could get so distant, so out of touch with life. No psychology class would ever help her understand her sister. "Come on." She waved Orla forward, around buildings and past the marching men.

"This must be it," Orla said, looking up at the building they were crouched by. The white building reached high into the air, a single tower at its point. A large veranda covered most of the garden, speckled with seating. Luscious bushes lined a cobbled walkway.

"How do we know where Aviva is?"

"I don't know," Orla muttered, searching the many windows for a sign of her sister. "Wait, Aviva called me somehow. Maybe we can call her."

They pulled their necklaces from their necks and placed them in their palms. "Aviva," Orla whispered. She leaned down close to the necklace as if it were a phone. "Aviva, are you there?"

"We need help finding you," Idalia said, copying Orla.

"Look, look," Orla said, swatting Idalia's arm and pointing to a window near the top of the building. A green light flooded the glass, shining out into the dark night. "That's gotta be Aviva, right?"

"Your guess is as good as mine," Idalia shrugged. "How are we going to get up there without being seen, though?"

They stared at the window, a good three stories high. "You can't, like, float us up there, can you?" Idalia asked, eyeing Orla.

"I don't know. I've never floated something that high before."

"Worth a shot," Idalia said.

Orla took Idalia's hand in hers and looked up at the tinted green window. She closed her eyes.

Idalia was wobbly beside her. She couldn't feel the current underneath her feet like Orla could. Her stomach lurched as they rose higher and higher, sifting through the air. She rocked too far forward, tipping over. Her hand was snatched from Orla's as she fell from the sky, landing hard on the snow. She grabbed her leg and pulled it to her chest. Her face contorted in pain, but she squeezed her lips shut to stop the whimper. Tears welled in her eyes. "Keep going," she whispered furiously to Orla, who was hanging in midair.

Orla tore her eyes away from Idalia on the ground and back up to the window. She climbed higher and higher, letting the cloud under her feet move her seamlessly through the air. She reached a hand out, pulling herself to the window with a green hue. She cupped her hands around her eyes and peered inside the room.

There was a figure sitting on the bed, a canopy obscuring the view. A green light emitted from beneath the fabric.

Orla tapped on the window lightly. The figure turned toward her slowly.

The canopy was swept away, and Aviva ran to the window.

"Orla?" she called through the window. Orla nodded, tears swam in her eyes.

Aviva pulled up the window, hot air blew into Orla's face.

"How'd you find me?"

Orla pointed to the glowing necklace.

"Of course," Aviva said, clutching the necklace in her palm. She slid it back onto her neck, the glow finally dissipating. "Where's Idalia?"

Orla looked down. She could barely make out Idalia sitting in the snow. "Down there. We gotta go before someone sees us."

Aviva poked her head out of the window. "I don't know about this," she said, her hands shaking on the window sill.

"It'll be fine," Orla said, reaching out her hand. "Just don't let go."

Aviva nodded and took her hand.

68

Aviva's feet touched the earth, finding solid ground underneath thick snow. "Well, that was something," Aviva said, looking back up at the window they had just flown out of. Her stomach flipped at the height.

"You couldn't have done that for me?" Idalia asked Orla, standing up on shaky legs. She tried putting weight on her foot. Her face pinched together, and she winced.

"You let go," Orla said in a hushed whisper. "Now, come on. We have to go before someone sees us."

Aviva went to Idalia's side. She wrapped one of Idalia's arms around her shoulders and hugged around her waist. She grunted at the weight Idalia put on her. She hadn't noticed just how much taller Idalia was than she. Orla came up on Idalia's other side. Aviva breathed in relief. All three of them hobbled away.

They stayed on the outskirts of Winter. Aviva held her breath every time a light from a house or a person's footsteps neared. She couldn't afford to be caught. She couldn't be a

prisoner again. But the longer they stayed on the inside of the wall, the longer that possibility remained. No matter how much Aviva wanted to go faster, to sprint from Winter, she couldn't. Idalia couldn't.

They made slow progress, hopping along behind buildings. Aviva's breaths escaped in harsh puffs of frozen air. She could feel the blood pool into her cheeks, flooding her face with redness. Idalia called warmth to her palms. Aviva sighed with relief as her bones began to unfreeze with the heat from Idalia.

"Hold up," Idalia said, standing straight up. "I need a break."

Orla looked around quickly. "We don't really have time for breaks," she said, trying to pull Idalia forward.

"Just a second," Idalia clipped, trying to catch her breath. "I just need to breathe."

Orla gave in and helped Idalia sit on a bench in the backyard of one of many houses lining the streets. Idalia took big breaths, folding in on herself.

Aviva wiped sweat from her brow. She turned away from them, heading toward the main road.

"Aviva," Orla whispered harshly. "Get back here."

Aviva didn't turn around. She looked low on the ground, digging through snow, until she found small branches and twigs. She gathered them up and sauntered back over to the bench. "Here," she said, laying the broken trees at Idalia's feet. She rolled her hands over them, concentrating. The twigs intertwined in the shape of a boot.

Aviva lifted Idalia's foot carefully. The twigs slithered around Idalia's foot, bracing it. "Thanks," Idalia said through clenched teeth.

"Mhmm," Aviva said, standing up. She slipped an arm

around Idalia and helped her stand. Orla took Idalia's other side. They started across the backyard, leaving footprints in their wake.

"Stop." Orla pulled Idalia and Aviva down onto the muggy ground. Orla covered Idalia's contorted mouth before she could get a sound out. Aviva followed Orla's pointed finger toward a house.

A light came on in the house, shining through the window. Aviva watched as two figures came into the room and walked toward the window. She could only see their outlines through the curtain. The figures grew larger as they drew near. One of them yanked the curtain away from the window.

Aviva gasped.

Orla pulled Idalia and Aviva behind a bush. She leaned back against the bush and closed her eyes. "There's no way," Orla muttered.

Aviva poked her head out from behind the bush, needing another look. She couldn't believe her eyes. It was the dark night, the street lights, something playing a trick on her.

Eira stood in the window, looking out over the backyard. She was talking, her hands flying wildly about her. And next to her, was an identical woman. Tall, blond, blue eyes. Queen Quinn.

"We need to go," Idalia whispered.

Aviva couldn't move. She couldn't feel her hands and feet in the snow. She couldn't catch a breath. She could only sit there, a feeling of dread washing over her, threatening to drown her. There was no way. No way she was alive. No way Eira was still working with her. No way she had lied about everything. Eira had been using her the whole time. She should have known better.

Idalia pushed Aviva. "Go," she whispered.

Aviva shook her head. Shivers ran down her spine.

"Now," Idalia said, pushing against her again.

Aviva shook her whole body, trying to free it from the shock of seeing their dead mother alive. She quickly crawled over to Orla at the edge of the property. Idalia followed behind, dragging her wrapped foot behind her.

Aviva sat with Orla, waiting for Idalia to reach them. She picked her up and half carried her toward the log wall. She was panting and sweating by the time she saw it.

"Wait," Aviva said, pulling away from the girls.

"What now?" Orla's hands flew up into the air, the snow surrounding them beginning to lift. Her face was bright red.

Aviva watched her take a big breath and put a hand back on Idalia to steady her.

"I gotta get Milo." Aviva disappeared into the barn. A few minutes later, she emerged with her small black horse covered in blankets. "Let's go," she said, spanking the horse's butt so he jumped through the broken-down border.

Aviva and Orla helped Idalia hobble through the wall. Idalia leaned against a tree while Orla and Aviva faced the wall, a big, gaping hole in the middle of it. Aviva made a lifting motion with her hands over the stack of logs to her side. She brought her hand up and over, setting it against the other logs of the structure. Tree trunks, one by one, floated into the air, stacking on top of one another. Orla stood alongside her, copying the motions. The wall was up in no time.

With the border sheltering them from Winter, the girls moved through the woods. Milo followed behind, his hooves kicking up the snow. Samson and Lady, still tied up to trees, came into view. Orla and Aviva gave Idalia a leg up, steadying her on top so she wouldn't topple off. Aviva and Orla mounted their own horses.

All three girls dug their heels into their horses' bellies and galloped toward Conformity Castle, their hair blowing fiercely in the frigid wind.

69

The flickering flame of several lampposts guided the horses back to Conformity Castle. Orla and Aviva jumped off their horses' backs, skidding to a stop just before the massive stairs leading up to the castle. Idalia wavered in the cold wind, slipping off Lady's back.

Orla ran to Idalia's side, reaching her hands out to catch her, but her hands slipped at the last moment, and Idalia fell onto the snow-covered ground. She rolled to her side, hugging her body with her arms.

"You okay?" Orla asked, kneeling down beside Idalia.

Idalia grunted as she sat up in the snow. She mumbled something Orla couldn't understand.

Aviva put an arm under Idalia's shoulder and lifted her up. Idalia stood on one shaky leg. "Thanks," she said to Aviva.

Aviva didn't say anything. She only nodded and slowly took steps forward, letting Idalia follow at her own pace. Orla went to Idalia's other side and helped them move up the stairs one step at a time.

"My ladies," a guy in a long coat said, opening the castle door. "Are you all right?"

They hobbled inside, dropping the blankets to the floor.

"Oh my," the guy said, looking down at Idalia's foot wrapped in vines. "Come, come," he said, taking Idalia from Orla and Aviva.

Idalia let the man lead her away. They weaved through the ground floor of the castle, passing doors Idalia had never opened. Sounds erupted from the large kitchen, pots banging against each other, cooks opening and closing drawers.

"Almost there," the man said. "You are so lucky Brey has decided to let us all come back. Otherwise, this wouldn't be such an easy fix."

Idalia didn't pay him any attention. She just kept putting her uninjured foot forward and letting him help her hop over her other foot.

The man stopped at a large wooden door. He pushed it open, the door creaking on its hinges. He set Idalia down on a long, flat chair and lifted her foot up. "I'll go get Gro," he said, bowing slightly and backing out of the room.

Idalia sat back, leaning against the wall. She brought a flame to her hand, illuminating the dark room. An unlit torch hung by the door. She slipped off the chair, reaching her hand out in front of her to steady herself. Idalia hopped across the floor, one small jump at a time. She reached the far wall and placed a fingertip on top of the torch. It burst into flames.

Idalia shook her hand out, the ball of fire disappearing. She hopped back across the floor to sit in the chair. A large bookcase was by the end of the chair. Idalia slid down the chair to reach the bookcase. Several dusty, leather-wrapped books were stacked on the shelves.

She pulled a red book out and flipped through it. Sketches

were scattered at the top of the pages. Different leaf patterns covered the worn pages with handwriting underneath the pictures. Idalia couldn't read the clumpy cursive writing. But she still flipped the pages, looking at all the plant life in Season. She dropped the book to her side when the door swung open.

A tiny woman with a long, white coat stepped into the room. Her hair was pulled tight against the back of her head. She was covered head to toe in white cloth.

The woman looked at Idalia, coming up to her side. "I'm Gro," she said simply. Gro pulled Idalia's foot into her hands. Idalia winced.

Gro turned her foot over and over and then dropped it, letting her foot dangle off the chair. She went to the other side of the room and ruffled through a small desk. She came back to Idalia with clippers in her hands. She held Idalia's foot again and began cutting the vines away.

Underneath the mess of vines, Idalia's foot was swollen and bruised. Gro swiveled her foot back and forth, side to side.

"Ow," Idalia said, clutching her leg.

Gro slapped Idalia's hands away. "Don't touch," she said gruffly.

Idalia moved her hands away and clutched the side of the chair. Her knuckles turned white as Gro continued looking over her foot.

Gro put Idalia's foot down and went back to the desk. She opened several drawers, pulling out materials. She bundled it up in her arms and dropped it next to Idalia on the chair. Gro set up a bowl, poured some liquid into it, and placed some bandages in the concoction.

Idalia wrinkled her nose up at the strong smell. "What is that?"

Gro kept her eyes down, busy wetting bandages. "Healing ointment," she said, her voice harsh. She placed a cold bandage on Idalia's ankle, wrapping it around and around. Once Idalia's foot was covered in wet strips of cloth, Gro placed her hands on each side of her ankle. She closed her eyes, and her lips began moving in words Idalia couldn't hear.

Idalia watched as a small flickering light seeped from beneath Gro's hands. The disc of light grew, blinding Idalia. She put her arm up to cover her eyes.

Her foot burned. She could feel the sweat beading underneath the bandages. But it wasn't a painful burn. It was warm, healing.

Idalia peeked through her fingers. Gro had removed her hands from her foot, and the bandages had disintegrated in the burning light. "All done," Gro said, patting Idalia's ankle rather hard. She motioned for Idalia to stand, but Idalia only raised an eyebrow.

"Let's go," she said, pulling on Idalia's arms. "I don't have all day."

Idalia slid off the chair, landing on the floor with both feet. She pushed her foot down onto the hard floor. No pain. As if her injury had never been there.

"Wha—" Idalia started. "How did you do that?"

"Practice," Gro said. She pushed Idalia out of the room. "Go on now," she said. Gro closed the door, leaving Idalia alone in the corridor.

Idalia turned away from the wooden door and headed down the hallway, trying to remember which way she had come earlier. She took each step gingerly, still not sure about her foot. But with each landfall, her foot became stronger, and she became confident.

70

Orla climbed the stairs, heading toward the chamber floor. She stepped off the landing, walking toward her room. Aviva followed close behind. They entered the golden room and sat on the bed.

Orla fell back against the mattress and closed her eyes. "It's been a long day," she murmured more to herself than Aviva.

But Aviva answered, "You're telling me."

They melted into silence, letting the cool air around them comfort them. "Thanks," Aviva said, not looking at Orla.

"For what?" Orla opened one eye to peek at Aviva. Aviva had leaned back against the wall, her eyes falling shut. The lamp next to Orla's bed flickered, casting eerie shadows across her bedroom.

Aviva's shoulders moved up and down, slowing with her breathing. "Saving me from Eira," she said.

"That's what sisters are for," Orla shrugged. She turned over to her side and watched Aviva closely.

"Yeah, I guess," Aviva said.

Orla reached out a hand toward Aviva. "What's that?" she

asked, brushing Aviva's shoulder and pointing toward her neck. A purplish ring wound around her neck. Purple and splotchy, like a bruise.

Aviva's eyes popped open, and she sank back against the wall. Aviva wrapped a hand around her neck.

"Did Eira do that?" Orla asked, sitting up and leaning in closer.

"No," Aviva said, shaking her head. "Of course she didn't. Eira wouldn't hurt me," Aviva said, rolling her eyes and turning away from Orla.

"Then what happened?"

Orla tried snatching Aviva's hand away so she could get a better look, but Aviva hopped up from the bed, putting distance between them. She pulled her jacket up around her shoulders to try to bury her bruise.

"We went by your house before we came here," Orla started slowly. Her mind was going in circles, blurring at the edges as she stared at her little sister across the room. "There were cops all around."

Aviva wouldn't meet her eyes.

"What happened to you?" Orla asked again, her voice barely above a whisper.

A tear threatened to sting Aviva's cheek, but she rubbed it clear and took a deep breath. They both turned to face the door.

Idalia strolled into the room, bouncing from one foot to the other, a smile spread wide on her face. She spun in a circle in the middle of the room, turning on a brand new heel. "The doc fixed my foot," she said. "Feels so much better." She twirled again. She stuck her foot out and stopped mid-turn.

"What's going on in here?" Idalia asked, finally noticing the solemn looks on her sisters' faces.

"Aviva was about to explain what caused that," Orla said, leaving the bed and walking over to Aviva. She pulled Aviva's collar down and exposed the bruise for Idalia to see.

"Oh, wow," Idalia said. She moved closer to them, peering at Aviva. "Are you okay?"

Aviva nodded. "Yeah, I'm fine," she said while shrugging Orla off.

Idalia and Orla both squinted at Aviva. "That looks nasty," Idalia said.

"No way you're fine," Orla said at the same time. "We saw Ted."

Aviva froze at the mention of her foster dad.

"They were rolling him out on a gurney. He's dead," Orla said.

Idalia nodded in agreement. "What happened over there?"

Aviva shrugged. "We got in a fight," she said, turning away from them. "Nothing unusual. But I lost control. Things got out of hand," she whispered. "I didn't mean to kill him."

Orla's heart beat hard, and the breath sucked from her chest. Then she lunged for Aviva, hugging her tight. Aviva tried protesting, but it was no use. Idalia joined the hug, shielding Aviva, as if protecting her from herself. Orla would always protect her. She would protect them. From here on out. She would be there. She would make sure they survived.

71

Aviva wiped the tears from her face, barely able to move with her sisters' arms wrapped around her.

"We know you didn't mean to kill him," Orla said, her mouth right next to Aviva's ear.

Aviva pulled away from Orla, taking a step back from her sisters. Orla and Idalia dropped their arms to their sides.

"Yeah," Idalia agreed. "I'm sure it was an accident," she said, bobbing her head.

They stood still, unmoving and not meeting one another's eyes. "We should probably go back to Texas," Orla said.

"I can't go back." Aviva's gaze snapped up from the floor. "The cops will come after me. They'll put me in jail." Her words were rushed as her eyes darted back and forth between Orla and Idalia. She could feel the panic set in. She could feel the heat rising in her face. Her hands went numb.

Idalia reached a hand out, placing it on her shoulder. "It's okay," she said. "It was self-defense. Just explain what happened." Idalia shrugged.

"But leave out the magic powers part," Orla interjected.

Idalia nodded. "Yeah, leave that out, but tell them everything else, and I'm sure they'd understand."

Aviva looked from one sister to the other. Their faces were hopeful, full of confidence in the system. She wished she could have that confidence. But she knew things would be different for her. There was no way she could go back. Kathy could've spun whatever story to make her look bad. She'd have her nails in the cops. Aviva would lose this battle just like the million other battles she'd lost. All the times she'd tried to tell her caseworker, all the times she was ignored. There was no way she could go back.

"Okay," she whispered. "But can we stay here tonight? I'm tired and would really like some sleep before figuring everything out."

Orla looked over at her bed. It was covered in warm blankets and soft pillows. "Yep, that's fine by me," she said, making her way across the room to the bed. She hopped on and made herself comfortable under the blanket. "I'm going to be in trouble either way," she said with a roll of her eyes.

Idalia shrugged. "I've got nowhere else to be," she said. Idalia climbed into the bed next to Orla and patted the spot next to her.

Aviva joined them and pulled the covers up tight. Orla blew the light from the lamp out with a gust of wind, and the room plunged into darkness.

"Goodnight," Orla said, her voice already drowsy.

"Night," Idalia said, rolling over and pulling the covers into her chest.

"Night," Aviva said, staring straight up at the ceiling.

Minutes went by, Aviva wasn't sure how many. Orla and Idalia's breathing had both slowed down. "What are we going to do about Queen Quinn?" Aviva whispered into the night.

Idalia rolled over, her back facing Aviva. "That's a problem for another day," she said, a big yawn escaping from her mouth. "Go to sleep."

Aviva nodded even though Idalia wouldn't be able to see. She hunkered down into the bed, trying to find sleep. But her mind was racing, and her eyes wouldn't shut.

The sky turned from black to a dusty pink, and Aviva watched every minute of the color change. She sat up, careful not to shake the bed too much. She peered over at her sisters. Both of them still had their eyes shut tightly.

Aviva scooted to the edge of the bed, leaving her sisters behind. She reached over to Orla's desk and scribbled a note on a piece of paper. Aviva slid it under Orla's pillow and stood. She quickly dressed and grabbed a blanket. She left the room without a sound.

At the bottom of the stairs, Aviva took a big coat off the rack and slipped it on. She pushed the castle doors open, revealing the cold winter day.

Aviva followed the path down the side of the castle to the stables. The smell of hay greeted her at the barn door. Soft sounds came from the stalls as she paced into the barn, looking for her horse. She found him near the back, laying in warm hay. She opened the stall door, slipping inside.

Milo's eyes rolled open.

"Hey," Aviva said, leaning down to her horse. She placed a hand on his head and stroked between his ears all the way to the tip of his nose. Milo nuzzled into her hand, his mane flipping around him. "Want to go for a ride?"

Milo bobbed his head. Aviva backed up, letting Milo stand. He shook out his whole body.

Aviva grabbed the saddle and reins that were hanging on the stall wall. She quickly got Milo ready. "Let's go," she said, leading him out of the stall and through the barn. She placed a foot in one stirrup and hoisted herself over Milo's back. She leaned down toward his ear. "Take me somewhere safe," she whispered.

Milo neighed, stomping at the ground. Aviva nudged her heels into his ribs, and Milo galloped away from the stables. He left Conformity Castle in his dust, taking Aviva far, far away from Eira, Queen Quinn, and her sisters.

72

Eira woke up with a smile on her face. She swung open the thick blue curtains, letting in streams of bright, burning light. She stretched her arms out over her head, rolling her shoulders back, and popping her neck side to side. *It's going to be a great day.*

Eira turned and sauntered out of her chambers, leaving a mess for the maids to clean. She walked down twisty hallways, following the same path Aviva had made several times since her stay. Eira knocked on Aviva's bedroom door.

"Aviva, are you awake?" Eira called through the wooden door. She waited for an answer but none came. Eira pressed her ear against the door, held her breath, and waited to hear any kind of sound in the room. "Aviva?" she called again.

There was nothing. No answer. No footsteps on the other side of the door.

Eira balled her fists. They turned white with rage. She grabbed the door handle, and it broke off in her hand, crumpling to the floor. The door swung open.

Eira stomped inside, looking from side to side. She ran over to the open window and looked down. In the snow, there were several sets of footsteps running away from the manor. She screamed, a loud, piercing sound erupting from within. Shards of ice exploded from her hand. The pointy daggers stuck to the walls. She whipped around, leaving Aviva's empty room.

Three guards met Eira outside. "We heard the scream," one guard said. Eira couldn't recall his name. Or any of their names.

"Are you injured, my queen?" another asked, eyeing her up and down.

Eira shook her head hard, her mouth in a tight line. "I'm fine," she said. "But my sister is missing."

"Missing?" the short brown-haired man who hadn't spoken asked.

"Yes, missing," Eira shouted, her hands raising into the air, waving all around. "Check the manor," she ordered. She turned her back on them and headed toward the stairway. "*Now,*" she called when they didn't move.

The three men scrambled away from Eira, spreading in each direction.

Eira barreled down the staircase, her face red with anger. The maids on the bottom floor dispersed when Eira's feet connected with the marbled floor. Eira burst out of the manor's front door, leaving them wide open behind her. She ran through the garden, past the gazebo, and down the streets. In the distance, she could hear footsteps stomping in the snow.

Her men were in lines before her, spaced equally from one another in all directions. They stood like stone: hard, cold, and unwavering. They didn't move when Eira approached in a flurry of kicked-up ice.

Jedrek was in the front of the army, his hands secured tightly behind his back. He paced, back and forth, down the lines of soldiers. He struck one of the men. The man slid his foot an inch. Jedrek nodded his head and moved on.

Jedrek ambled back to the top of the army. "They look good, don't they?" he asked Eira.

Eira turned a furious eye on him. "Aviva is missing. We need to find her," she said. Her callous words hung in the air around them.

Jedrek snapped his head over to Eira. "Missing? Where could she have gone?"

"With the others," Eira said shortly. "Fetch my horse. I'll go to Conformity Castle and see if they are there. You and your men tear this place apart looking for her. The woods included."

Eira barely gave him time to nod before turning around, her coat billowing out behind her. She made it back to the manor and waited on the porch for Jedrek to return with her horse.

It was several minutes before he shuffled up to the porch empty handed. "Willow is gone, my queen," he said with his head bowed and his eyes on the ground.

"Gone?" Eira asked, barely breathing.

Jedrek nodded. "Yes, my queen. She was let out."

"Find her," Eira screamed. Ice shot out from her hands in every direction, smothering Winter.

73

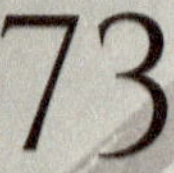

Orla groaned and covered her eyes with her palms. She rolled over, turning her back away from the bright light streaming through the window. "Sorry," she muttered when her elbow connected with her sister's back.

"Mhmm," Idalia mumbled, sitting up and rubbing the sleep from her eyes. She looked around the room. "Where's Aviva?" she asked.

Orla shot up out of the bed. She swiveled back and forth, searching the room. Idalia walked into the bathroom, still rubbing her eyes as she went. "She's not in here," she called to Orla. A loud *bang* rang out as the toilet seat fell, and a swooshing sound filled the bathroom.

Orla padded over to the desk. It was clean, books stacked to the side, pushed all the way to the wall. Pencils lined on one edge. Everything was in its place. She turned on her heel, surveying her room. Floating to the ground next to the bed was one sheet of paper with Aviva's handwriting all over it.

"She's gone," Orla whispered, reading the note.

"What?" Idalia asked, coming back into the room. Orla handed her the note, a solemn expression frozen on her face. "What is it?"

Orla nodded to the piece of paper. Idalia held it up and began reading it.

Orla and Idalia,

I really wish there was some other way to do this, but I can't go home. I killed Ted. And I can't go to jail. I know y'all said I wouldn't since it was self-defense, but I'm a foster kid. The system doesn't care about us. So I'm leaving. I don't know where I'm going, but I'm getting far away from Texas. And Queen Quinn. I really can't face her again. I thought we were done dealing with her. But now we have to get through her and Eira. And the other trials. I can't do it. I'm done fighting.

Love y'all,
Aviva

Idalia balled-up the piece of paper and threw it on the floor. "She's just going to bail like that?" she asked, her voice rising.

"Can you blame her?"

Idalia rubbed a hand over her face, a deep sigh escaping

her lips. "I guess not," she admitted. "So what do we do? Go after her?"

Orla chewed on her lip. Aviva was her little sister. She needed to protect her. She had to make sure she was safe. But that would mean staying in Season longer. Searching everywhere for her. Who knew how long that would take? "I can't. My parents are going to kill me as it is. I gotta get home," Orla sighed.

Idalia nodded. "Yeah, I should, too. Classes are starting soon."

Orla didn't want to leave. She didn't want to abandon Aviva in Season. But she'd made the choice. She'd left them. Sometimes protecting someone meant letting them leave. Sometimes being the big sister meant letting mistakes happen. Right?

She stepped up to Idalia, lifting her hands for Idalia to clasp onto. They both closed their eyes, envisioning the cool air of Winter in Texas.

74

In the Land of Texas

The sides of Idalia's car appeared around Idalia and Orla. The metal roof materialized above them. Green lawns and small houses lined the street around them. "I don't think I'll ever get used to that," Orla said, shaking the blurry vision away.

"Me either," Idalia said, buckling her seatbelt across her lap.

The car started, bursting to life under Orla. Her seat vibrated in time with the engine. Idalia pulled into the street, and Orla watched as Aviva's house disappeared in her side-view mirror.

Idalia skidded to a stop in front of Orla's house. Two cars were sitting in the driveway, despite it being a weekday.

"I'm in so much trouble." Orla watched the house. She didn't want to get out. She didn't want to face the fury that her parents were bound to feel at yet another disappearance. A curtain moved, and Orla's mother peeked through the window.

"Good luck," Idalia said.

Orla's parents came outside. They stood at the top of the driveway, a foot away from the front door, with narrowed eyes and pursed lips. Her mother placed her hands on her hips, and her father tapped his foot against the pavement. Orla looked back at Idalia. "If you don't hear from me in a little while, call the cops."

"Will do," Idalia said, a smile breaking out on her lips.

Orla stepped out of the car and watched as Idalia drove away. She took a big breath and finally met her parents' eyes.

"And where exactly have you been?" her father asked when she reached them. His lips were so tight the words were hardly able to escape his mouth. Creases around his eyes deepened as he stared daggers at Orla. "Did we not just unground you?" he asked before Orla could answer his first question.

Orla nodded. "Yes, you did. I'm sorry."

"You're sorry?" Orla's mother said, throwing her hands in the air. She inhaled deeply, trying to suck in the tears forming in her eyes. "She's sorry," she said to Orla's father. Her mother turned and walked back into the house. She shook her head the whole way.

Orla's father turned on his heel and followed her mother inside the house. Orla took a deep breath and made her feet move.

She closed the front door behind her. Her father paced in the living room. Her mother sat on the couch, her hands covering her face, and sniffles coming from her nose.

"Oh, no you don't," Orla's father said as she tried snaking

around the living room furniture unseen. "You can take a seat right over there," he said, pointing to the couch.

Orla hung her head and followed his finger to the couch. Her father didn't stop his pacing. A few minutes passed. The only sound was her mother's sniffles and her father's steps.

"Orla," her father started, running a hand over his face. "What has gotten into you lately? You stay out late, don't come home when you're supposed to, don't call to let us know anything."

"It's not like any of this is planned. It just happens. It's out of my control," she burst out, interrupting his monologue.

"How is it out of your control?" her father yelled. His cheeks were flushed. Orla could imagine tiny puffs of smoke coming out of his ears.

"I can't say," Orla whispered.

Her father laughed. The noise sounded foreign in the hostile room.

Orla's mother finally picked her head up from her hands and moved beside Orla. She took Orla's hand in hers and looked at her with teary eyes. "We're worried about you, sweetheart. You haven't been acting like yourself lately."

Orla clenched her lips together to stop from speaking. She wanted to tell them everything. Tell them about Season and her sisters. Tell them why she kept disappearing. But they wouldn't believe her. Why would they? She still had a hard time believing it herself.

Orla's father sat on her other side. "Just tell us why," he said. His eyes were desperate. Orla could see the concern hidden in them.

Orla opened her mouth to speak, but no words came out. She clamped it shut again.

What could she tell them to help them understand? Would they even understand?

"I've just been hanging out with Aviva and Idalia a lot lately," she said with a shrug. She didn't look up at her parents' faces, but she could tell they were staring at her.

"Well, maybe that needs to stop," her father said.

Her mother nodded. "They must not be very good influences for you to be behaving like this."

Orla's head shot up. "What? No," she said, her voice rising. She snatched her hand from her mother's grasp and stood in front of her parents. "You can't make me stop hanging out with them."

Her parents glanced at one another but didn't say anything.

Orla turned her backs on them and took a few steps away from the couch. She took a huge breath, her shoulders rising and falling heavily. "Look," she said, running a hand over her face just as her father had done minutes before. "They're my sisters. We have to be together. We have to help each other."

"We understand that y'all are friends," her mother said softly.

"No, not friends," Orla interrupted. "We're sisters. Biological sisters."

Her mother's jaw snapped shut, and her father's eyes bulged. "How do you know?" her mother whispered.

"We each got a letter after our biological father died," Orla said, trying to keep as close to the truth as possible.

Her mother covered her mouth with her hand in shock.

"There's a lot going on right now," Orla said. "We're just trying to figure everything out. But I'm sorry for being MIA, and I'm sorry for not telling you sooner."

"Oh, Orla," her mother said, standing up and gathering her

in a hug. "Sweetheart, that is a lot to handle by yourself. You should've told us."

Orla nodded. "I know. I just didn't know how to."

Orla's father joined the hug and laid his head on hers. "This still doesn't excuse your behavior, young lady."

Orla nodded.

"But we love you," he said.

"I love y'all, too."

The three of them stood in the middle of their living room entangled in one another's arms. Orla felt the warmth radiating from her parents. But deep down, in the pit of her stomach, she felt guilt. Guilt for still holding back the truth.

75

Idalia parked her car in the driveway of her parents' house. She leaned her head back against the headrest and closed her eyes. She was tired. But not physically tired; although, getting a good night's sleep in a different world than the one she was used to wasn't as easy as she had hoped. No, she was mentally exhausted.

Everything she thought she knew was wrong. Her evil mother had somehow managed to survive Eira's fatal blow. And not only that, Eira was protecting her. Keeping her hidden, safe.

And Aviva ran away, unable to come back to Texas for fear of the cops. Who knew where she would end up in Season, or even if she would be able to stay alive?

Idalia rubbed a harsh hand over her face and blew out a sigh of frustration. She was so over the back and forth. Texas, her real world. And Season, the world she had been thrust into. She just wanted a break. But that wasn't going to happen.

Something clacked against the window.

Idalia jumped, her eyes flying open. She looked to her left, clutching the edge of the seat.

"Sorry," her mother said through the wall of glass, her fingers resting on the window. "I didn't mean to scare you," she said with a guilty smile.

Idalia turned the ignition off and pushed the car door open. Her mother stepped out of the way. "It's okay," Idalia said after closing the door behind her.

"What were you doing in there?"

Idalia followed her mother inside the house. "Nothing. Just thinking."

Her mother nodded. "I didn't know if you were coming back. You left so suddenly the other day."

"Yeah, sorry about that," Idalia said, sinking down into the couch.

"Oh, it's no problem," her mother said with a wave of her hand. "You're grown; you can come and go as you please." She straightened a pillow and sat opposite Idalia. "Anyway, I knew you'd be back when I went to tidy up the guest room and your bags were all over the place. You never were one to be organized, huh?"

Idalia forced a smile across her lips, and her mother stopped laughing. She reached a hand across the couch and placed it on Idalia's knee.

"What's wrong, honey?"

Idalia shook her head and looked away from her mother's worried eyes. "It's nothing, Mom. Just a lot on my plate right now."

"Would you like to talk about it?"

Idalia wished she could. But the only people she could talk to about Season and everything going on in her life were her sisters. And one of them wasn't even on their side.

"No thanks, Mom."

Her mother nodded and removed her hand from Idalia's knee. "Okay," she said. She stood and walked out of the living room and into the kitchen. Idalia could hear her combing through the cabinets.

"Have you registered for the Spring semester?" her mother called through the house. "What classes are you taking?" she asked when she walked back into the living room with two glasses of tea in her hand. She handed one to Idalia.

Idalia took a sip, gulping past the knot in her throat. She nodded. "I don't know yet. Haven't looked at classes."

One of her mother's eyebrows raised as she peered over her glass. "Don't you think you should do that soon?"

"I think I may take a break."

"A break?"

"Yeah." Idalia nodded, forcing a smile. "There's a lot going on, and I don't want to waste money by possibly failing classes I can't focus on."

"Mhmm," she said. "I guess," she mumbled disapprovingly. "Get ready for dinner," Idalia's mother said, not meeting her eyes. "Your father will be home shortly."

Idalia nodded slowly and stood. She left her mother sitting on the couch, sipping her cup of iced tea, looking off into the distance.

76

Eira looked out the frosty window. Winter was covered in spears of ice. Her soldiers carefully maneuvered around them, making sure not to touch the frigid knives. Her hands grasped the cold ledge of her window, nails digging into the wet brick. Her gaze darted back and forth, watching her town. Looking for any sign of her missing horse or sisters.

But she didn't see anything out of the ordinary. It was just the same townspeople she had grown accustomed to watching as she ruled over Winter.

"My queen?" a voice said from behind Eira.

She turned to look at the maidservant.

"Yes?" Eira asked, rolling her eyes at the frail girl. The servant's skirt swallowed her up, making her look ten years old.

"You have a visitor," she said, bowing her head and taking a step backward, away from the door.

Behind the servant, a woman clad in a golden dress came slithering into Eira's room. Tresses to match her dress snuck out from underneath a hood. Her feet glided confidently across the floor, her steps light but strong. The woman let the hood fall around her shoulders.

"Quinn?" Eira said, eyeing her mother up and down. "What are you doing here?"

"Coming to see my daughter, of course," she said with a flip of her hair.

"Do you think that's wise? I thought you were staying hidden for a while?" Eira crossed her arms in front of her body.

"Well." Quinn stepped up to Eira and placed her hands on her shoulders. "Your sisters have disappeared and set your horse free. What is there to hide from now that they know what you've done?"

Eira shrugged off her hands and stepped back. "What I've done?" she asked, her voice rising. She didn't care that Quinn was her mother. No one was allowed to talk to her like that. Not in Winter. *Her* Winter.

"Well, yes." Quinn nodded. "You faked my death, Eira. Do you really think you can come back from that?"

"That was your idea," Eira said, blowing hot air through her teeth. Seeing Quinn in her manor, standing in her room, she wished she'd had a different plan. One that hadn't included saving her. Why had she listened to her?

"Of course it was," she said, a small laugh escaping from her taut lips. She turned around, her back facing Eira. "But you played along. Your sisters will never forgive you for that."

The maidservant quickly picked up her skirt and excused herself from the room.

Eira huffed. "I don't need their forgiveness. I don't need anything from them." She faced the window, ignoring her mother. "Especially not when I'm going to be the only one alive by the end of this."

Eira jumped when Quinn placed a hand on her arm.

"Are you sure about that?"

Eira hated the sickening sweetness that coated Quinn's words. Hated how easily she could force emotion onto her words. How easily she could mask herself.

"Sure about what?" Eira asked, whipping around to come face to face with her mother.

"If you're going to be the last one alive, you have to do things the others won't."

"Like what?"

Quinn leaned forward until her lips were level with Eira's ear, "Kill your sisters."

Eira backed up. "And you think I won't be able to do that?" A snarl spread across her lips.

Quinn shrugged and let Eira pass. "You will. If you take after your mother and not the weak King Quilo."

"Weak?" she asked, one eyebrow rising on her forehead. "He killed his brothers to become king."

"Or they all killed each other while he laid in wait," Quinn shrugged, looking out the window.

Eira waved her hand in the air. "It doesn't matter. I'll do whatever it takes to make Season my home. Even if I have to do all the killing myself. It's not like I really know them anyway."

"That's my girl," Quinn said, a glow in her eyes Eira had never seen before.

Eira turned away from her and walked toward the door.

"Where are you going?" Quinn asked, stopping Eira in her tracks.

"To make my next move."

77

"I'm sorry about your father, honey," Idalia's mother said while shutting Idalia's car door. "But you know he's right. College is too important to put off."

"Yeah, Mom." Idalia rolled her eyes. She buckled her seatbelt across her chest. "Whatever you say," she whispered underneath her breath.

Her mom pretended not to hear. Instead, she closed the door and stepped away from the car. "I love you, honey," she called through the door.

Idalia shook her head and put the car in reverse, backing out of the driveway. She waved just as she pulled out of view.

Idalia stopped the car, leaving it idling in front of her building. She looked up at the brown bricks she had just left a few weeks ago. She wasn't ready to be back, but at least she didn't have to switch dorms.

Idalia rolled her eyes. She sighed, her shoulders lifting and dropping heavily. She had a feeling the semester was going to be a waste. But it was her parents' money, and they'd pushed her to go back.

No, that wasn't right. They forced her to go back.

If only they knew the real reason she didn't want to come back. The reason she wanted to forget about school and just be done with it. But they wouldn't believe her if she told them there was a chance she'd never finish college. There was a chance she'd be dead within the year. No, they would just send her to a different school. A school for crazy people.

Idalia turned the car off, unbuckled her seatbelt, and slid out of the car. She grabbed a box from the back seat and headed up the stairs. She juggled the box on her knee as she tried jiggling the key into the doorknob. The box fell and broke, her comforter spilling out of its torn edges. Idalia let out a huge breath through her nose and pushed the door open.

She bent down and tried stuffing the contents of the box into her arms. But there was too much stuff, and she kept dropping items. She turned her head at the sound of footsteps reverberating off the steps.

"Oh, hi, Idalia," Katie said.

Brittany raised an eyebrow at her. "We didn't know if you were going to come back. Or if you had switched dorms, or something."

Idalia nodded against her comforter and forced a smile. "Of course not. Why would I switch?"

Katie shrugged. "I don't know. We hadn't heard from you all break. And you weren't here on move-in day."

"Had a last minute family vacation," Idalia lied. Well, sort of. She had gone away with her family, and it was last minute. Idalia shook her head free of Season and her sisters. If her parents were going to force her to be here, she needed to take it seriously. She needed good grades. Just in case.

"Want to go grab coffee or something then?" Brittany asked.

"Yeah, sounds good. I just have to bring in a couple of boxes." She walked through the open door and threw her comforter onto the bed. Katie and Brittany followed her with the items she had dropped along the way. "Thanks," Idalia muttered.

"We'll help," said Katie, following Idalia down the steps and to her car. Idalia handed them each a small box. She reached into the car and pulled out the last box, setting it on her hip as she closed the door.

Brittany plopped a fry into her mouth and noisily chewed it. Katie leaned forward across the table. "So what did you do over the break?" she asked Idalia.

Idalia sipped her coffee, letting the warmth soak into her body. It wasn't as warm as her fire, but it'd do in its absence. "Just hung out with family," she said shortly. She didn't want to get into the whole mess of Season and her sisters, especially since her friends didn't even know about her sisters.

"Oh, you said you went somewhere," Brittany said, eyeing Katie.

"Right, right." Idalia chewed her lip. "We just went to the lake for a few days, nothing too grand," she said.

"Sounds so fun," Katie said, finally sitting back in her chair and letting Idalia have her space back. "After Christmas, we went to the mountains. It was so fun," Katie said with a bright smile. "You should've come with us."

Idalia nodded. "Sorry, I meant to text you. Things just got so busy with the holidays," she lied.

"Of course," Katie said, nodding her head in fake understanding.

Brittany muttered something beside her.

Idalia didn't pay Brittany any attention. She kept the conversation going with as little effort as possible, nodding and asking questions as Katie told her all about their time in the mountains. "Sounds like it was a blast," Idalia said, forcing a smile onto her lips.

"It really was." Katie sighed. "I can't wait for our next trip," she said, reaching a hand out to touch Brittany's arm.

Brittany nodded enthusiastically. "As long as I get to choose the destination this time," she said. They both laughed, the sound so foreign to Idalia's ears.

Had it really been that long since she had been around her friends? Had it really been that long since she was a normal college student just trying to pass her classes?

Idalia sighed, wishing she could go back to a few months before. Before she knew about Season and her sisters. Before she knew about the five trials that were going to end up killing her and her new family.

Idalia glanced outside. The streetlamps had clicked on as the sun lowered in the sky. A few students walked across the campus, all in groups of people. Idalia felt alone, even with the company of her best friends. Or her ex best friends. Since apparently they had moved on without her. She didn't blame them. It was good they were used to her not being around, especially since in a few months, she might not be.

"I'm gonna go," Idalia said, standing abruptly.

Brittany and Katie held their mouths open, in the middle of a conversation. Brittany was the first to recover. She looked down at her phone. "Oh, it's getting late. We can walk back with you," she offered.

Katie looked up at her, her eyes bright.

"No, it's fine," Idalia said. "Y'all stay. Finish eating. I gotta get back to the dorm and decide what classes to take. Last minute registering." She pushed in her chair and left without giving them another chance to stop her. She could feel their stares on her back.

She opened the door of the coffee shop and stepped out into the darkened night. She followed the pathway back to the dorm, staying under the streetlamps.

How many more times would she get to walk at night? Get to leave a coffee shop? How much longer did she have in Texas? With her family? With her friends? She didn't know. And maybe it was better to put space between herself and all those things anyway. Maybe it would be better if she just disappeared. Like Aviva. Like Eira.

She rubbed her fingertips together, letting the hot burn of flames run through her hand. At least she had this connection. This power. At least she had something to comfort her as her end drew nearer.

78

"**M**s. Fletcher," Orla's teacher said, tapping a pencil against her desk.

Orla lifted her head off her arms and looked up at Mrs. Phillips.

"Yes?" Orla answered lazily.

"Didn't you get enough sleep during Winter Break?" Mrs. Phillips asked, turning on her heel and walking back to the front of the class.

Orla shook her head even though Mrs. Phillips had her back turned and couldn't see. She had not had enough sleep, not even close.

"This is not the time to catch up on sleep," Mrs. Phillips said, her voice rising to cover the noise in her classroom. "This is the time to get serious about your studies. Finals will be upon us before we know it. And you must pass my class if you want to graduate."

Orla stopped listening to Mrs. Phillips' monologue, her voice a nice melody in the back of her head as she stared out the window.

The windows lined the room, leaving a clear view of the school's parking lot. Orla saw her car sitting out front, and she wanted nothing more than to fake being sick so she could get in it and drive away. Her head fell back onto her arms. Her eyes kept falling shut and snapping back open.

"You okay, Orla?" Angela said, leaning over the aisle.

Orla could barely keep her eyes open, but she turned to look at Angela. "Yeah," she said. "I'm just tired."

Angela laughed. "Yeah, everyone can see that. Hear it, too, with all that snoring."

Orla faked a laugh. "I don't snore."

Angela reached across the other aisle and started whispering with Samantha. Orla turned around, facing forward. Trying to pay attention. Her eyes wouldn't focus on the words on the board. Or on Mrs. Phillips as she stomped around the front of the class. She was tired. Bone tired. And frankly, she didn't much care about school. What was the point?

"Samantha wants to know why you never texted us back over the break," Angela said, leaning back toward Orla.

"Dad had my phone." Orla rolled her eyes.

Angela relayed the message. Samantha leaned forward on her desk to see around Angela.

She mouthed words, but Orla couldn't understand. Angela busted out laughing, trying to cover the noise with her hand, but it didn't work. Everyone in the class turned to look at them. Orla's face turned red. She sat back and slid down in her chair. She covered her eyes with her hands.

"Girls, that's quite enough," Mrs. Phillips said, wagging her finger.

"Sorry, Mrs. Phillips," Samantha said. She, too, covered her face to hide the laughter.

The bell rang, the sound piercing the room. Students

jumped from their chairs, slung backpacks over their shoulders, and bolted through the door.

"The bell doesn't dismiss you. I do," Mrs. Phillips yelled, following the students into the hall.

Orla stood and gathered her stuff.

Another bell, the final bell rang, and Orla exhaled. It had been a long, boring day. But at least it was over, and she could go home and do nothing. She would welcome her grounding. Maybe then she'd have some time to figure things out. Figure out how to fix everything that was going wrong in her world. Figure out how to protect Aviva. How to stop Eira. What to do next. There was so much to figure out and so little time.

79

In the Land of Season

Aviva scraped the bottom of a tin can, scooping up the little remains of beans with her fingers. She savored the taste, closing her eyes, and dreaming the beans were pizza. Her stomach growled in protest as she swallowed the last bite. She was hungry. And she had nothing left.

She threw the can across the room. It landed on a pile of dirt.

Milo neighed beside her, nuzzling his nose against her arm. "You're hungry too, huh?" she asked the horse.

He bobbed his head.

"I guess we'll have to go find some food then."

Aviva stood on shaky legs. She placed a hand on a dirty wall to brace herself as her vision went dark and her head swam. She should be used to being on the brink of starvation, but it still surprised her. All of her time in broken homes with horrible foster parents hadn't prepared her for being out on her own. Especially not in Season.

The horse stood beside her and brushed against her side. "Thanks, Milo," she said, resting an arm around the horse's neck. She was glad Milo was small.

Aviva grabbed Milo's reins and led him outside. His hooves clicked across the cabin floor. She pulled him through the tall grass, leaving the scattered remains of the cabin she had called home for a few days behind.

She trudged through the forest, stopping every once in a while for Milo to bend his head and nibble at the ground.

A few miles out, Aviva heard the clattering of pots and pans being smacked against a metal fire pit. "Stay here," she whispered to Milo. She slid the blanket off Milo's back and wrapped it around her shoulders, covering her face. She peered through a fence of shrubs.

A small village was busy before her eyes. Men surrounded the fire pit, poking sticks of meat into a fire while women cleaned up behind them. She could smell the burnt flesh of the meat. Smoke assaulted her nose. She covered her mouth to hide the coughs that came over her. She ducked down when a few men eyed her hiding place.

She needed that meat, but she wasn't going to be able to get it in broad daylight.

Aviva went back to Milo and tied him around a tree. "It's gonna be a while, bud," she whispered to the horse. Milo continued grazing, getting his fill of the grass around them. Aviva slid down the trunk of the tree. She dozed off, waiting for darkness.

Aviva opened her eyes. She could barely see in front of her, it was so dark in the forest. She stood and patted Milo's head, making her way back to the edge of the forest. The fire pit was still burning, but the men were no longer standing over it. Instead, all of the people had gathered near a small cabin to eat. Aviva watched in silence, hoping they would leave some food for her.

Her stomach growled as she watched them devour the food, juices running down their jaws. A while later, the men went inside and left the women to clean. Aviva watched as they picked up the remains and threw it into the fire.

Her heart sank as the food went up in flames.

The rest of the village moved inside, leaving her to watch the food burn before her eyes.

Aviva stepped closer to the fire, letting her growling stomach lead the way. She left the cover of the forest and moved into the open field. She swung her head side to side, careful not to step on a fallen twig or make any noise.

She reached the fire. The heat hit her in the face. Her skin reddened and beads of sweat broke out on her forehead. Despite the heat, she pulled the blanket closer.

She peered into the fire. A small smoldering piece of meat was just at its edge, slowly burning. Aviva held her hand out toward the flame. It licked her fingers, and she pulled it back quickly, wincing in pain.

Aviva put her hand down, palm toward the earth. Grass, vines, and twigs slithered to her. They made their way up her leg, over her stomach, around her shoulder, and down her arm.

A protective layer of earth surrounded her entire hand and forearm.

She reached out gingerly. The flames surrounded her hand, but she couldn't feel the burn. She reached down and grabbed the meat, bringing it out of the fire and dropping it on the ground. It was smoking, too hot to eat. She reached back in to grab another piece.

Her arm was pulled from the fire and hoisted over her head. The vines covering her arm and body snaked away before he noticed them. "And what do you think you're doing, little thief?" a tall man said. He towered over her. His face was scrunched up in a snarl.

"I-I—" Aviva tried to speak, but only mutters and half words came out of her mouth. Looking up into the man's face reminded her of all the times her foster dad had looked at her the same. Ted's face flashed before her eyes, and she cowered away from the unknown man. She covered her face with her free arm, preparing for a blow to the cheek.

"Castor," a woman's voice rang out into the night. Small footsteps sounded against the ground, closing in on them. "What is going on here?" the woman asked, looking from the man to Aviva.

"This little thief," the man said, dragging Aviva clean off the ground by her arm, "was trying to steal the food."

"The food we threw out?" the woman said, one eyebrow raising on her forehead.

The man, Castor, nodded.

"It is not stealing if it has been thrown out. Let her go."

The man obliged, dropping Aviva's arm. She fell to the ground. She rubbed her shoulder, trying to get the feeling back into her arm.

"I'm sorry, darling," the woman said, leaning down to

Aviva. "Castor doesn't know any better. Always trying to protect what's ours."

Aviva only nodded. She still couldn't get her mouth to form words.

"Come, let's eat. There's plenty of fresh food inside," the woman said, pointing to the cabins.

"No, that's all right," Aviva said finally. "I should get going." Aviva stood, careful not to fall over in her dizziness. She started walking back toward the forest where Milo waited for her. Her vision twinkled in front of her, making it hard for her to walk straight. She tipped over, and the blanket fell away from her shoulders.

The woman ran up to her, placing steadying hands on each of Aviva's arms.

"Thank you," Aviva said, looking at the woman.

"My-my," the woman stammered. She let Aviva go and fell to her knees. "My princess. Princess Aviva," she said, lifting her hands into the air.

"Oh, no," Aviva said, reaching down to pull the lady up to her feet. "There's no need for all of that."

"Come, let us prepare a place for you to stay," the woman said, pulling Aviva back toward the cabins. "It would give us much honor."

Aviva looked behind her, into the forest. "Milo," she called out and clucked her tongue. Her horse emerged a few seconds later.

"Right this way," the woman said, leading Aviva into a warm cabin.

80

In the Land of Texas

Orla pulled into her driveway. Her parents' cars were out front, and they were inside rustling around. Orla went around the house, through the back door, hoping her parents wouldn't see her come in. She wanted to be alone, needed time to think. Needed time alone. She snuck down the hall, and just as she opened her bedroom door, her mother popped her head into the hallway.

"Sweetheart," she said, coming down the hallway toward Orla. "How was your day at school?"

"Fine," Orla answered as her mother pulled her into a hug.

Her mother stretched out her arms, holding Orla away from her. "It feels like we haven't seen you in a while," she said with a soft smile.

"Mom," Orla said, rolling her eyes and trying to pull away. "I was only at school."

"I know," her mother said, letting Orla's arms go. "I just missed you, but you need your space. I understand," she said, wiping at her eyes as they brimmed with tears.

"I still love you, Mom," Orla said. "I'm just dealing with some things right now."

"I know, I know." Her mother turned her back and headed toward the living room. "Oh," she said, stopping and facing Orla again. "A package came for you. I put it on your bed."

Orla nodded. She turned the knob and went into her room. She closed the door behind her and went over to her bed where the big brown box was waiting. A tight knot kept the box closed. She tried loosening it, but it wouldn't budge. Whoever tied it had some serious skill. Orla grabbed her scissors from her desk and clipped the sides of the rope.

The box finally popped open underneath Orla's hands. She screamed, covering her mouth with her hands trying to muffle the sound. She couldn't stop screaming. But she couldn't look away either.

Brey's dead eyes looked up at her.

Orla grabbed her stomach, lurching to the side as vomit escaped her mouth. It splashed into her small trash can. She heard footsteps in the hall, running toward her room. She rushed to the door and clicked the lock into place.

"Sweetheart, are you all right?" her mother called through the door.

Orla leaned against it, putting all her weight on the wooden door.

She shook her head and took a huge gulp of air. "Yes, Mom, I'm fine."

"Let me in," she said, jiggling the doorknob.

"It's fine, Mom. Just a bug."

"Orla," her mother warned.

Orla closed her eyes and tried to breathe evenly. "Really, Mom. I'm fine. I killed it. It's all good."

Orla could feel her heart beating furiously, blood rushing through her body so fast she was sweating. All she could hear was pounding in her ears. She slid down the door and sat on the floor. She rested her head on shaky arms. And she waited. Waited for her mom to finally leave. Waited to regain feeling in her legs. Waited for the headache to stop.

After an eternity, Orla crawled across her floor, back to her bed. She pulled herself up. She quickly flipped the box's sides up, trying with all her might to get the dead look of Brey's eyes out of her mind.

She held her mouth, the vomit etching to come up again. She put her back to her bed, to the box, and grabbed her phone.

"Hello?" she whispered.

"Orla?" Idalia asked. "Are you okay?" she said, her voice rising in concern.

"No. Not really." Orla paused. Her brain was scattered, and she couldn't form a thought. Couldn't figure out what to say or do. "I think I may need your help."

81

Idalia sped over to Orla's house, barely stopping at stop signs. She rushed to the front door and knocked. She drummed her fingers as she waited for someone to answer.

"Oh, hello, Idalia," Orla's father said with a smile on his face.

"Hi, Mr. Fletcher," Idalia said hurriedly. "Orla called me. Can I come in?"

"Of course, of course," he said, stepping aside so she could pass him.

She wandered through the house until she got to the back hallway. She padded down the hall, stopping at Orla's bedroom door.

Idalia raised her hand to knock. "Orla?" she said through the door. She put her ear to the door, trying to hear what was happening on the other side. The way her sister had sounded on the phone, something was wrong. Very wrong.

The door fell away from Idalia, and she stumbled inside Orla's bedroom. Orla shut the door and turned the lock.

"Finally," Orla said under her breath. "What took you so long?" Orla said, staring daggers at Idalia.

"I got here as fast as I could. Now, what is it?" Idalia asked. "What's wrong?"

Orla pointed toward a half-open box on her bed. Idalia raised an eyebrow and took a few steps toward Orla's bed. She put her hand on one side of the box and started lifting the flap.

"I don't know if you want to do that," Orla said quickly, staying as far back as she could get from the box.

Idalia dropped the flap and turned to look at Orla. "Then what is it?"

"It's—it's um," Orla stammered. "It's Brey," she finally got out, her words choking.

"Brey?" Idalia asked, her eyebrow raising in disbelief again. Brey? What was she talking about? Maybe this was it. Maybe Orla was going crazy. She certainly felt like she was. Maybe it was going around.

Orla nodded. "His head," she whispered.

Idalia glanced back at the box. "What do you mean it's his head?" she said, a breath between each word.

"His head," Orla said again. "His head is in the box. Eira must have..." Tears streamed down her cheeks.

"Eira had his head chopped off?" Idalia asked, her breath catching in her throat. She threw the flap to the side, exposing Brey's bloody head. Blood stained the wool blanket around the head. His eyes stared straight at Idalia. His neck was a mangled mess. Idalia slowly backed away. "Why? Why would she do that?"

Idalia fell against the wall next to Orla. "I don't know," Orla whispered. "She's insane."

"Brey didn't deserve this," Idalia said. "He was helping us," she whispered harshly. "He was the only one helping us." Tears pooled in her eyes and fell in streams down her face. She put her head in her hands and sobbed.

"What are we going to do with it?" Idalia asked, her voice too loud in her ringing ears.

Orla sucked in a huge breath. "It?" she said, turning to look at Idalia. There was fire behind her eyes, anger.

"Him," Idalia corrected herself. "What are we going to do with him?"

Orla took slow breaths. They sat in silence for a few minutes, both of them staring at the box on the bed. "I don't know," Orla finally whispered. "I was hoping you would have an idea."

"We have to get rid of it. Him," Idalia said, forcing herself to stand on shaky legs. "Come on." She reached down to Orla.

Orla slid her hand into Idalia's, and Idalia lifted her up.

Idalia turned in circles in the middle of Orla's room. Thinking. "We can't be here with that. Someone could find him. Your mom or dad." She looked toward Orla's door.

Her head spun in a million directions. This was too much. Too much to deal with.

"We'll go to Season. Dispose of him there. No one can trace it back to us that way. Right?" Idalia stopped turning circles.

Orla nodded curtly, but she didn't move.

Idalia held her breath and walked toward the bed. She tried closing the box, but the flaps wouldn't stay shut. Tears stung her eyes again. Why wouldn't it just shut? She wanted to scream. She wanted to burn something.

She took a deep breath and lifted the box, turning her eyes away.

The box was heavier than she had expected. Heavier than she knew a human head was. She stepped closer to Orla. Brey's head fell from beneath the box. Orla gasped.

"Just turn around," Idalia snapped, grabbing the wool blanket and wrapping the head up again. She smashed the box with her foot and held it in her armpit. She held the head away from her body.

"What do I need to do?" Orla asked, her voice sounding far away as Idalia got everything into place.

"Get us to Season."

Orla nodded, turning back to face Idalia with her eyes closed. She placed her hands on Idalia's shoulders, connecting them. Making sure they went together. "Season," Orla whispered.

In a blink, they stood in an open field. The Tree of Season sparkled into view. It was a big, beautiful shining mass. Idalia was sick to her stomach looking at it. Brey shouldn't be here. Not like this.

"Sorry, it was the first thing that came to mind," Orla whispered, solemn. She stepped away and kept her eyes downcast.

Idalia didn't mind her. She placed the box on the ground near the trunk. On top of it she put Brey's head. A tear slipped from her eye as she raised her hand.

Flames licked at the box, growing as it reached the wool-wrapped head. Every inch of box and flesh melted underneath her fire. Her throat closed when the pungent smell filled the air.

She raised her other hand, putting all her might into her flames. All her anger. All her frustration. She was glad when all that remained of Brey was a deeply singed spot of earth. A reminder of the man who'd helped them. A reminder of the only man who had answers to questions they'd never be able to ask.

82

In the Land of Season

"Marge, you don't need to do that," Aviva said, standing back as the older woman replaced the sheets on Aviva's bed. "I can do it myself," she said.

Marge shook her head fiercely. "Oh, no, no. A princess of mine will not be doing her own bedding," Marge said, not even bothering to look over at Aviva. Instead, she made quick work of the bed.

"It was enough of you to let me stay here," Aviva said.

Marge waved her hand dismissively. "No princess of mine will be left out in the woods when we have a perfectly fine room."

"Thank you," Aviva said. "And you can stop calling me *princess.*" Aviva blushed as Marge turned to face her with a disapproving look.

Marge wagged her finger in Aviva's face. "Now, haven't I told you? You are a princess, and that is what I will call you."

Aviva nodded. "Yes, ma'am. I was just saying it's unnecessary."

Marge made a clicking sound with her tongue and finished up Aviva's room in silence. "Go on into the kitchen," Marge instructed Aviva, all but pushing her out of the room. "Breakfast is ready."

Aviva didn't fight the woman. It had been a constant battle for days, and Aviva was giving up. Marge would never stop taking care of her.

Aviva pulled out a chair and sat in front of a big plate. She didn't say a word as she shoveled food into her mouth. Her stomach had never been so happy or full as it had been these last few days. She couldn't remember one instant where a parent cared and worried over her as much as Marge, a stranger, had.

Marge came into the room as she ate and watched over her with piercing eyes. "You've never been properly loved, have you?"

Aviva choked on the eggs. Marge pushed her glass of water closer to her. Aviva took it and drank down the eggs. Her face was flushed, and she couldn't meet Marge's eyes.

"Sorry for the intrusion," Marge said, standing up and clearing off the table.

Aviva turned around in her chair and watched Marge wash off the plate and clean the spotless kitchen again. "No, it's fine," Aviva said, finally able to speak again. "And to answer your question, I guess not."

"Oh, you would know if you had," Marge said, not looking at Aviva. "It's sad really," she said more to herself than Aviva.

"You've gone your whole life with no one on your side, and now you have to kill the only family you have left if you want to survive. It shouldn't be this way," she said, shaking her head.

Aviva watched as a small tear rolled down Marge's face and plopped onto the counter. Marge wiped her face and sighed before finally looking up and smiling at Aviva.

"But it's okay," Marge said. "I know you'll do what you think is right."

Marge walked back over to Aviva, reached down a hand, and pulled her to a stand. "Come, come," she said, leading Aviva outside.

Aviva loved her time spent outdoors in Spring. The air was fresh and just the right temperature. It wasn't cold like in Winter where snow blew in flurries all around. No, here in Spring, flowers were blooming, the grass was green, and the trees swayed in the light brush of wind.

Aviva felt connected. And strong.

She could feel the earth underneath her feet, feel it as the power rose up inside of her and strengthened every inch of her body. She closed her eyes and breathed in a huge breath.

Laughter erupted in the air, a little ways away. Aviva opened her eyes and found the source. A few of the village kids were running around, kicking a ball. Aviva smiled. She loved it here. She could stay forever.

A horn blew, almost knocking Aviva off her feet. Marge steadied her by her arm.

"Get inside, quick," Marge said, pushing Aviva back toward the cabins.

"What? Why?" Aviva asked, trying to tear her arm away. All of the villagers were running around, hiding things, guarding things.

Marge pushed her hard. Aviva tripped and fell onto the ground, mud caking her hands.

"Go," Marge shouted, her face full of terror. "Keep yourself hidden."

Aviva pushed herself to her feet and skidded into the nearest cabin. She ducked under the window, her back on the wall, breathing heavily. All she could hear was the sound of the horn blaring in her ears. It was minutes before the sound disappeared.

She pulled herself up, crouching under the window. She pushed the curtain to the side just an inch to see the yard. All of the villagers were standing side by side, shoulders touching. And they all were facing the fence of shrubs at the front of the clearing.

No one was making any noise. No one moved. They just waited.

Aviva pushed up on one leg to stand before crashing back to the floor. She held her breath. Her heart pounded. She shook her head. *No, no, no,* was all she could think to herself. This couldn't be happening.

She finally turned back around and looked out the window. Queen Quinn was standing at the head of an army.

Marge had stepped forward, ahead of the villagers. Aviva could see Quinn's lips moving, but she couldn't hear anything they said. Marge shook her head fiercely and waved her hands in the air in a sweeping motion.

Quinn stepped back. One of the soldiers leaned down so that she could whisper in his ear. The soldier nodded. He turned his back, facing the army. And then, all of a sudden, the army exploded.

They coated the small village, every inch covered with soldiers. They kicked in barrels, spilling water and food over the ground. Rummaged through cabins, throwing furniture out the windows and doors. They bashed any and everything they could get their hands on. Pushed small children out of the way. Raised a bat to an elderly man who cowered to the ground. Set fire to a stack of logs. All while Quinn stepped back and watched with a faint smile on her lips.

Aviva gripped the windowsill, watching the scene with desperation. She was frozen to her spot and couldn't move. Couldn't even think of what she would do if she could move away from the window.

A soldier ran toward the cabin, directly in Aviva's line of sight. Marge rushed over, putting her hands up to ward off the soldier. Marge looked over her shoulder, meeting Aviva's eyes. A look of terror crossed her face.

The soldier reared back before smashing his wooden baton across Marge's face. The wood splintered with the force, and Marge fell into a lifeless lump on the ground. Her eyes were open, staring at Aviva, but she was dead. Blood poured out of the side of her head, covering the fresh green grass with red.

Aviva ran from the cabin, finally able to move. She met the soldier, a bloodied baton at his side, with her hands raised in the air. One of the fiery logs came rushing through the clearing, knocking the soldier to the ground. "No," Aviva shouted at the soldier. She piled more and more burning logs on top of him. He writhed underneath the weight before finally giving up and dying right next to Marge.

"No," Aviva shouted, walking toward the middle of the clearing. Toward Queen Quinn.

Queen Quinn hadn't noticed her yet. Hardly anyone did. She was just a young, small child to them. But not anymore. Not when they were trying to destroy the only home she had felt safe in.

She raised her hands above her head, pulling the earth from its roots. She used all her might, all of the strength she felt in Spring, and pushed it toward Quinn and the soldiers running around.

Logs, branches, whole trees uplifted and flew through the air toward the edge of the clearing. Soldiers were covered with the earth, dying underneath its weight. The soldiers who weren't directly affected by Aviva's earth storm ran from the village, barely stopping to get their queen out of the ambush.

When the last of the soldiers were gone, Aviva dropped her hands, and the earth fell back to the ground. Aviva panted. Her face was red, sweat beading on her forehead. Her hands shook at her side. She stared at the woods, looking for any sign of a returning soldier. Looking for any reason to release some more power.

"Princess," a small girl said, tugging on Aviva's pant leg.

Aviva looked down at her. The girl was covered with mud and her other arm hung loosely at her side.

"What do we do now?"

Aviva turned to look at her village. She couldn't take her gaze away from the destruction.

Cabins were half torn down, ablaze in fire. All the food and water was ruined. There was hardly anything left of the village.

Aviva knelt next to the little girl, holding her hand tightly. She whispered to the little girl, a determined look in her eyes, "We rebuild."

83

Orla stepped forward, through the edge of a forest. She put her hand on a tree trunk and peered across the makeshift road.

"Where are we?" Idalia asked, coming to her side.

Orla shrugged. "I'm not sure. I meant to take us home." Orla placed her foot outside the tree line and slowly crossed the road. She held her hands out, ready. The air shifted around her.

"Stop," Idalia said, putting a hand around her arm. "Listen."

Orla did. Clinking and clanking sounds were not far off. The earth trembled underneath her feet. Voices. She could hear it all. And most importantly, she could hear the soft, yet strong voice of her littlest sister. "Aviva," Orla breathed. Her legs propelled her forward.

Aviva stood in the middle of a broken down village. Orla rushed to her, not stopping until her arms were around her. "Aviva," she said again, tears spilling over her cheeks. "You're here."

"Orla?" Aviva said before Idalia crushed into them, too. "Idalia? How did y'all find me?"

Orla detached herself and wiped her eyes. "We didn't. Not really. I tried portaling us home, and it brought us here." She stopped, looking around again. If it weren't for the vandalized village, she'd be in the middle of a beautiful and lush town. "Where are we?"

"Spring."

"What happened here?" Idalia asked, surveying the damage. The still burning cabins. The emptied barrels.

"Quinn is what happened," Aviva said. Her mouth was set in a straight, hard line.

"She came here? Why?" Orla asked. She stayed beside Aviva, not wanting her to get too far away. Not wanting to lose her again. If she had portaled home, and this is where it took her, then this is where she needed to be. Here, next to Aviva with Idalia. Home. With her sisters.

Aviva shrugged. "I don't know. She just showed up not long ago."

Quinn had been in Spring. Eira had sent them Brey's head. What were they planning next? Orla didn't want to find out.

"What are y'all doing in Season?"

"Brey," Orla started. His face flashed in her mind. Her stomach turned over again.

"He sent another letter? I haven't gotten anything, but then again, Quinn just destroyed this place."

Orla shook her head. Aviva raised her eyebrow, confusion washing over her face.

"Eira sent Orla Brey's head," Idalia said. "Sent a box to her doorstep with him in it."

Orla turned away, putting a hand over her mouth.

Aviva whipped toward Idalia. "What? What did you say?"

Idalia gulped. "Eira decapitated Brey and sent us his head. He's dead. Brey's dead."

Silence enveloped them. Orla forced her eyes to remain open, not wanting to chance another image of Brey's severed head. Not wanting to be reminded yet again of what Eira was capable of. Who Eira had become.

"Brey's dead," Aviva whispered.

Orla and Idalia nodded.

Aviva reached out her hands, taking Orla's in one and Idalia's in the other. Orla grabbed it, thankful for the warmth it gave her. For the strength. For the love she could feel growing each day between the three of them.

Eira was lost. She didn't know if they'd ever get her back. But at least she had Idalia and Aviva. At least she had someone to go through this with. At least she wasn't alone.

Orla looked at Aviva's village. Spring. She knew Aviva wasn't going to leave. Not when she'd found her home. And she knew she couldn't stay. Not yet. Not until she got out from under her parents. Not until graduation. Then, she could act like she was moving off for college. Then, she could come to Season. She could help Aviva. They could find Eira. They could fix her. Or deal with her. Whichever it took to keep Aviva safe.

"We'll help," Orla said around the lump in her throat. "We'll help fix this. But then, I have to go home. Just until graduation."

Aviva squeezed her hand.

"I'm coming back to stay. We can figure out what to do with Eira and Quinn. The trials and everything," Orla said.

Idalia nodded in agreement. "I have to go back, too. My parents are making me go back to college. I'll wear them down though, hopefully. And then we can all be here. We can all fix the mess our father created when he sent us away and changed everything."

Tears welled in Orla's eyes. She looked out over Spring. And just like they had with Autumn, with her little home away from Texas, they rebuilt. All three of them. Together. Stronger than ever. Stronger because they were one.

ACKNOWLEDGMENTS

Reworking my previously published books (The Ebb of Winter and The Frost of Spring) into this beauty would not have been possible alone. I have many people to thank. Without these people and their support, this new version would've never made it onto bookshelves. Thank you so much for everything you did for me and my book!

To Victoria Smart, my best friend, my book bestie. I am so grateful you allow me to talk your ear off about my books. I don't make friends easily, so having and keeping you as a friend is something I cherish. Thank you for all you do for me and for your continued support of my author dreams.

To Megan Dollarhide, my step sister who I have more in common with than my biological sisters. I don't know what I'd do if I didn't have a sister I could talk books and writing with. I appreciate your time and feedback on this thing.

To my cover designer at Selkkie Designs, I absolutely adore what you created. This cover fits so nicely with the story and genre. I am proud to have it displayed on my shelves. I cannot wait to work with you again.

To my editor, Claire Ashgrove, I am amazed at your work. You were absolutely needed on this project. You changed this story for the better. Without you, my story would not be its best. So thank you again for your criticism and expertise.

Lastly, to my beta and ARC readers, thank you for your early support and comments.

ABOUT THE AUTHOR

H.E. Shows (Shows like cows, not TV shows) has always dreamed of being a best-selling fantasy author. Actually, her ultimate dream is to star in a TV or movie based on one of her novels. (Gotta have big dreams, kiddos!) She has been reading and writing for as long as she can remember. She earned a bachelor's degree in Creative Writing and English from SNHU. Then, she went on to teach English for a year and a half at the high school level and two years at the middle school level. Although she enjoyed teaching (for the most part), she has decided to stay-at-home with her newest child. This will hopefully give her the time she wants to focus on becoming the author she's always wanted to be.

H.E. Shows currently lives in the Dallas area with her three wonderful children who take up a majority of the free time she believed she would be getting without a traditional job. You can follow H.E. Shows on Facebook, TikTok, Instagram, Goodreads, and Amazon.